Dame Ngaio Marsh was born in New Zealand in 1899 and died in February 1982.

She wrote over twenty-five detective novels and many of her stories have theatrical settings, for Ngaio Marsh's real passion was the theatre. She was both actress and producer and almost single-handedly revived the New Zealand public's interest in live theatre. It was for this work that she received what she called her 'damery' in 1966.

Available in Fontana by the same author

Artists in Crime
Black as He's Painted
Colour Scheme
Clutch of Constables
Dead Water
Death at the Bar
Death at the Dolphin
Death and the Dancing Footman
Death in Ecstacy
Death in a White Tie
Died in the Wool
Enter a Murderer
False Scent
Final Curtain
Grave Mistake
Hand in Glove
Last Ditch
Light Thickens
A Man Lay Dead
The Nursing Home Murder
Off With His Head
Overture to Death
Photo-finish
Scales of Justice
Singing in the Shrouds
Spinsters in Jeopardy
Surfeit of Lampreys
Swing Brother, Swing
Tied Up in Tinsel
Vintage Murder
When in Rome

NGAIO MARSH

Opening Night

FONTANA/Collins

To The Management and Company of
The New Zealand
Student Players
of 1949
in love and gratitude

First published by William Collins Sons & Co. Ltd 1951
First issued in Fontana Paperbacks 1963
Ninth impression October 1987

Printed and bound in Great Britain by
William Collins Sons & Co. Ltd, Glasgow

CONTENTS

I	The Vulcan	page 7
II	In a Glass Darkly	22
III	First Dress-Rehearsal	44
IV	Second Dress-Rehearsal	60
V	Opening Night	79
VI	Performance	92
VII	Disaster	106
VIII	After-Piece	129
IX	The Shadow of Otto Brod	150
X	Summing Up	168
XI	Last Act	185

CAST OF CHARACTERS

Of the Vulcan Theatre

MARTYN TARNE	
BOB GRANTLEY	*Business Manager*
FRED BADGER	*Night Watchman*
CLEM SMITH	*Stage Director*
BOB CRINGLE	*Dresser to Adam Poole*
ADAM POOLE	*Actor-manager*
HELENA HAMILTON	*Leading Lady*
CLARK BENNINGTON	*Her husband*
GAY GAINSFORD	*His niece*
J. G. DARCEY	*Character actor*
PARRY PERCIVAL	*Juvenile*
JACQUES DORÉ	*Designer and assistant to Adam Poole*
DR. JOHN JAMES RUTHERFORD	*Playwright*

Of the C.I.D. New Scotland Yard

CHIEF DETECTIVE-INSPECTOR ALLEYN	
DETECTIVE-INSPECTOR FOX	
DETECTIVE-SERGEANT GIBSON	
DETECTIVE-SERGEANT BAILEY	*Finger-print expert*
DETECTIVE-SERGEANT THOMPSON	*Photographer*
P.C. LORD MICHAEL LAMPREY	
DR. CURTIS	

CHAPTER I

MARTYN AT THE VULCAN

As she turned into Carpet Street the girl wondered at her own obstinacy. To what a pass it had brought her, she thought. She lifted first one foot and then the other, determined not to drag them. They felt now as if their texture had changed: their bones, it seemed, were covered by sponge and burning wires.

A clock in a jeweller's window gave the time as twenty-three minutes to five. She knew, by the consequential scurry of its second-hand, that it was alive. It was surrounded by other clocks that made mad dead statements of divergent times as if, she thought, to set before her the stages of that day's fruitless pilgrimage. Nine o'clock, the first agent. Nine thirty-six, the beginning of the wait for auditions at the Unicorn; five minutes past twelve, the first dismissal. " Thank you, Miss—ah—— Thank you, dear. Leave your name and address. Next, please." No record of her flight from the smell of restaurants but it must have been about ten-to-two, a time registered by a gilt carriage-clock in the corner, that she had climbed the stairs to Garnet Marks' Agency on the third floor. Three o'clock exactly at the Achilles where the auditions had already closed, and the next hour in and out of film agencies. " Leave your picture if you like, dear. Let you know if there's anything." Always the same. As punctual as time itself. The clocks receded, wobbled, enlarged themselves and at the same time spread before their dials a tenuous veil. Beneath the arm of a bronze nude that brandished an active swinging dial, she caught sight of a face: her own. She groped in her bag and presently in front of the mirrored face, a hand appeared and made a gesture at its own mouth with the stub of a lipstick. There was a coolness on her forehead, something pressed heavily against it. She discovered that this was the shop-window.

Behind the looking-glass was a man who peered at her from the shop's interior. She steadied herself with her hand against the window, lifted her suitcase and turned away.

The Vulcan Theatre was near the bottom of the street. Although she did not at first see its name above the entry, she had, during the past fortnight, discovered a sensitivity to theatres. She was aware of them at a distance. The way was downhill: her knees trembled and she resisted with difficulty an impulse to break into a shamble. Among the stream of faces that approached and sailed past there were now some that, on seeing hers, sharpened into awareness and speculation. She attracted notice.

The stage-door was at the end of an alley-way. Puddles of water obstructed her passage and she did not altogether avoid them. The surface of the wall was crenellated and damp.

"She knows," a rather shrill uncertain voice announced inside the theatre, "but she *mustn't* be told." A second voice spoke unintelligibly. The first voice repeated its statement with a change of emphasis: "She *knows* but she mustn't be *told*," and after a further interruption added dismally: "Thank you very much."

Five women came out of the stage-door and it was shut behind them. She leant against the wall as they passed her. The first two muttered together and moved their shoulders petulantly, the third stared at her and at once she bent her head. The fourth passed by quickly with compressed lips. She kept her head averted and heard, but did not see, the last girl halt beside her.

"Well, for God's sake!" She looked up and saw, for the second time that day, a too-large face, over-painted, with lips that twisted downwards, tinted lids, and thickly mascaraed lashes.

She said: "I'm late, aren't I?"

"You've had it, dear. I gave you the wrong tip at Marks's. The show here, with the part I told you about, goes on this week. They were auditioning for a tour: 'That'll be all for to-day, ladies, thank you. What's the hurry, here's your hat.' For what it's worth, it's all over."

"I lost my way," she said faintly.

"Too bad." The large face swam nearer. "Are you all right?" it demanded.

She made a slight movement of her head. "A bit tired. All right, really."

"You look shocking. Here: wait a sec. Try this."

"No, no. Really. Thank you so much but——"

"It's O.K. A chap who travels for a French firm gave it to me. It's marvellous stuff: cognac. Go *on*."

A hand steadied her head. The cold mouth of the flask opened her lips and pressed against her teeth. She tried to say: "I've had nothing to eat," and at once was forced

8

to gulp down a burning stream. The voice encouraged her:
" Do you a power of good. Have the other half."

She shuddered, gasped and pushed the flask away. " No,
please!"

" Is it doing the trick?"

" This is wonderfully kind of you. I am so grateful. Yes,
I think it must be doing the trick."

" Gra-a-a-nd. Well, if you're sure you'll be O.K. . . ."

" Yes, indeed. I don't even know your name."

" Trixie O'Sullivan."

" I'm Martyn Tarne."

" Look nice in the programme, wouldn't it? If there's
nothing else I can do . . ."

" Honestly. I'll be fine."

" You look better," Miss O'Sullivan said doubtfully. " We
may run into each other again. The bloody round, the
common task." She began to move away. " I've got a date,
actually, and I'm running late."

" Yes, of course. Good-bye, and thank you."

" It's open in front. There's a seat in the foyer. Nobody'll
say anything. Why not sit there for a bit?" She was half-
way down the alley. "Hope you get fixed up," she said.
" God, it's going to rain. What a life!"

" What a life," Martyn Tarne echoed and tried to sound
gay and ironic.

" I hope you'll be all right. 'Bye."

" Good-bye and thank you."

The alley was quiet now. Without moving she took stock
of herself. Something thrummed inside her head and the tips
of her fingers tingled but she no longer felt as if she was going
to faint. The brandy glowed at the core of her being, sending
out ripples of comfort. She tried to think what she should do.
There was a church, back in the Strand: she ought to know
its name. One could sleep there, she had been told, and
perhaps there would be soup. That would leave two and
eightpence for to-morrow: all she had. She lifted her
suitcase, it was heavier than she had remembered, and walked
to the end of the alley-way. Half a dozen raindrops plopped
into a puddle. People hurried along the footpath with
upward glances and opened their umbrellas. As she hesitated,
the rain came down suddenly and decisively. She turned
towards the front of the theatre and at first thought it was
shut. Then she noticed that one of the plate-glass doors was
ajar.

She pushed it open and went in.

The Vulcan was a new theatre, fashioned from the shell of an old one. Its foyer was an affair of geranium-red leather, chromium steel and double glass walls housing cacti. The central box-office marked " Reserved Tickets Only " was flanked by doors and beyond them, in the corners, were tubular steel and rubber-foam seats. She crossed the heavily carpeted floor and sat in one of these. Her feet and legs, released from the torment of supporting and moving her body, throbbed ardently.

Facing Martyn, on a huge easel, was a frame of photographs under a printed legend: " Opening at this Theatre on Thursday, May 11th: *Thus to Revisit,* a New Play by John James Rutherford." She stared at two large familiar faces and four strange smaller ones. Adam Poole and Helena Hamilton: those were famous faces. Monstrously enlarged, they had looked out at the New Zealand and Australian public from hoardings and from above cinema entrances. She had stood in queues many times to see them, severally and together. They were in the centre and surrounding them were Clark Bennington with a pipe and stick and a look of faded romanticism in his eyes, J. G. Darcey with pince-nez and hair enbrosse, Gay Gainsford, young and intense, and Parry Percival, youngish and dashing. The faces swam together and grew dim.

It was very quiet in the foyer and beginning to get dark. On the other side of the entrance doors the rain drove down slantways half blinding her vision of homeward-bound pedestrians and the traffic of the street beyond them. She saw the lights go on in the top of a bus, illuminating the passive and remote faces of its passengers. The glare of headlamps shone pale across the rain. A wave of loneliness, excruciating in its intensity, engulfed Martyn and she closed her eyes. For the first time since her ordeal began, panic rose in her throat and sickened her. Phrases drifted with an aimless rhythm on the tide of her desolation: " You're sunk, you're sunk, you're utterly sunk, you asked for it, and you've got it. What'll happen to you now?"

She was drowning at night in a very lonely sea. She saw lights shine on some unattainable shore. Pieces of flotsam bobbed indifferently against her hands. At the climax of despair, metallic noises, stupid and commonplace, set up a clatter in her head.

Martyn jerked galvanically and opened her eyes. The whirr and click of her fantasy had been repeated behind an obscured-glass wall on her left. Light glowed beyond the wall and she was confronted by the image of a god, sand-blasted across the surface of the glass and beating at a forge under the surprising supervision, it appeared, of Melpomene and Thalia. Farther along, a notice in red light: "Dress Circle and Stalls," jutted out from an opening. Beyond the hammer-blows of her heart a muffled voice spoke peevishly.

"... Not much use to *me*. What? Yes, I know, old boy, but that's not the point."

The voice seemed to listen. Martyn thought: "This is it. In a minute I'll be turned out."

"... Something pretty bad," the voice said irritably. "She's gone to hospital. ... They *said* so but nobody's turned up. ... Well, you know what she's like, old boy, don't you? We've been snowed under all day and *I* haven't been able to do anything about it ... auditions for the northern tour of the old piece ... yes, yes, that's all fixed but ... Look, another thing: *The Onlooker* wants a story and pictures for this week ... yes, on stage. In costume. Nine-thirty in the morning and everything still in the boxes. ... Well, can't you think of *anyone*? ... Who? ... O, God, I'll give it a pop. All right, old boy, thanks."

To Martyn, dazed with brandy and sleep, it was a distortion of a day-dream. Very often had she dreamt herself into a theatre where all was confusion because the leading actress had laryngitis and the understudy was useless. She would present herself modestly: "I happen to know the lines. I could perhaps ..." The sudden attentiveness, when she began to speak the lines ... the opening night ... the grateful tears streaming down the boiled shirts of the management ... the critics ... no image had been too gross for her.

"Eileen?" said the voice. "Thank God! Listen, darling, it's Bob Grantley here. Listen, Eileen, I want you to do something terribly kind. I know it's asking a hell of a lot but I'm in trouble and you're my last hope. Helena's dresser's ill. Yes, indeed, poor old Tansey. Yes, I'm afraid so. Just this afternoon, and we haven't been able to raise anybody. First dress-rehearsal to-morrow night and a photograph call in the morning and nothing unpacked or anything. I know what a good soul you are and I wondered ... O, God! I see. Yes, I see. No, of course. Oh, well, never mind. I know you would. Yes. 'Bye."

Silence. Precariously alone in the foyer, she meditated an advance upon the man beyond the glass wall and suppressed a dreadful impulse in herself towards hysteria. This was her day-dream in terms of reality. She must have slept longer than she had thought. Her feet were sleeping still. She began to test them, tingling and pricking, against the floor. She could see her reflection in the front doors, a dingy figure with a pallid face and cavernous shadows for eyes.

The light behind the glass wall went out. There was, however, still a yellow glow coming through the box-office door. As she got to her feet and steadied herself, the door opened.

"I believe," she said, "you are looking for a dresser."

II

As he had stopped dead in the lighted doorway she couldn't see the man clearly but his silhouette was stocky and trim.

He said with what seemed to be a mixture of irritation and relief: "Good Lord, how long have you been here?"

"Not long. You were on the telephone. I didn't like to interrupt."

"Interrupt!" he ejaculated as if she talked nonsense.

He looked at his watch, groaned, and said rapidly: "You've come about this job? From Mrs. Greenacres, aren't you?"

She wondered who Mrs. Greenacres, could be? An employment agent? She hunted desperately for the right phrase, the authentic language.

"I understood you required a dresser and I would be pleased to apply." Should she have added "sir"?

"It's for Miss Helena Hamilton," he said rapidly. "Her own dresser who's been with her for years—for a long time —has been taken ill. I explained to Mrs. Greenacres. Photograph call for nine in the morning and first dress-rehearsal to-morrow night. We open on Thursday. The dressing's heavy. Two quick changes and so on. I suppose you've got references?"

Her mouth was dry. She said: "I haven't brought——" and was saved by the telephone bell. He plunged back into the office and she heard him shout "Vulcan" into the receiver. "Grantley, here," he said. "Oh, hallo, darling. Look, I'm desperately sorry, but I've been held up or I'd have rung you before. For God's sake apologise for me. Try and keep them going till I get there. I know, I know. Not a smell of one until——" the voice became suddenly muffled. She caught isolated words. "I think so . . . yes, I'll ask . . . yes . . . Right. 'Bye, darling."

12

He darted out, now wearing a hat and struggling into a raincoat. "Look," he said, "Miss——"

"Tarne."

"Miss Tarne. Can you start right away? Miss Hamilton's things are in her dressing-room. They need to be unpacked and hung out to-night. There'll be a lot of pressing. The cleaners have been in but the room's not ready. You can finish in the morning but she wants the things that can't be ironed—I wouldn't know—hung out. Here are the keys. We'll see how you get on and fix up something definite to-morrow if you suit. The night-watchman's there. He'll open the room for you. Say I sent you. Here!"

He fished out a wallet, found a card and scribbled on it. "He is a bit of a stickler: you'd better take this."

She took the card and the keys. "To-night?" she said. "Now?"

"Well, can you?"

"I—yes. But——"

"Not worrying about after-hours are you?"

"No."

For the first time he seemed, in the darkish foyer, to be looking closely at her. "I suppose," he muttered, "it's a bit——" and stopped short.

Martyn said in a voice that to herself sounded half-choked: "I'm perfectly trustworthy. You spoke of references. I have——"

"Oh, yes, yes," he said. "Good. That'll be O.K. then. I'm late. Will you be all right? You can go through the house. It's raining outside. Through there, will you? Thank you. Good night."

Taking up her suitcase, she went through the door he swung open and found herself in the theatre.

She was at the back of the stalls, standing on thick carpet at the top of the ramp and facing the centre aisle. It was not absolutely dark. The curtain was half-raised and a bluish light filtered in from off-stage through some opening —a faintly-discerned window—in the scenery. This light was dimly reflected on the shrouded boxes. The dome was invisible, lost in shadow, and so far above that the rain, hammering on the roof beyond it, sounded much as a rumour of drums to Martyn. The deadened air smelt of naphthalene and plush.

She started off cautiously down the aisle. "I forgot," said Mr. Grantley's voice behind her. She managed to choke back a yelp. " You'd better get some flowers for the dressing-room. She likes roses. Here's another card."

" I don't think I've——"

" Florain's at the corner," he shouted. " Show them the card."

The door swung to behind him and, a moment later, she heard a more remote slam. She waited for a little while longer, to accustom herself to the dark. The shadows melted and the shape of the auditorium filtered through them like an image on a film in the darkroom. She thought it beautiful: the curve of the circle, the fan-like shell that enclosed it, the elegance of the proscenium and modesty of the ornament—all these seemed good to Martyn, and her growing sight of them refreshed her. Though this encouragement had an unreal, rather dream-like character, yet it did actually dispel something of her physical exhaustion so that it was with renewed heart that she climbed a little curved flight of steps on the prompt side of the proscenium, pushed open the pass-door at the top and arrived back-stage.

She was on her own ground. A single blue working-light, thick with dust, revealed a baize letter-rack and hinted at the baton and canvas backs of scenery fading upwards into yawning blackness. At her feet a litter of flex ran down into holes in the stage. There were vague, scarcely dis-cernible shapes that she recognised as stacked flats, light bunches, the underside of perches, a wind machine and rain box. She smelt paint and glue-size. As she received the assurance of these familiar signs she heard a faint scuffling noise, a rattle of paper, she thought. She moved forward.

In the darkness ahead of her a door opened on an oblong of light which widened to admit the figure of a man in an overcoat. He stood with bent head, fumbled in his pocket and produced a torch. The beam shot out, hunted briefly about the set and walls and found her. She blinked into a dazzling white disk and said: " Mr. Grantley sent me round. I'm the dresser."

" Dresser?" the man said hoarsely. He kept his torch-light on her face and moved towards her. " I wasn't told about no dresser," he said.

She held Mr. Grantley's card out. He came closer and flashed his light on it without touching it. " Ah," he said with a sort of grudging cheerfulness, " that's different. Now I know where I am, don't I?"

" I hope so," she said, trying to make her voice friendly.

14

" I'm sorry to bother you. Miss Hamilton's dresser has been taken ill and I've got the job."

" *Aren't* you lucky," he said with obvious relish and added: " Not but what she isn't a lady when she takes the fit for it."

He was eating something. The movement of his jaws, the succulent noises he made and the faint odour of food were an outrage. She could have screamed her hunger at him. Her mouth filled with saliva.

" He says to open the star room," he said. " Come on froo while I get the keys. I was 'avin' me bitter supper."

She followed him into a tiny room choked with junk. A kettle stuttered on a gas-ring by a sink clotted with dregs of calcamine paint and tea leaves. His supper was laid out on a newspaper: bread and an open tin of jam. He explained that he was about to make a cup of tea and suggested she should wait while he did so. She leant against the door and watched him. The fragrance of freshly brewed tea rose above the reek of stale size and dust. She thought: " If he drinks it now I'll have to go out."

" Like a drop of char?" he said. His back was turned to her.

" Very much."

He rinsed out a stained cup under the tap.

Martyn said loudly: " I've got a tin of meat in my case. I was saving it. If you'd like to share it and could spare some of your bread. . . ."

He swung round and for the first time she saw his face. He was dark and thin and his eyes were brightly impertinent. Their expression changed as he stared at her.

" Hallo, 'allo!" he said. " Who give *you* a tanner and borrowed 'alf a crahn? What's up?"

" I'm all right."

" *Are* you? Your looks don't flatter you, then."

" I'm a bit tired and——" Her voice broke and she thought in terror that she was going to cry. " It's nothing," she said.

" 'Ere!" He dragged a box out from under the sink and not ungently pushed her down on it. " Where's this remarkable tin of very perticerlar meat? Give us a shine at it?"

He shoved her suitcase over and while she fumbled at the lock busied himself with pouring out tea. " Nothing to touch a drop of the old char when you're browned off,"

15

he said. He put the reeking cup of dark fluid beside her and turned away to the bench.

"With any luck,'" Martyn thought folding back the garments in her case, "I won't have to sell these now."

She found the tin and gave it to him. "Coo!" he said, "looks lovely, don't it? Tongue and veal and a pitcher of sheep to show there's no deception. Very tempting."

"Can you open it?"

"Can I open it? Oh, dear."

She drank her scalding tea and watched him open the tin and turn its contents out on a more than dubious plate. Using his clasp knife he perched chunks of meat on a slab of bread and held it out to her. "You're in luck," he said. "Eat it slow."

She urged him to join her but he said he would set his share aside for later. They could both, he suggested, take another cut at it to-morrow. He examined the tin with interest while Martyn consumed her portion. She had never before given such intense concentration to a physical act. She would never have believed that eating could bring so fierce a satisfaction.

"Comes from Australia, don't it?" her companion said, still contemplating the tin.

"New Zealand."

"Same thing."

Martyn said: "Not really. There's quite a big sea in between."

"Do you come from there?"

"Where?"

"Australia."

"No. I'm a New Zealander."

"Same thing."

She looked up and found him grinning at her. He made the gesture of wiping the smile off his face. "Oh, dear," he said.

Martyn finished her tea and stood up. "I must start my job," she said.

"Feel better?"

"Much, much better."

"Would it be quite a spell since you ate anything?"

"Yesterday."

"I never fancy drinking on an empty stomach, myself."

Her face burnt against the palms of her hands. "But I don't . . . I mean, I know. I mean I was a bit faint and somebody . . . a girl . . . she was terribly kind. . . ."

"Does yer mother know you're aht?" he asked ironically and took a key from a collection hung on nails behind the door. "If you *must* work," he said.

"Please."

"Personally escorted tour abaht to commence. Follow in single file and don't talk to the guide. I thank you."

She followed him to the stage and round the back of the set. He warned her of obstructions by bobbing his torchlight on them and, when she stumbled against a muffled table, took her hand. She was disquieted by the grip of his fingers, calloused, and wooden, and by the warmth of his palm which was unexpectedly soft. She was oppressed with renewed loneliness and fear.

"End of the penny section," he said, releasing her. He unlocked a door, reached inside and switched on a light.

"They call this the greenroom," he said. "That's what it was in the old days. It's been done up. Guvnor's idea."

It was a room without a window, newly painted in green. There were a number of arm-chairs in brown leather, a round table littered with magazines, a set of well-stocked book-shelves and a gas-fire. Groups of framed Pollock's prints decorated the walls: "Mr. Dale as Claude Amboine," "Mr. T. Hicks as Richard I," "Mr. S. French as Harlequin." This last enchanted Martyn because the diamonds of Mr. French's costume had been filled in with actual red and green sequins and he glittered in his frame.

Above the fire-place hung a largish sketch—it was little more than that—of a man of about thirty-five in medieval dress, with a hood that he was in the act of pushing away from his face. The face was arresting. It had great purity of form being wide across the eyes and heart shaped. The mouth, in particular, was of a most subtle character, perfectly masculine but drawn with extreme delicacy. It was well done: it had both strength and refinement yet it was not these qualities that disturbed Martyn. Reflected in the glass that covered the picture she saw her own face lying ghost-wise across the other; their forms intermingled like those in a twice-exposed photograph. It seemed to Martyn that her companion must be looking over her shoulder at this double image and she moved away from him and nearer to the picture. The reflection disappeared. Something was written faintly in one corner of the sketch. She drew closer and saw that it was a single word: "Everyman."

"Spitting image of him, ain't it?" said the doorkeeper behind her.

"I don't know," she said quickly; "is it?"

"*Is* it! Don't you know the guvnor when you see 'im?"

"The governor?"

"Streuth you're a caution and no error. Don't you know who owns this show? That's the great Mr. Adam Poole, that is."

"Oh," she murmured after a pause and added uneasily, "I've seen him in the pictures, of course."

"Go on!" he jeered. "Where would that be? Australia? Fancy!"

He had been very kind to her but she found his remorseless vein of irony exasperating. It would have been easier and less tedious to have let it go but she found herself embarked on an explanation. Of course she knew all about Mr. Adam Poole, she said. She had seen his photograph in the foyer. All his pictures had been shown in New Zealand. She knew he was the most distinguished of the younger contemporary actor-managers. She was merely startled by the painting, because . . . But it was impossible to explain why the face in the painting disturbed her and the unfinished phrase trailed away into an embarrassed silence.

Her companion listened to this rigmarole with an equivocal grin and when she gave it up merely remarked: "Don't apologise. It's the same with all the ladies: 'E fair rocks 'em. Talk about 'aving what it takes."

"I don't mean that at all," she shouted angrily.

"You should see 'em clawing at each other to get at 'im rahnd the stage-door, first nights. Something savage! Females of the speeches? Disgrace to their sexes more like. There's an ironing-board etceterer in the wardrobe-room farther along. You can plug in when you're ready. 'Er Royal 'Ighness is over the way."

He went out, opened a further door, switched on a light and called to her to join him.

III

As soon as she crossed the threshold of the star dressing-room she smelt greasepaint. The dressing-shelf was bare, the room untenanted, but the smell of cosmetics mingled with the faint reek of gas. There were isolated dabs of colour on the shelves and the looking-glass; the lamp-bulbs were smeared with cream and red where sticks of greasepaint had been warmed at them and on a shelf above the wash-basin

18

somebody had left a miniature frying-pan of congealed mascara in which a hair-pin was embedded.

It was a largish room, windowless and dank, with an air of submerged grandeur about it. The full-length cheval-glass swung from a gilt frame. There was an Empire couch, an arm-chair and an ornate stool before the dressing-shelf. The floor was carpeted in red with a florid pattern that use had in part obliterated. A number of dress-boxes bearing the legend " Costumes by Pierrot et Cie " were stacked in the middle of the room and there were two suitcases on the shelf. A gas-heater stood against one wall and there was a caged jet above the wash-basin.

" Here we are," said the doorkeeper. " All yer own."

She turned to thank him and encountered a speculative stare. " Cosy," he said, " ain't it?" and moved nearer. " Nice little hidey-hole, ain't it?"

" You've been very kind," Martyn said, " I'll manage splendidly now. Thank you very much, indeed."

" Don't mention it. Any time." His hand reached out clumsily to her. " Been arht in the rain," he said thickly. " Naughty girl."

" I'll soon dry off. I'm quite all right."

She moved behind the pile of dress-boxes and fumbled with the string on the top one. There was a hissing noise. She heard him strike a match and a moment later was horribly jolted by an explosion from the gas heater. It forced an involuntary cry from her.

" 'Allo, 'allo!" her companion said. " Ain't superstitious, are we?"

" Superstitious?"

He made an inexplicable gesture towards the gas-fire. " You know," he said, grinning horridly at her.

" I'm afraid I don't understand."

" Don't tell me you never 'eard abaht the great Jupiter case! Don't they learn you nothing in them anti-podes?"

The heater reddened and purred.

" Come to think of it," he said, " it'd be before your time. I wasn't here myself when it occurred, a-course, but them that was don't give you a chance to forget it. Not that they mention it direct-like but it don't get forgotten."

" What was it?" Martyn asked against her will.

" Sure yer not superstitious?"

" No, I'm not."

" You ain't been long in this business, then. Nor more am I. Shake 'ands." He extended his hand so pointedly that she was obliged to put her own in it and had some difficulty in releasing herself.

"It must be five years ago," he said, "all of that. A bloke in number four dressing-room did another bloke in, very cunning, by blowing dahn the tube of 'is own gas-fire. Like, if I went nex' door and blew dahn the tube, this fire'd go aht. And if you was dead drunk like you might of been if this girl friend of yours'd been very generous with 'er brandy you'd be commy-toes and before you knew where you was you'd be dead. Which is what occurred. It made a very nasty impression and the theatre was shut dahn for a long time until they 'ad it all altered and pansied up. The guvnor won't 'ave it mentioned. 'E changed the name of the 'ouse when 'e took it on. But call it what you like the memory, as they say, lingers on. Silly, though, ain't it? You and me don't care. That's right, isn't it? We'd rather be cosy. Wouldn't we?" He gave a kind of significance to the word "cosy." Martyn unlocked the suitcases. Her fingers were unsteady and she turned her back in order to hide them from him. He stood in front of the gas-fire and began to give out a smell of hot dirty cloth. She took sheets from the suitcase, hung them under the clothes pegs round the walls, and began to unpack the boxes. Her feet throbbed cruelly and, with a surreptitious manipulation, she shuffled them out of her wet shoes.

"That's the ticket," he said. "Dry 'em orf, shall we?"

He advanced upon her and squatted to gather up the shoes. His hand, large and prehensile, with a life of its own, darted out and closed over her foot. "'Ow abaht yer stockings?"

Martyn felt not only frightened but humiliated and ridiculous: wobbling, dead tired, on one foot. It was as if she were half caught in some particularly degrading kind of stocks.

She said: "Look here, you're a good chap. You've been terribly kind. Let me get on with the job."

His grip slackened. He looked up at her without embarrassment, his thin London face sharp with curiosity. "O.K.," he said. "No offence meant. Call it a day, eh?"

"Call it a day."

"You're the boss," he said and got to his feet. He put her shoes down in front of the gas-fire and went to the door. "Live far from 'ere?" he asked. A feeling of intense desolation swept through her and left her without the heart to prevaricate.

"I don't know," she said. "I've got to find somewhere. There's a women's hostel near Paddington, I think."

"Broke?"

"I'll be all right, now I've got this job."

His hand was in his pocket: "'Ere," he said.

"No, no. Please."

"Come orf it. We're pals ain't we?"

"No, really. I'm terribly grateful but I'd rather not. I'm all right."

"You're the boss," he said again, and after a pause: "I can't get the idea, honest I can't. The way you speak and be'ave and all. What's the story? 'Ard luck or what?"

"There's no story, really."

"Just what you say yourself. No questions asked." He opened the door and moved into the passage. "Mind," he said over his shoulder, "it's against the rules but I won't be rahnd again. My mate relieves me at eight ack emma but I'll tip 'im the wink if it suits you. Them chairs in the greenroom's not bad for a bit of kip and there's the fire. I'll turn it on. Please yerself a-course."

"Oh," she said, "could I? *Could* I?"

"Never know what you can do till you try. Keep it under your titfer, though, or I'll be in trouble. So long. Don't get down'earted. It'll be all the same in a fahsand years."

He had gone. Martyn ran into the passage and saw his torchlight bobbing out on the stage. She called after him: "Thank you—thank you so much. I don't know your name—but thank you and good night."

"Badger's the name," he said, and his voice sounded hollow in the empty darkness. "Call me Fred."

The light bobbed out of sight. She heard him whistling for a moment and then a door slammed and she was alone.

With renewed heart she turned back to her job.

IV

At ten o'clock she had finished. She had traversed with diligence all the hazards of fatigue: the mounting threat of sleep, the clumsiness that makes the simplest action an ordeal, the horror of inertia and the temptation to let go the tortured muscles and give up, finally and indifferently, the awful struggle.

Five carefully ironed dresses hung sheeted against the

21

walls, the make-up was laid out on the covered dressing-shelf. The boxes were stacked away, the framed photographs set out. It only remained to buy roses in the morning for Miss Helena Hamilton. Even the vase was ready and filled with water.

Martyn leant heavily on the back of a chair and stared at two photographs of the same face in a double leather-case. They were not theatre photographs but studio portraits and the face looked younger than the face in the greenroom: younger and more formidable, with the mouth set truculently and the gaze withdrawn. But it had the same effect on Martyn. Written at the bottom of each of these photographs, in a small incisive hand, was " Helena from Adam. 1950." " Perhaps," she thought, " he's married to her."

Hag-ridden by the fear that she had forgotten some important detail, she paused in the doorway and looked round the room. No, she thought, there was nothing more to be done. But as she turned to go she saw herself, cruelly reflected in the long cheval-glass. It was not, of course, the first time she had seen herself that night ; she had passed before the looking-glasses a dozen times and had actually polished them, but her attention had been ruthlessly fixed on the job in hand and she had not once focused her eyes on her own image. Now she did so. She saw a girl in a yellow sweater and dark skirt with black hair that hung in streaks over her forehead. She saw a white, heart-shaped face with smudges under the eyes and a mouth that was normally firm and delicate but now drooped with fatigue. She raised her hand, pushed the hair back from her face and stared for a moment or two longer. Then she switched off the light and blundered across the passage into the greenroom. Here, collapsed in an arm-chair with her overcoat across her, she slept heavily until morning.

CHAPTER II

IN A GLASS DARKLY

Martyn slept for ten hours. A wind got up in the night and found its way into the top of the stagehouse at the Vulcan. Up in the grid old back-cloths moved a little and, since the Vulcan was a hemp-house, there was a soughing among the forest of ropes. Flakes of paper, relics of some

Victorian snowstorm, were dislodged from the top of a batten and fluttered down to the stage. Rain, driven fitfully against the theatre, ran in cascades down pipes and dripped noisily from ledges into the stage-door entry. The theatre mice came out, explored the contents of paste-pots in the sink-room and scuttled unsuccessfully about a covered plate of tongue and veal. Out in the auditorium there arose at intervals a vague whisper and in his cubby-hole off the dock Fred Badger dozed and woke uneasily. At one o'clock he went on his rounds. He padded down corridors, flicking his torchlight on framed sketches for décor and costumes, explored the foyer and examined the locked doors of the offices. He climbed the heavily carpeted stairs and, lost in meditation, stood for a long time in the dress-circle among shrouded rows of seats and curtained doorways. Sighing dolorously he returned back-stage and made a stealthy entrance on to the set. Finally he creaked to the greenroom door and impelled by who knows what impulse furtively opened it.

Martyn lay across the chair, her knees supported underneath by one of its arms and her head by the other. The glow from the gas-fire was reflected in her face. Fred Badger stood for quite a long time eyeing her and scraping his chin with calloused fingers. At last he backed out, softly closed the door and tiptoed to his cubby-hole, where he telephoned the fire-station to make his routine report.

At dawn the rain stopped and cleaning vans swept the water down Carpet Street with their great brushes. Milk-carts clinked past the Vulcan and the first bus roared by. Martyn heard none of them. She woke to the murmur of the gas-fire, and the confused memory of a dream in which someone tapped gently at a door. The windowless room was still dark but she looked at her watch in the fire-glow and found it was eight o'clock. She got up stiffly, crossed the room and opened the door on grey diffused daylight. A cup of tea with a large sandwich balanced on it had been left on the floor of the passage. Underneath it was a torn scrap of paper on which was scrawled: " Keep your pecker up matey see you some more."

With a feeling of gratitude and timid security she breakfasted in the greenroom, and afterwards explored the empty passage, finding at the far end an unlocked and unused dressing-room. To this room she brought her own suitcase and here, with a chair propped under the door handle, she stripped and washed in icy water. In clean clothes, with her toilet complete, and with a feeling of detachment, as if she herself looked on from a distance at these proceedings, she crossed the stage and went out through the side door and up the alley-way into Carpet Street.

It was a clean sunny morning. The air struck sharply at her lips and nostrils and the light dazzled her. A van had drawn up outside the Vulcan and men were lifting furniture from it. There were cleaners at work in the foyer and a telegraph boy came out whistling. Carpet Street was noisy with traffic. Martyn turned left and walked quickly downhill until she came to a corner shop called Florian. In the window a girl in a blue overall was setting out a large gilt basket of roses. The door was still locked, but Martyn, emboldened by fresh air and a sense of freedom and adventure, tapped on the window and when the girl looked up, pointed to the roses and held up Mr. Grantley's card. The girl smiled and, leaving the window, came to let her in.

Martyn said: " I'm sorry to bother you but Mr. Grantley at the Vulcan told me to get some roses for Miss Helena Hamilton. He didn't give me any money and I'm afraid I haven't got any. Is all this very irregular and tiresome?"

"That will be quayte O.K.," the girl said in a friendly manner. "Mr. Grantley has an account."

"Perhaps you know what sort of roses I should get," Martyn suggested. She felt extraordinarily light and rather loquacious. "You see, I'm Miss Hamilton's dresser but I'm new and I don't know what she likes."

"Red would be quayte in order, I think. There are some lovely Bloody Warriors just in." She caught Martyn's eye and giggled. "Well, they do think of the weirdest names, don't they? Look: aren't they lovelies?"

She held up a group of roses with drops of water clinging to their half-opened petals. "Gorgeous," she said, ' aren't they? Such a colour."

Martyn, appalled at the price, took a dozen. The girl looked curiously at her and said: "Miss Hamilton's dresser. Fancy! Aren't you lucky?" and she was vividly reminded of Fred Badger.

"I feel terribly lucky this morning," she said and was going away when the girl, turning pink under her make-up, said: "Pardon me asking but I don't suppose you could get me Miss Hamilton's autograph. I'd be ever so thrilled."

"I haven't even seen her yet but I'll do my best."

"You are a ducks. Thanks a million. Of course," the girl added, "I'm a real fan. I never miss any of her pictures and I do think Adam Poole—pardon me, Mr.

24

Poole—is simply mawvellous. I mean to say I just think he's mawvellous. They're so mawvellous together. I suppose he's crazy about her in real life, isn't he? I always say they couldn't ect together like that—you know—so gorgeously—unless they had a pretty hot clue on the sayde. Don't you agree?"

Martyn said she hadn't had a chance of forming an opinion as yet and left the florist in pensive contemplation of the remaining Bloody Warriors.

When she got back to the theatre its character had completely changed; it was alive and noisy. The dock-doors were open and sunlight lay in incongruous patches on painted canvas and stacked furniture. Up in the grid there was a sound of hammering. A back-cloth hung diagonally in mid-air and descended in jerks, while a man in shirt sleeves shouted " Down on yer long. Now yer short. Now bodily. Right-oh. Dead it. Now find yer Number Two."

A chandelier lay in a heap in the middle of the stage and, above it, was suspended a batten of spotlights within reach of an elderly mechanist who fitted pink and straw-coloured mediums into their frames. Near the stage-door a group of men stared at a small empire desk from which a stage-hand had removed a cloth wrapping. A tall young man in spectacles, wearing a red pullover and corduroy trousers, said irritably: " It's too bloody chi-chi. Without a shadow of doubt, he'll hate its guts."

He glanced at Martyn and added: " Put them in her room, dear, will you?"

She hurried to the dressing-room passage and found that here too, there was life and movement. A vacuum-cleaner hummed in the greenroom, a bald man in overalls was tacking cards on the doors, somewhere down the passage an unseen person sang cheerfully and the door next to Miss Hamilton's was open. These signs of preparation awakened in Martyn a sense of urgency. In a sudden fluster she unwrapped her roses and thrust them into the vase. The stalks were too long and she had nothing to cut them with. She ran down the passage to the empty room, and reflected as she rootled in her suit-case that she would be expected to have sewing materials at hand. Here was the housewife an aunt had given her when she left New Zealand but it was depleted and in a muddle. She ran back with it, sawed at the rose stems with her nail-scissors and when someone in the next room tapped on the wall, inadvertently jammed the points into her hand.

25

"And how," a disembodied voice inquired, "is La Belle Tansey this morning?"

Sucking her left hand and arranging roses with her right, Martyn wondered how she should respond to this advance. She called out, tentatively: "I'm afraid it's not Miss Tansey."

"What's that?" the voice said vaguely, and a moment later she heard the brisk sound of a clothes-brush at work.

The roses were done at last. She stood with the ends of the stalks in her hand and wondered why she had become so nervous.

"Here we go again," a voice said in the doorway. She spun round to face a small man in an alpaca coat with a dinner-jacket in his hands. He stared at her with his jaw dropped. "Pardon me," he said. "I thought you was Miss Tansey."

Martyn explained.

"Well!" he said. "That'll be her heart, that will. She ought to have given up before this. I warned her. In hospital, too? T'ch, t'ch, t'ch." He wagged his head and looked, apparently in astonishment, at Martyn. "So that's the story," he continued, "and you've stepped into the breach? Fancy that! Better introduce ourselves, hadn't we? The name's Cringle but Bob'll do as well as anything else. I'm 'is lordship's dresser. How are you?"

Martyn gave him her name and they shook hands. He had a pleasant face covered with a cobweb of fine wrinkles. "Been long at this game?" he asked and added: "Well, that's a foolish question, isn't it? I should have said: will this be your first place or are you doing it in your school holidays or something of that sort."

"Do you suppose," Martyn said anxiously, "Miss Hamilton will think I'm too young?"

"Not if you give satisfaction you won't. She's all right if you give satisfaction. Different from my case. Slave meself dizzy, I can, and if 'is lordship's in one of 'is moods, what do I get for it? Spare me days, I don't know why I put up with it and that's a fact: But *she's* all right if she likes you." He paused and added tentatively: "but you know all about that, I dare say." Martyn was silent and felt his curiosity reach out as if it was something tangible. At last she said desperately: "I'll try. I want to give satisfaction."

He glanced round the room. "Looks nice," he said. "Are you pressed and shook out? Yes, I can see you are.

26

Flowers too. Very nice. Would you be a friend of hers? Doing it to oblige, like?"

"No, no. I've never seen her. Except in the pictures, of course."

"Is that a fact?" His rather bird-like eyes were bright with speculation. "Young ladies," he said, "have to turn their hands to all sorts of work these days, don't they?"

"I suppose so. Yes."

"No offence, I hope, but I was wondering if you come from one of these drama schools. Hoping to learn a bit, watching from the side, like."

A kind of sheepishness that had hardened into obstinacy prevented her from telling him in a few words, why she was there. The impulse of a fortnight ago to rush to somebody—the ship's captain, the High Commissioner for her own country, anyone—and unload her burden of disaster, had given place almost at once to a determined silence. This mess was of her own making, she had decided, and she herself would see it out. And throughout the loneliness and panic of her ordeal, to this resolution she had stuck. It had ceased to be a reasoned affair with Martyn: the less she said, the less she wanted to say. She had become crystallised in reticence.

So she met the curiosity of the little dresser with an evasion. "It'd be wonderful," she said, "if I did get the chance."

A deep voice with an unusually vibrant quality called out on the stage. "Bob! Where the devil have you got to? Bob!"

"Cripes!" the little dresser ejaculated. "Here we are *and* in one of our tantrums. *In here, sir! Coming, sir.*"

He darted towards the doorway but before he reached it a man appeared there, a man so tall that for a fraction of a second he looked down over the dresser's head directly into Martyn's eyes.

"This young lady," Bob Cringle explained with an air of discovery, "is the new dresser for Miss Hamilton. I just been showing her the ropes, Mr. Poole, sir."

"You'd much better attend to your work. I want you." He glanced again at Martyn. "Good morning," he said and was gone. "Look at this!" she heard him say angrily in the next room. "Where *are* you!"

Cringle paused in the doorway to turn his thumbs down and his eyes up. "Here we are, sir. What's the little trouble?" he said pacifically, and disappeared.

Martyn thought: "The picture in the greenroom is more like him than the photographs." Preoccupied with this discovery she was only vaguely aware of a fragrance in the air and a new voice in the passage. The next moment her employer came into the dressing-room.

II

An encounter with a person hitherto only seen and heard on the cinema screen is often disconcerting. It is as if the two-dimensional and enormous image had contracted about a living skeleton and in taking on substance had acquired an embarrassing normality. One is not always glad to change the familiar shadow for the strange reality.

Helena Hamilton was a blonde woman. She had every grace. To set down in detail the perfections of her hair, eyes, mouth and complexion, her shape and the gallantry of her carriage would be to reiterate merely, that which everyone had seen in her innumerable pictures. She was, in fact, quite astonishingly beautiful. Even the circumstance of her looking somewhat older than her moving shadow could not modify the shock of finding her its equal in everything but this.

Coupled with her beauty was her charm. This was famous. She could reduce press conferences to a conglomerate of eager, even naïve, males. She could make a curtain-speech that every leading woman in every theatre in the English-speaking world had made before her and persuade the last man in the audience that it was original. She could convince bit-part actresses playing maids in first acts that there, but for the grace of God, went she.

On Martyn, however, taken off her balance and entirely by surprise, it was Miss Hamilton's smell that made the first impression. At ten guineas a moderately sized bottle, she smelt like Master Fenton, all April and May. Martyn was very much shorter than Miss Hamilton but this did not prevent her from feeling cumbersome and out of place, as if she had been caught red-handed with her own work in the dressing-room. This awkwardness was in part dispelled by the friendliness of Miss Hamilton's smile and the warmth of her enchanting voice.

"You've come to help me, haven't you?" she said. "Now, that *is* kind. I know all about you from Mr. Grantley

28

and I fully expect we'll get along famously together. The only thing I *don't* know, in fact, is your name."

Martyn wondered if she ought to give only her Christian name or only her surname. She said: "Tarne. Martyn Tarne."

"But what a charming name!" The brilliant eyes looked into Martyn's face and their gaze sharpened. After a fractional pause she repeated: "Really charming," and turned her back.

It took Martyn a moment or two to realise that this was her cue to remove Miss Hamilton's coat. She lifted it from her shoulders—it was made of Persian lamb and smelt delicious—and hung it up. When she turned round she found that her employer was looking at her. She smiled reassuringly at Martyn and said: "You've got everything arranged very nicely. Roses, too. Lovely."

"They're from Mr. Grantley."

"Sweet of him but I bet he sent you to buy them."

"Well——" Martyn began and was saved by the entry of the young man in the red sweater with a dressing-case for which she was given the keys. While she was unpacking it the door opened and a middle-aged, handsome man with a raffish face and an air of boldness came in. She remembered the photographs in the foyer. This was Clark Bennington. He addressed himself to Miss Hamilton.

"Hallo," he said, "I've been talking to John Rutherford."

"What about?" she asked and sounded nervous.

"About that kid. Young Gay. He's been at her again. So's Adam."

He glanced at Martyn. "I wanted to talk to you," he added discontentedly.

"Well, so you shall. But I've got to change, now, Ben. And, look, this is my new dresser, Martyn Tarne."

He eyed Martyn with more attention. "Quite a change from old Tansey," he said. "And a very nice change, too." He turned away. "Is Adam down?" He jerked his head at the wall.

"Yes."

"I'll see you later, then."

"All right, but—yes, all right."

He went out, leaving a faint rumour of alcohol behind him. She was quite still for a moment after he had gone. Martyn heard her fetch a sigh, a sound half-impatient, half-anxious. "Oh well," she said, "let's get going, shall we?"

Martyn had been much exercised about the extent of her duties. Did, for instance, a dresser undress her employer? Did she kneel at her feet and roll down her stockings? Did she unhook and unbutton? Or did she stand capably aside while these rites were performed by the principal herself. Miss Hamilton solved the problem by removing her dress, throwing it to Martyn and waiting to be inserted into her dressing-gown. During these operations a rumble of male voices sounded at intervals in the adjoining room. Presently there was a tap at the door. Martyn answered it and found the little dresser with a florists' box in his hands. "Mr. Poole's compliments," he said and winked broadly before retiring.

Miss Hamilton by this time was spreading a yellow film over her face. She asked Martyn to open the box and, on seeing three orchids that lay, crisp and fabulous on their mossy bed, sang "Darling!" on two clear notes.

The voice beyond the wall responded. "Hallo?"

"They're quite perfect. Thank you, my sweet."

"Good," the voice said. Martyn laid the box on the dressing-table and saw the card: "Until to-morrow. Adam."

She got through the next half-hour pretty successfully, she hoped. There seemed to be no blunders and Miss Hamilton continued charming and apparently delighted. There were constant visitors. A tap on the door would be followed by a head looking round and always by the invitation to come in. First there was Miss Gay Gainsford, a young and rather intense person with a pretty air of deference who seemed to be in a state of extreme anxiety.

"Well, darling," Miss Hamilton said, glancing at her in the glass: "Everything under strict control?"

Miss Gainsford said unevenly: "I suppose so. I'm trying to be good and sort of *biddable,* do you know, but underneath I realise that I'm seething like a cauldron. Butterflies the size of *bats* in the stomach."

"Well, of course. But you mustn't be terrified really, because whatever happens we all know John's written a good play, don't we?"

"I suppose we do."

"We do indeed. And Gay—you're going to make a great personal success in this part. I want you to tell yourself you are. Do you know? *Tell* yourself."

"I wish I could believe it." Miss Gainsford clasped her hands and raised them to her lips. "It's not very easy," she said, "when he—John—Dr. Rutherford—so obviously

30

thinks I'm a misfit. Everybody keeps telling me it's a marvellous part but for me it's twenty sides of hopeless hell. Honestly, it is."

"Gay, what *nonense*. John may seem hard——"

"*Seem?*"

"Well, he may *be* hard, then. He's famous for it, after all. But you'll get your reward, my dear, when the time comes. Remember," said Miss Hamilton with immense gravity, "we all have faith in you."

"Of course," said Miss Gainsford with an increased quaver in her voice, "it's too marvellous your feeling like that about it. You've been so miraculously kind. And Uncle Ben, of course. Both of you. I can't get over it."

"But, my dear, that's utter nonsense. You're going to be one of our rising young actresses."

"You do *really* think so!"

"But yes. We all do." Her voice lost a little colour and then freshened. "We all do," she repeated firmly and turned back to her glass.

Miss Gainsford went to the door and hesitated there. "Adam doesn't," she said loudly.

Miss Hamilton made a quick expressive gesture toward the next dressing-room and put her fingers to her lips. "He'll be *really* angry if he hears you say that," she whispered and added aloud with somewhat forced casualness: "Is John down this morning?"

"He's on-stage. I think he said he'd like to speak to you."

"I want to see him particularly. Will you tell him, darling?"

"Of course, Aunty Ella," Miss Gainsford said rather miserably and added, "I'm sorry. I forgot. Of course, Ella, darling." With a wan smile she was gone.

"Oh, dear!" Miss Hamilton sighed and catching Martyn's eye in the looking-glass made a rueful face. "If only——" she began and stopped unaccountably, her gaze still fixed on Martyn's image. "Never mind," she said.

There was a noisy footfall in the passage followed by a bang on the door, and, with scarcely a pause for permission, by the entry of a large, florid and angry-looking man wearing a sweater, a leather waistcoat, a muffler and a very old duffel coat.

"Good morning, John darling," said Miss Hamilton gaily and extended her hand. The new-comer planted a smacking kiss on it and fixed Martyn with a china-blue and bulging pair of eyes. Martyn turned away from this embarrassing regard.

"What have we here?" he demanded. His voice was loud and rumbling.

"My new dresser. Dr. Rutherford, Martyn."

"Stay me with flagons!" said Dr. Rutherford. He turned on Miss Hamilton. "That fool of a wench Gainsford said you wanted me," he said. "What's up?"

"John, *what* have you been saying to that child?"

"I? Nothing. Nothing to what I could, and, mark you, what I ought to say to her. I merely asked her if, for the sake of my sanity she'd be good enough to play the central scene without a goddam simper on her fat and wholly unsuitable dial."

"You're frightening her."

"She's terrifying me. She may be your niece, Ella——"

"She's not my niece. She's Ben's niece."

"If she was the Pope's niece she'd still be a goddam pain in the neck. I wrote this part for an intelligent actress who could be made to look reasonably like Adam. What do you give me? A moronic amateur who looks like nothing on God's earth."

"She's extremely pretty."

"Lollypops! Adam's too damn' easy on her. The only hope lies in shaking her up. Or kicking her out and I'd do that myself if I had my way. It ought to have been done a month back. Even now——"

"Oh, my *dear* John! We open in two days you might remember."

"An actress worth her salt'd memorise it in an hour. I told her——"

"I do beg you," she said, "to leave her to Adam. After all he is the producer, John, and he's very wise."

Dr. Rutherford pulled out of some submerged pocket a metal box. From this he extracted a pinch of snuff which he took with loud and uncouth noises.

"In a moment," he said, "you'll be telling me the author ought to keep out of the theatre."

"That's utter nonsense."

"Let them try to keep *me* out," he said and burst into a neighing laugh.

Miss Hamilton slightly opened her mouth, hardened her upper lip, and with the closest attention, painted it a purplish red. "Really," she said briskly, "you'd much better behave prettily, you know. You'll end by having her on your hands with a nervous breakdown."

"The sooner the better if it's a good one."

"Honestly, John, you are the rock *bottom* when you get like this. If you didn't write the plays you do write—if you weren't the greatest dramatist since——"

"Spare me the raptures," he said, "and give me some actors. And while we're on the subject I may as well tell you that I don't like the way Ben is shaping in the big scene. If Adam doesn't watch him he'll be up to some bloody leading-man hocus-pocus and by God if he trys that on I'll wring his neck for him."

She turned and faced him. "John, he *won't*. I'm sure he won't."

"No, you're not. You can't be sure. Nor can I. But if there's any sign of it to-night, and Adam doesn't tackle him, I will. I'll tickle his catastrophe, by God I will. As for that Mongolian monstrosity, that discard from the wax-works, Mr. Parry Percival; what devil—will you answer me—what inverted sadist foisted it on my play?"

"Now, look here, John——" Miss Hamilton began with some warmth and was shouted down.

"Have I not stipulated from the beginning of my disastrous association with this ill-fated playhouse that I would have none of these abortions in my works? These Things. These foetid Growths. These Queers."

"Parry isn't one."

"Yah! He shrieks it. I have an instinct, my girl. I nose them as I go into the lobby."

She made a gesture of despair: "I give up," she said.

He helped himself to another pinch of snuff. "Hooey!" he snorted. "You don't do anything of the sort, my sweetiepie. You're going to rock 'em, you and Adam. Think of that and preen yourself. And leave all the rest—to *me*."

"Don't quote from Macbeth. If Gay Gainsford heard you doing that she really would go off at the deep end."

"Which is precisely where I'd like to push her."

"Oh, go away," she cried out impatiently but with an air of good nature. "I've had you. You're wonderful and you're hopeless. Go away."

"The audience is concluded?" He scraped the parody of a regency bow.

"The audience is concluded. The door, Martyn."

Martyn opened the door. Until then, feeling wretchedly in the way, she had busied herself with the stack of suitcases in the corner of the room and now, for the first time, came absolutely face to face with the visitor. He eyed her with an extraordinary air of astonishment.

"Here!" he said. "Hi!"

"No, John," Miss Hamilton said with great determination. "No!"

"*Eureka!*"

"Nothing of the sort. Good morning."

He gave a shrill whistle and swaggered out. Martyn turned back to find her employer staring into the glass. Her hands trembled and she clasped them together. "Martyn," she said, "I'm going to call you Martyn because it's such a nice name. You know, a dresser is rather a particular sort of person. She has to be as deaf as a post and as blind as a bat to almost everything that goes on under her very nose. Dr. Rutherford is, as I expect you know, a most distinguished and brilliant person. Our Greatest English Playwright. But like many brilliant people," Miss Hamilton continued in what Martyn couldn't help thinking a rather too special voice, "he is *eccentric*. We all understand and we expect you to do so too. Do you know?"

Martyn said she did.

"Good. Now, put me into that pink thing and let us know the worst about it, shall we?"

When she was dressed she stood before the cheval-glass and looked with cold intensity at her image. "My God," she said, "the lighting had better be good."

Martyn said: "Isn't it right? It looks lovely to me."

"My poor girl!" she muttered. "You run to my husband and ask him for cigarettes. He's got my case. I need a stimulant."

Martyn hurried into the passage and tapped at the next door. "So they are married," she thought. "He must be ten years younger than she is but they're married and he still sends her orchids in the morning."

The deep voice shouted impatiently: "Come in!" and she opened the door and went in.

The little dresser was putting Poole into a dinner jacket. Their backs were turned to Martyn. "Yes?" Poole said.

"Miss Hamilton would like her cigarette-case, if you please."

"I haven't got it," he said and shouted: "Ella!"

"Hallo, darling?"

"I haven't got your case."

There was a considerable pause. The voice beyond the

wall called: " No, no. Ben's got it. Mr. Bennington, Martyn."

" I'm so sorry," Martyn said, and made for the door, conscious of the little dresser's embarrassment and of Poole's annoyance.

Mr. Clark Bennington's room was on the opposite side of the passage and next the greenroom. On her entrance Martyn was abruptly and most unpleasantly transported into the immediate past—into yesterday with its exhaustion, muddle and panic, to the moment of extreme humiliation when Fred Badger had smelt brandy in her breath. Mr. Bennington's flask was open on his dressing-shelf and he was in the act of entertaining a thick-set gentleman with beautifully groomed white hair, wearing a monocle, in a strikingly handsome face. This person set down his tumbler and gazed in a startled fashion at Martyn.

" It's not," he said, evidently picking up, with some difficulty, the conversation she had interrupted, " it's not that I would for the world interfere, Ben, dear boy. Nor do I enjoy raising what is no doubt a delicate subject in these particular circumstances. But I feel for the child damnably, you know. Damnably. Moreover, it does rather appear that the doctor never loses an opportunity to upset her."

" I couldn't agree more, old boy, and I'm bloody angry about it. Yes, dear, wait a moment, will you?" Mr. Bennington rejoined, running his speeches together and addressing them to no one in particular. " This is my wife's new dresser, J. G."

" Really?" Mr. J. G. Darcey responded and bowed politely to Martyn. " Good morning, child. See you later, Ben, my boy. Thousand thanks."

He rose, looked kindly at Martyn, dropped his monocle, passed his hand over his hair and went out, breaking into operatic song in the passage.

Mr. Bennington made a half-hearted attempt to put his flask out of sight and addressed himself to Martyn.

" And what," he asked, " can I do for the new dresser?" Martyn delivered her message. " Cigarette-case? Have I got my wife's cigarette-case? God, I don't know. Try my overcoat, dear, will you? Behind the door. Inside pocket. No secrets," he added obscurely. " Forgive my asking you. I'm busy."

But he didn't seem particularly busy. He twisted round in his chair and watched Martyn as she made a fruitless search of his overcoat pockets. " This your first job?" he asked.

She said it was not and he added: " As a dresser, I mean."

" I've worked in the theatre before."

" And where was that?"

" In New Zealand."

"*Really?*" he said as if she had answered some vitally important question.

" I'm afraid," Martyn went on quickly, " it's not in the overcoat."

" God, what a bore! Give me my jacket then, would you? The grey flannel."

She handed it to him and he fumbled through the pockets. A pocket-book dropped on the floor, spilling its contents. Martyn gathered them together and he made such a clumsy business of taking them from her that she was, obliged to put them on the shelf. Among them was an envelope bearing a foreign stamp and postmark. He snatched it up and it fluttered in his fingers. " Mustn't lose track of that one, must we?" he said and laughed. " All the way from Uncle Tito." He thrust it at Martyn. " Look," he said and steadied his hand against the edge of the shelf. " What d'you think of *that*? Take it."

Troubled at once by the delay and by the oddness of his manner Martyn took the envelope and saw that it was addressed to Bennington.

" Do you collect autographs?" Bennington asked with ridiculous intensity—" or signed letters?"

" No, I'm afraid I don't," she said and put the letter face down on the shelf.

" There's someone," he said with a jab of his finger at the envelope, " who'd give a hell of a lot for *that* one in there. A hell of a lot."

He burst out laughing, pulled a cigarette-case out of the jacket and handed it to her with a flourish. " Purest gold," he said. " Birthday present but not from me. I'm her husband you know. What the hell! Are you leaving me! Don't go."

Martyn made her escape and ran back to Miss Hamilton's room where she found her in conference with Adam Poole and a young man of romantic appearance whom she recognised as the original of the last of the photographs in the foyer—Mr. Parry Percival. The instinct that makes us aware of a conversation in which we ourselves have in our absence been involved, warned Martyn that they had been talking about her and had broken off on her entrance. After a moment's silence, Mr. Percival, with far too elaborate a nonchalance, said: "Yes: well there you have it," and it was obvious that there was a kind of double significance in this remark. Miss Hamilton said: "My poor Martyn, where *have* you been?" with a lightness that was not quite cordial.

"I'm sorry," Martyn said: "Mr. Bennington had trouble in finding the case." She hesitated for a moment and added, "Madam."

"That," Miss Hamilton rejoined, looking at Adam Poole, "rings dismally true. Would you believe it, darling, I became so furious with him for taking it that, most reluctantly, I gave him one for himself. He lost it instantly of course and now swears he didn't and mine is his. If you follow me."

"With considerable difficulty," Poole said, "I do."

Parry Percival laughed gracefully. He had a winning, if not altogether authentic air of ingenuousness, and at the moment seemed to be hovering on the edge of some indiscretion. "I am afraid," he said ruefully to Miss Hamilton, "I'm rather in disgrace myself."

"With me, or with Adam?"

"I hope not with either of you. With Ben." He glanced apologetically at Poole, who did not look at him. "Because of the part, I mean. I suppose I spoke out of turn, but I really did think I could play it—still do for a matter of that, but there it is."

It was obvious that he was speaking at Poole. Martyn saw Miss Hamilton look from one man to the other before she said lightly, "I think you could too, Parry, but as you say, there it is. Ben *has* got a flair, you know."

Percival laughed. "He has indeed," he said, "he has had it for twenty years. Sorry. I shouldn't have said that. Honestly, I *am* sorry."

Poole said, "I dislike post-mortems on casting, Parry."

"I know, I *do* apologise." Percival turned ingratiatingly, and the strong light caught his face sideways. Martyn saw with astonishment that under the thin film of greasepaint there was a system of incipient lines, and she realised that he was not, after all a young man. "I know," he repeated, "I'm being naughty."

Poole said, "We open on Thursday. The whole thing was thrashed out weeks ago. Any discussion now is completely fruitless."

"That," said Miss Hamilton, "is what I have been trying to tell the doctor."

"John? I heard him bellowing in here," Poole said. "Where's he gone? I want a word with him. And with you, Parry, by the way. It's about that scene at the window in the second act. You're not making your exit line. You must top Ben there. It's most important."

"Look, old boy," Mr. Percival said with agonised intensity, "I *know*. It's just another of those things. Have you *seen* what Ben does? Have you seen that business with my handkerchief? He won't take his hands off me. The whole exit gets messed up."

"I'll see what can be done."

"John," said Miss Hamilton, "is worried about it too, Adam."

Poole said: "Then he should talk to me."

"You know what the doctor is."

"We all do," said Parry Percival, "and the public, I fear, is beginning to find out. God, there I go again."

Poole looked at him. "You'll get along better, I think, Parry, if you deny yourself these cracks against the rest of the company. Rutherford has written a serious play. It'd be a pity if any of us should lose faith in it."

Percival reddened and made towards the door. "I'm just being a nuisance," he said, "I'll take myself off and be photographed like a good boy." He made an insinuating movement of his shoulders towards Miss Hamilton, and fluttered his hand at her dress. "Marvellous," he said, "a triumph, if the bit-part actor may be allowed to say so."

The door shut crisply behind him, and Miss Hamilton said: "Darling, aren't you rather high and grand with poor Parry?"

"I don't think so. He's behaving like an ass. He couldn't play the part. He was born to be a feed."

"He'd *look* it."

"If all goes well Ben will *be* it."

"If all goes well! Adam, I'm terrified. He's——"

"Are you dressed, Ella? The cameras are ready."

"Shoes, please, Martyn," said Miss Hamilton. "Yes, darling. I'm right."

Martyn fastened her shoes and then opened the door. Miss Hamilton swept out, lifting her skirts with great elegance. Martyn waited for Poole to follow, but he said: "You're meant to be on-stage. Take make-up and a glass and whatever Miss Hamilton may need for her hair."

She thanked him and in a flurry gathered the things together. Poole took the Persian lamb coat and stood by the door. She hesitated, expecting him to precede her, but found that he was looking at the cheval-glass. When she followed his gaze

38

it was to be confronted by their images, side by side in the glass.

"Extraordinary," he said abruptly, "isn't it?" and motioned her to go out.

When Martyn went out on the stage she was able for the first time to see the company assembled together, and found it consisted, as far as the players were concerned, of no more than the six persons she had already encountered: first in their fixed professional poses in the show-frame at the front of the house, and later in their dressing-rooms. She had attached mental tags to them and found herself thinking of Helen Hamilton as the Leading Lady, of Gay Gainsford as the Ingenue, of J. G. Darcey as the Character Actor, of Parry Percival as the Juvenile, of Clark Bennington regrettably, perhaps unjustly, as the Drunken Actor, and of Adam Poole— but as yet she had found no label for Poole, unless it was the old-fashioned one of "Governor," which pleased her by its vicarious association with the days of the Victorian actor-managers.

To this actual cast of six she must add a number of satellite figures—the author, Dr. John Rutherford, whose eccentricities seemed to surpass those of his legend, with which she was already acquainted, the man in the red sweater who was the stage-manager, and was called Clem Smith, his assistant, a morose lurking figure, and the crew of stage-hands who went about their business or contemplated the actors with equal detachment.

The actors were forming themselves now into a stage "picture," moving in a workmanlike manner, under the direction of Adam Poole, and watched with restless atten- tiveness by an elderly, slack-jointed man, carrying a paint pot and brushes. This man, the last of all the figures to appear upon the stage that morning, seemed to have no recognisable job but to be concerned in all of them. He was dressed in overalls and a tartan shirt, from which his long neck emerged, bird-like and crapulous, to terminate in a head that wobbled slightly as if its articulation with the top of the spine had loosened with age. He was constantly addressed with exas- perated affection as Jacko. Under his direction, bunches of lights were wheeled into position, camera men peered and muttered, and at his given signal the players, by an easy transition in behaviour and appearance, became larger than life. A gap was left in the middle of the group, and into this when all was ready floated Helena Hamilton, ruffling her plumage, and becoming at once the focal point of the picture.

" Darling," she said, " it's not going to be a flash, is it, with all of you looking like village idiots, and me like the Third Witch on the morning after the cauldron scene?"

" If you can hold it for three seconds," Adam Poole said, " it needn't be a flash."

" I can hold anything, if you come in and help me."

He moved in beside her. " All right," he said, " let's try it. The end of the first act," and at once she turned upon him a look of tragic and burning intensity. The elderly man wandered across and tweaked at her skirts. Without changing pose or expression, she said, " Isn't it shameful the way Jacko can't keep his hands off me." He grinned and ambled away. Adam Poole said " Right," the group froze in postures of urgency that led the eye towards the two central figures and the cameras clicked.

Martyn tried, as the morning wore on, to get some idea of the content of the play but was unable to do so. Occasionally the players would speak snatches of dialogue leading up to the moment when a photograph was to be taken, and from these she gathered that the major conflict of the theme was between the characters played by Adam Poole and Clark Bennington and that this conflict was one of ideas. About a particular shot there was a great deal of difficulty. In this Poole and Gay Gainsford confronted each other and it was necessary that her posture, the arrested gesture of her hand and even her expression should be an exact reflection of his.

To Martyn, Poole had seemed to be a short-tempered man, but with Gay Gainsford he showed exemplary patience. " It's the old story, Gay," he said, " you're over-anxious. It's not enough for you to look like me. Let's face it," he hesitated for a moment and said quickly, " we've had all this, haven't we—but it's worth repeating—you can't look strikingly like me, although Jacko's done wonders. What you've got to do is to *be* me. At this moment, don't you see, you're my heredity, confronting me like a threat. As far as the photograph is concerned, we can cheat—the shot can be taken over your shoulder, but in the performance there can be no cheating, and that is why I'm making such a thing of it. Now let's take it with the line. Your head's on your arms, you raise it slowly to face me. Ready now. Right, up you come."

Miss Gainsford raised her face to his as he leaned across the writing-desk and whispered: "*Don't you like what you see?*" At the same moment there was a cascade of laughter from Miss Hamilton. Poole's voice cracked like a whip-lash, " Helena, please," and she turned from Parry Percival to say, " Darling, I'm so sorry," and in the same breath spoke her line of dialogue: "*But it's you, don't you see, you can't escape from it, it's you.*" Gay Gainsford made a hopeless little gesture and Poole said: " Too late, of course. Try again."

They tried several times, in an atmosphere of increasing tension. The amiable Jacko was called in to make an infinitesimal change in Gay's make-up, and Martyn saw him blot away a tear. At this juncture a disembodied voice roared from the back of the circle: "*Sister, have comfort. All of us have cause to wail the dimming of our shining star.*"

Poole glanced into the auditorium. " Do shut up like a good chap, John," he said.

"*Pour all your tears! I am your sorrows nurse*
And I will pamper it with la-men-ta-ti-ons."

The man called Jacko burst out laughing and was instantly dismissed to the dressing-rooms by Poole.

There followed a quarter of an hour of mounting hysteria on the part of Gay Gainsford and of implacable persistence from Adam Poole. He said suddenly, " All right, we'll cheat. Shift the camera."

The remaining photographs were taken without a great deal of trouble. Miss Gainsford, looking utterly miserable, went off to her dressing-room. The man called Jacko reappeared and ambled across to Miss Hamilton. There was an adjustment in make-up while Martyn held up the mirror.

" Maybe it's lucky," he said, " you don't have to look like somebody else."

" Are you being nice or beastly, Jacko?"

He put a cigarette between her lips and lit it. " The dresses are good," he said. He had a very slight foreign accent.

" You think so, do you?"

" Naturally. I design them for *you.*"

" Next time," she said gently, " you'd better write the play as well."

He was a phenomenally ugly man but a smile of extraordinary sweetness broke across his face.

" All these agonies!" he murmured, " and on Thursday night everyone will be kissing everyone else and at the

Combined Arts Ball we are in triumph and on Friday morning you will be purring over your notices. And you must not be unkind about the play. It is a good play." He grinned again, more broadly. His teeth were enormous and uneven. " Even the little niece of the great husband cannot entirely destroy it."

" Jacko!"

" You may say what you like, it is not intelligent casting."

" Please, Jacko."

" All right, all right. I remind you instead of the Combined Arts Ball, and that no one has decided in what costume we go."

" Nobody has any ideas. Jacko, you must invent something marvellous."

" And in two days I must also create out of air eight marvellous costumes."

" Darling Jacko, how beastly we are to you. But you know you love performing your little wonders."

" I suggest then, that we are characters from Tchekov as they would be in Hollywood. You absurdly gorgeous, and the little niece still grimly ingenue. Adam perhaps as Vanya if he were played by Boris Karloff. And so on."

" Where shall I get my absurdly gorgeous dress?"

" I paint the design on canvas and cut it out and if I were introduced to your dresser I would persuade her to sew it up." He took the glass frm Martyn and said, " No one makes any introductions in this theatre, so we introduce ourselves to each other. I am Jacques Doré, and you are the little chick whom the stork has brought too late, or dropped into the wrong nest. Really," he said, rolling his eyes at Miss Hamilton, " it is the most remarkable coincidence, if it is a coincidence. I am dropping bricks," he added. " I am a very privileged person but one day I drop an outsize brick, and away I go." He made a circle of his thumb and forefinger and looked through it, as though it were a quizzing glass, at Martyn. " All the same," he said, " it is a pity you are a little dresser and not a little actress."

IV

Between the photograph call and the dress-rehearsal, which was timed for seven o'clock, a state of uneven ferment prevailed at the Vulcan. During the rare occasions on which she had time to reflect, Martyn anticipated a sort of personal zero hour, a moment when she would have to take stock, to come to a decision. She had two and fourpence and no place of abode, and she had no idea when she would be paid, or how much she would get. This moment of reckoning, however, she continually postponed. The problem of food was answered for the moment by the announcement that it would be provided for everyone whose work kept them in the theatre throughout the day. As Miss Hamilton had discovered a number of minor alterations to be made in her dresses, Martyn was of this company. Having by this time, realised the position of extraordinary ubiquity held by Jacko, she was not surprised to find him cooking a mysterious but savoury mess over the gas-ring in Fred Badger's sink-room.

This concoction was served in enamel mugs, at odd intervals, to anyone who asked for it and Martyn found herself eating her share in company with Bob Cringle, Mr. Poole's dresser. From him she learnt more about Mr. Jacques Doré. He was responsible for the décor and dressing of all Poole's productions. His official status was that of assistant to Mr. Poole but in actual fact he seemed to be a kind of superior odd-job man. " General dogsbody," Cringle gossiped, " that's what Mr. Jacko is. ' Poole's Luck ' people call him, and if the guv'nor was superstitious about anything, which 'e is *not*, it would be about Mr. Jacko. The lady's the same. Can't do without 'im. As a matter of fact it's on 'er account 'e sticks it out. You might say 'e's 'er property, a kind of pet, if you like to put it that way. Joined up with 'er and 'is nibs when they was in Canada and the guv'nor still doing the child-wonder at 'is posh college. 'E's a Canadian-Frenchy, Mr. Jacko is. Twenty years ago that must 'ave been, only don't say I said so. It's what they call dog-like devotion, and that's no error. To 'er, *not* to 'is nibs."

" Do you mean Mr. Bennington?" Martyn ventured.

" Clark Bennington, the distinguished character actor, that's right," said Cringle dryly. Evidently he was not inclined to elaborate this theme. He entertained Martyn, instead, with a lively account of the eccentricities of Dr. John Rutherford. " My oaff," he said, " what a daisy! Did you 'ear 'im chi-ikeing from the front this morning? Typical! We done three of 'is pieces up to date and never a dull moment. Rows and ructions, ructions and rows from the word go. The guvnor puts up with it on account he likes the pieces and what a time 'e has with 'im, oh, dear. It's something shocking the way doctor cuts up. Dynamite! This time it's the little lady and 'is nibs and Mr. Parry Profile Percival 'e's got it in for. Can't do nothing to please 'im. You should 'ear 'im at rehearsals. ' You're bastardising my play,' e' 'owls. ' Get the 'ell art of it,' 'e shrieks. You never seen such an exhibition. Shocking! Then the guv'nor shuts 'im up, 'e 'as an attack of the willies or what-have-you and keeps aht of the theaytre for a couple of days. Never longer, though, which is very unfortunate for all concerned."

To Martyn, held as she was in a sort of emotional suspension, the lives and events enclosed within the stage walls and curtain of the Vulcan Theatre assumed a greater reality than her own immediate problem. Her existence since five o'clock the previous afternoon when she had walked into the theatre, had much of the character and substance of a dream with all the shifting values, the passages of confusion and extreme clarity which make up the texture of a dream. She was in a state of semi-trauma and found it vaguely agreeable. Her jobs would keep her busy all the afternoon and to-night there was the first dress-rehearsal.

She could, she thought, tread water indefinitely, half in and half out of her dreams, as long as she didn't come face to face with Mr. Adam Poole in any more looking-glasses.

CHAPTER III

FIRST DRESS-REHEARSAL

" I wish," Martyn said, " I knew what the play was about. Is it really a modern morality and do you think it good?"

" All good plays are moralities," said Jacko sententiously, and he leant so far back on the top of his step-ladder that Martyn hurriedly grasped it. " And this is a good play with a very old theme." He hesitated for a moment and she wondered if she only imagined that he looked worried. " Here is a selected man with new ideas in conflict with people who have very old ones. Adam plays the selected man. He has been brought up on an island by a community of idealists ; he represents the value of environment. By his own wish he returns to his original habitat, and there he is confronted by his heredity, in the persons of his great uncle, who is played by J. G. Darcey, his brilliant but unstable cousin, who is played by Clark Bennington, this cousin's wife, who is

Helena, and with whom he falls in love, and their daughter who is freakishly like him, but vicious and who represents therefore his inescapable heredity. This wretched girl," Jacko continued with great relish, looking at Martyn out of the corner of his eyes, " is engaged to a nonentity but finds herself drawn by a terrible attraction to Adam himself. She is played by Gay Gainsford. Receive again from me the pink pot, and bestow upon me the brown. As I have recited it to you so baldly, without nuance and without detail, you will say perhaps if Ibsen or Kafka or Brecht or even Sartre had written this play it would be a good one.

Inexplicably, he again seemed to be in some sort of distress. " It has, in fact," he said, " a continental flavour. But for those who have ears to hear and eyes to see, it has a wider implication than I have suggested. It is a tale, in point of fact, about the struggle of the human being in the detestable situation in which from the beginning he has found himself. Now I descend." He climbed down his step-ladder, groaning lamentably. " And now," he said, " we have some light and we see if what I have done is good. Go out into the front of the house and in a moment I join you."

By the time Martyn reached the sixth row of the stalls the stage was fully illuminated, and for the first time she saw the set for Act II as Jacko had intended it.

It was an interior, simple in design and execution, but with an air of being over-civilised and stale. " They are," Jacko explained, slumping into a seat beside her, " bad people who live in it. They are not bad of their own volition, but because they have been set down in this place by their heredity and cannot escape. And now you say, all this is pretentious nonsense, and nobody will notice my set except perhaps a few queers who come to first nights and in any case will get it all wrong. And now we wash ourselves and go out to a place where I am known, and we eat a little, and you tell me why you look like a puppy who has found his tail but dare not wag it. Come."

The restaurant where Jacko was known turned out to be hard by the theatre, and situated in a basement. He insisted on paying for a surprisingly good meal, and Martyn's two and fourpence remained in her pocket. Whereas the curiosity of Fred Badger and Bob Cringle, and in some degree of the actors, had been covert and indirect, Jacko's was unblushing and persistent.

" Now," he said, over their coffee, " I ask you my questions. If there is a secret you tell me so, and with difficulty I shut myself up. If not, you confide in me, because everybody in the Vulcan makes me their confidant and I am greatly flattered by this. In any case we remain friends, no bones broken, and we repeat our little outings. How old do you think I am?"

With some embarrassment, Martyn looked at his scrawny neck, at the thin lichen-like growth of fuzz on his head, and at his heavily scored and indented face. "Fifty-seven," she ventured.

"Sixty-two," said Jacko complacently. "I am sixty-two years old, and a bit of a character. I have not the talent to make a character of myself for the people who sit in front, so instead I play to actors. A wheel within wheels. For twenty years I have built up my role of confidant and now, if I wanted to I couldn't leave off. For example I can speak perfect English, but my accent is a feature of the role of Papa Jacko, and must be sustained. Everybody knows it is a game and, amiably, everyone pretends with me. It is all rather ham and *jejune,* but I hope that you are going to play too."

Martyn thought, "It would be pleasant to tell him: I'm sure he's very nice and so why don't I do it? I suppose it's because he looks so very old." And whether with uncanny prescience or else by a queer coincidence, he said, "I'm not nearly as peculiar as I look."

Martyn said tentatively, "But I honestly don't know what you want me to tell you."

On the opposite wall of the restaurant there was a tarnished looking-glass, upon the surface of which someone had half-heartedly painted a number of water-lilies and leaves. Among this growth, as if drowned in Edwardiana, Jacko's and Martyn's faces were reflected. He pointed to hers.

"See," he said. "We rehearse a play for which it is necessary a secondary-part actress should resemble, strikingly, the leading man. We have auditions, and from the hundreds of anxious ingénues we select the one who is least unlike him, but she is still very unlike him. Incidentally," Jacko continued, looking Martyn very hard in the eye "she is the niece of Clark Bennington. She is not very like him either which is neither here nor there and perhaps fortunate for her. It is her unlikeness to Adam that we must deplore. Moreover, although I am a genius with make-up, there is very little I can do about it. So we depend instead on reflected emotions and echoed mannerisms. But although she is a nice little actress with a nice small talent, she cannot do this very

46

well either. In the meantime our author who is a person of unbridled passion where his art is in question, becomes incensed with her performance and makes scenes and everybody except her Uncle Bennington retires into corners and tears pieces of their hair out. The little actress also retires into corners and weeps and is comforted by her Uncle Bennington, who never the less knows she is no good.

"Upon this scene there enters, in the guise of a dresser," he jabbed his finger at the fly-blown glass, "this. Look at it. If I set out to draw the daughter or the young sister of the leading man, that is what I should draw. Everybody has a look at her and retires again into corners to ask what it is about. Because obviously, she is not a dresser. Is she perhaps—and there are many excited speculations. 'A niece for a niece?' we ask ourselves, and there is some mention of Adam's extreme youth, you must excuse me, and the wrong side of the rose bush, and everybody says it cannot be an accident and waits to see, except Papa Jacko whose curiosity will not permit him to wait."

Martyn cried out, "I've never seen him before, except in films in New Zealand. He knows nothing about me at all. Nothing. I came here from New Zealand a fortnight ago and I've been looking for a job ever since. I came to the Vulcan looking for a job, that's all there is about it."

"Did you come looking for the job of dresser to Miss Hamilton?"

"For any job," she said desperately. "I heard by accident about the dresser."

"But it was not to be a dresser that you came all the way from New Zealand, and yet it was to work in the theatre, and so perhaps after all you hoped to be an actress."

"Yes," Martyn said, throwing up her hands, "all right, I hoped to be an actress. But please let's forget all about it. You can't imagine how thankful I am to be a dresser, and if you think I'm secretly hoping Miss Gainsford will get laryngitis or break her leg, you couldn't be more mistaken. I don't believe in fairy tales."

"What humbugs you all are."

"Who?" she demanded indignantly.

"All you Anglo-Saxons. You humbug even yourselves. Conceive for the moment the *mise en scène*, the situation, the coincidence, and have you the cheek to tell me again that you came thirteen thousand miles to be an actress and yet do not wish to play this part. Are you a good actress?"

"Don't," Martyn said, "don't. I've got a job and I'm

in a sort of a trance. It makes everything very simple and I don't want to come out of it."

Jacko grinned fiendishly. " Just a little touch of laryngitis?" he suggested.

Martyn got up. " Thank you very much for my nice dinner," she said, " I ought to be getting on with my job."

" Little hypocrite. Or perhaps after all you know already you are a very bad actress."

Without answering she walked out ahead of him, and they returned in silence to the Vulcan.

II

Timed to begin at seven, the dress-rehearsal actually started at ten-past eight. Miss Hamilton had no changes in the first act, and told Martyn she might watch from the front. She went out and sat at the back of the stalls near the other dressers.

Suddenly the lights went up along the fringe of the curtain, Martyn's flesh began to creep. Throughout the auditorium other little flames sprang up, illuminating from below, like miniature footlights, the faces of the watchers in front. A remote voice said " O.K. Take it away," a band of gold appeared below the fringe of the curtain, widened and grew to a lighted stage. Parry Percival spoke the opening line of Dr. Rutherford's new play.

Martyn liked the first act. It concerned itself with the group of figures Jacko had already described—the old man, his son, his son's wife, their daughter and her fiancé. They were creatures of convention, the wife alone possessed of some inclination to reach out beyond her enclosed and aimless existence.

Gay Gainsford's entry as the daughter was a delayed one, and try as she might not to anticipate it, Martyn felt a sinking in her midriff when at last towards the end of the act Miss Gainsford came on. It was quite a small part but one of immense importance. Of the entire group the girl represented the third generation, the most completely lost, and in the writing of her part Rutherford displayed the influence of Existentialism. It was clear that with a few lines to carry her she must make her mark, and clever production was written over everything she did. Agitated as she was by Jacko's direct attack, Martyn wondered if she only imagined that there was nothing more than production
48

there, and if Miss Gainsford was really as ill at ease as she herself supposed. A specific gesture had been introduced and was evidently important, a sudden thrust of her fingers through her short hair, and she twice used a phrase: ": That was not what I meant " where in the context it was evidently intended to plant a barb of attention in the minds of the audience. When this moment came, Martyn sensed uneasiness among the actors. She glanced at Poole and saw him make the specific gesture he had given Miss Gainsford, a quick thrust of his fingers through his hair.

At this juncture the voice in the circle ejaculated: " Boo!"

" Quiet!" said Poole.

Miss Gainsford hesitated, looked wretchedly into the auditorium, and lost her words. She was twice prompted before she went on again. Bennington crossed the stage put his arm about her shoulder and glared into the circle. The prompter once more threw out a line, Miss Gainsford repeated it and they were off again. Poole got up and went back-stage through the pass-door. The secretary leant forward and shakily lit one cigarette from the butt of another. For the life of her, Martyn couldn't resist glancing at Jacko. He was slumped back in his stall with his arms folded—deliberately imperturbable, she felt—putting on an act. The light from the stage caught his emu-like head and as if conscious of her attention, he rolled his eyes round at her. She hastily looked back at the stage.

With Gay Gainsford's exit, Martyn could have sworn, a wave of relaxation blessed the actors. The dialogue began to move forward compactly with a firm upward curve towards some well-designed climax. There was an increase in tempo corresponding with the rising suspense. Martyn's blood tingled and her heart thumped. Through which door would the entrance be made? The players began a complex circling movement accompanied by a sharp crescendo in the dialogue. Up and up it soared. " Now," she thought, " now!" The action of the play was held in suspense, poised and adjusted, and into the prepared silence, with judgment and precision, at the head of Jacko's twisted flight of steps, came Adam Poole.

" Is that an entrance," thought Martyn, pressing her hands together, " or is it an entrance?"

The curtain came down almost immediately. The secretary gathered his notes together and went back-stage.

Dr. Rutherford shouted: " Hold your horses," thundered out of the circle, reappeared in the stalls, and plunged through the pass-door to back-stage where he could be heard cruelly apostrophising the Almighty and the actors. Jacko stretched elaborately and slouched down the centre aisle, saying into the air as he passed Martyn, " You had better get round for the change."

Horrified, Martyn bolted like a rabbit. When she arrived in the dressing-room she found her employer, with a set face, attempting to unhook an elaborate back fastening. Martyn bleated an apology which was cut short.

" I hope," said Miss Hamilton, " you haven't mistaken the nature of your job, Martyn. You are my dresser and as such are expected to be here, in this dressing-room, whenever I return to it. Do you understand?"

Martyn, feeling very sick, said that she did, and with trembling fingers effected the complicated change. Miss Hamilton was completely silent, and to Martyn, humiliated and miserable, the necessary intimacies of her work were particularly mortifying.

A boy's voice in the passage chanted: " Second Act, please. Second Act," and Miss Hamilton said, " Have you got everything on-stage for the quick change?"

" I think so, madam."

" Very well." She looked at herself coldly and searchingly in the long glass and added, " I will go out."

Martyn opened the door. Her employer glanced critically at her. " You're as white as a sheet," she said, " what's the matter?"

Martyn stammered, " Am I? I'm sorry, madam. It must have been the first act."

" Did you like it?"

" Like it?" Martyn repeated, " oh yes, I liked it."

" As much as that?" As easily as if she had passed from one room into another, Miss Hamilton re-entered her mood of enchantment. " What a ridiculous child you are," she said. " It's only actresses who are allowed to have temperaments."

She went out to the stage, and as Martyn followed her she was surprised to feel in herself a kind of resistance to this woman who could so easily command her own happiness or misery.

An improvised dressing-room had been built on the stage for the quick change, and in or near it Martyn spent the whole of the second act. She was not sure when the quick change came, and didn't like to ask anybody. She therefore spent the first quarter of an hour on tenterhooks, hearing the dialogue, but not seeing anything of the play.

After a short introductory passage the act opened with a long scene between Helena Hamilton and Adam Poole in which their attraction to each other was introduced and established, and her instinctive struggle against her environment made clear and developed. The scene was admirably played by both of them, and carried the play strongly forward. When Miss Hamilton came off she found her dresser bright eyed and excited. Martyn effected the change without any blunders and in good time. Miss Hamilton's attention seemed to be divided between her clothes and the scene which was now being played between J. G. Darcey, Poole and her husband. This scene built up into a quarrel between Poole and Bennington which at its climax was broken by Poole saying in his normal voice, " I dislike interrupting dress-rehearsals, Ben, but we've had this point over and over again. Please take the line as we rehearsed it."

There was complete silence, perhaps for five seconds, and then, unseen, so that Martyn formed no picture of what he was doing or how he looked, Bennington began to giggle. The sound wavered and bubbled into a laugh. Helena Hamilton whispered: " Oh, my *God*!" and went out to the stage. Martyn followed. A group of stage-hands who had been moving round the set stopped dead as if in suspended animation. Parry Percival, waiting off-stage, turned with a look of elaborate concern to Miss Hamilton and mimed bewilderment.

Bennington's laughter broke down into ungainly speech. " I always say," he said, " there is no future in being an actor-manager unless you arrange things your own way. I want to make this chap a human being. You and John say he's to be a monster. All right, all right, dear boy, I won't offend again. He shall be less human than Caliban, and far less sympathetic."

Evidently Poole was standing inside the entrance nearest to the dressing-room, because Martyn heard Bennington cross the stage and when he spoke again he was quite close to her, and had lowered his voice. " You're grabbing everything, aren't you?" the voice wavered. " On— and off-stage, as you might say—domestically and professionally. The piratical Mr. Poole."

Poole muttered, " If you are not too drunk to think, we'll go on," and pitching his voice, threw out a line of dialogue: "*If you knew what you wanted, if there was any object, however silly, behind anything you say or do, I could find some excuse for you——*"

Martyn heard Helena Hamilton catch her breath in a sob. The next moment she had flung open the door and made her entrance.

III

Through the good offices of Jacko, Martyn was able to watch the rest of the act from the side. Evidently he was determined she should see as much as possible of the play. He sent her round a list, scribbled in an elaborate hand, of the warnings and cues for Miss Hamilton's entrances and exits and times when she changed her dress. "Stand in the O.P. corner," he had written across the paper, "and think of your sins." She wouldn't have dared to follow his advice if Miss Hamilton, on her first exit, had not said with a sort of irritated good nature: "You needn't wait in the dressing-room perpetually. Just be ready for me: that's all."

So she stood in the shadows of the O.P. corner and saw the one big scene between Adam Poole and Gay Gainsford. The author's intention was clear enough. In this girl, the impure flower of her heredity, the most hopelessly lost of all the group, he sought to show the obverse side of the character Poole presented. She was his twisted shadow, a spiritual incubus. In everything she said and did the audience must see a distortion of Poole himself, until at the end they faced each other across the desk, as in the scene that had been photographed, and Helena Hamilton re-entered to speak the line of climax: "*But it's you, don't you see? You can't escape it. It's you,*" and the curtain came down.

Gay Gainsford was not good enough. It was not only that she didn't resemble Poole closely; her performance was too anxious, too careful a reproduction of mannerisms without a flame to light them. Martyn burnt in her shadowy corner. The transparent covering in which, like a sea-creature, she had spent her twenty-four hours' respite, now shrivelled away and she was exposed to the inexorable hunger of an unsatisfied player.

She didn't see Bennington until he put his hand on her arm as the curtain came down, and he startled her so much that she cried out and backed away from him.

"So you think you could do it, dear, do you?" he said.

Martyn stammered: "I'm sorry. Miss Hamilton will want me," and dodged past him towards the improvised dressing-room. He followed and with a conventionally showy movement, barred her entrance.

"Wait a minute, *wait* a minute," he said. "I want to talk to you."

She stood there, afraid of him, conscious of his smell of greasepaint and alcohol and thinking him a ridiculous as well as an alarming person.

"I'm *so* angry," he said conversationally, "just literally *so* angry that I'm afraid you're going to find me quite a difficult man. And now we've got that ironed out perhaps you'll tell me who the bloody hell you are."

"You know who I am," Martyn said desperately. "Please let me go in."

"M'wife's dresser?"

He took her chin in his hand and twisted her face to the light. Poole came round the back of the set. Martyn thought: "He'll be sick of the sight of me. Always getting myself into stupid little scenes." Bennington's hand felt wet and hot round her chin.

"M'wife's dresser," he repeated. "And m'wife's lover's little by-blow. That the story?"

The edge of Poole's hand dropped on his arm. "In you go," he said to Martyn, and twisted Bennington away from the door. Martyn slipped through and he shut it behind her. She heard him say: "You're an offensive fellow in your cups, Ben. We'll have this out after rehearsal. Get along and change for the third act."

There was a moment's pause. The door opened and he looked in.

"Are you all right?" he asked.

"Perfectly, thank you." Martyn said and in an agony of embarrassment added, "I'm sorry to be a nuisance, sir."

"Oh, don't be an ass," he said with great ill-humour. The next moment he had gone.

Miss Hamilton, looking desperately worried, came in to change for the third act.

IV

The dress-rehearsal ended at midnight in an atmosphere of acute tension. Because she had not yet been paid, Martyn proposed to sleep again in the greenroom. So easily do our standards adjust themselves to our circumstances that whereas on her first night at the Vulcan the greenroom had a blessed haven, her hours of precarious security had bred a longing for a bed and ordered cleanliness, and she began to dread the night.

In groups and singly, the actors and stage-staff drifted away. Their voices died out in the alley and passages, and she saw, with dismay, that Fred Badger had emerged from the door of his cubby-hole and now eyed her speculatively. Desolation and fear possessed Martyn. With a show of preoccupation, she hurried away to Miss Hamilton's dressing-room which she had already set in order. Here she would find a moment's respite. Perhaps in a few minutes she would creep down the passage and lock herself in the empty room and wait there until Fred Badger had gone his rounds. He would think she had found a lodging somewhere and left the theatre. She opened the door of Miss Hamilton's room and went in.

Adam Poole was sitting in front of the gas-fire.

Martyn stammered, " I'm sorry," and made for the door.

" Come in," he said and stood up. " I want to see you for a moment."

" Well," Martyn thought sickly, " this is it. I'm to go."

He twisted the chair round and ordered rather than invited her to sit in it. As she did so she thought: " I won't be able to sleep here to-night. When he's sacked me I'll get my suitcase and ask my way to the nearest women's hostel. I'll walk alone through the streets and when I get there the hostel will be shut."

He had turned his back to her and seemed to be examining something on the dressing-shelf.

" I would very much rather have disregarded this business," he said irritably, " but I suppose I can't. For one thing, someone should apologise to you for Bennington's behaviour. He's not likely to do it for himself."

" It really didn't matter."

" Of course it mattered," he said sharply. " It was insufferable. For both of us."

She was too distressed to recognise as one of pleasure the small shock this last phrase gave her.

" You realise, of course, how this nonsense started," he was saying. " You've seen something of the play. You've seen me. It's not a matter for congratulation, I dare say, but you're like enough to be my daughter. You're a New Zealander, I understand. How old are you?"

" Nineteen, sir."

" You needn't bother to pepper your replies with this
' sir ' business. It's not in character and it's entirely unconvincing. I'm thirty-eight. I toured New Zealand in my first
job twenty years ago, and Bennington was in the company.
That, apparently, is good enough for him. Under the circumstances I hope you won't mind my asking you who your
parents are and where you were born."

" I've no objection whatever," said Martyn with spirit.
" My father was Martin Tarne. He was the son and grand-
son of a high-country run-holder—a sheep-farmer—in the
South Island. He was killed on Crete."

He turned and looked directly at her for the first time since
she had come into the room.

" I see. And your mother?"

" She's the daughter of a run-holder in the same district?"

" Do you mind telling me her maiden name, if you please?"

Martyn said: " I don't see what good this will do."

" Don't you, indeed? Don't you, after all, resent the
sort of conjecture that's brewing among these people?"

" I certainly haven't the smallest desire to be thought your
daughter."

" And I couldn't agree more. Good Lord!" he said.
" This is a fatheaded way for us to talk. Why don't you
want to tell me your mother's maiden name? What was the
matter with it?"

" She always thought it sounded silly. It was Paula Poole
Passington."

He brought the palm of his hand down crisply on the
back of her chair. " And why in the world," he asked,
" couldn't you say so at once?" Martyn was silent. " Paula
Poole Passington," he repeated. " All right. An old cousin
of my father's—cousin Paula—married someone called Passington and disappeared. I suppose to New Zealand. Why
didn't she look me up when I went out there?"

" I believe she didn't care for theatricals," said Martyn.
" She was my grandmother. The connection is really quite
distant."

" You might at least have mentioned it."

" I preferred not to."

" Too proud?"

" If you like," she said desperately.

" Why did you come to England?"

" To earn my living."

" As a dresser?" She was silent. " Well?" he said.

"As best I could."

"As an actress? Oh, for God's sake," he added, "it's damnably late and I'll be obliged if you'll behave reasonably. I may tell you I've spoken to Jacko. Don't you think you're making an ass of yourself? All this mystery act!"

Martyn got up and faced him. "I'm sorry," she said. "It's a silly business but it's not an act. I didn't want to make a thing of it. I joined an English touring company in New Zealand a year ago and they took me on with them to Australia."

"What company was this? What parts did you play?" She told him.

"I heard about the tour," he said. "They were a reasonably good company."

"They paid quite well and I did broadcasting too. I saved up enough to keep me in England for six months and got a job as an assistant children's minder in a ship. Perhaps I should explain that my father lost pretty well everything in the slump, and we are poor people. I had my money in traveller's cheques and the day we landed they were stolen out of my bag, together with my letters of introduction. The bank will probably be able to stop them and let me have it back but until they decide, I'm hard up. That's all."

"How long have you been here?"

"A fortnight."

"Where have you tried?"

"Agencies. All the London theatres, I think."

"This one last? Why?"

"One of them had to be last."

"Did you know of this—connection—as you call it?"

"Yes. My mother knew of it."

"And the resemblance?"

"I—we saw your pictures—people sometimes said——" They looked at each other, warily, with guarded interest.

"And you deliberately fought shy of this theatre because you knew I was playing here?"

"Yes."

"Did you know about this piece? The girl's part?"

Martyn was beginning to be very tired. A weariness of spirit and body seeped up through her being in a sluggish tide. She was near to tears and thrust her hand nervously through her short hair. He made some kind of ejaculation and she said at once: "I didn't mean to do that."

"But you knew about the part when you came here?"

"There's a lot of gossip at the agencies when you're

56

waiting. A girl I stood next to in the queue at Garnet Marks' told me they wanted someone at the Vulcan who could be made-up to look like you. She'd got it all muddled up with yesterday's auditions for the touring company in another piece."

"So you thought you'd try?"

"Yes. I was a bit desperate by then. I thought I'd try."

"Without, I suppose, mentioning this famous 'connection'?"

"Yes."

"And finding there was nothing for you in the piece you applied for the job of dresser?"

"Yes."

"Well," he said, "it's fantastic, but at least it's less fantastic than pure coincidence would have been. One rather respects you by the way, if it's not impertinent in a second cousin once removed to say so."

"Thank you," she said vaguely.

"The question is: What are we going to do about it?"

Martyn turned away to the ranks of dresses and with business-like movements of her trembling hands, tweaked at the sheets that covered them. She said briskly: "I realise of course that I'll have to go. Perhaps Miss Hamilton——"

"You think you ought to go?" his voice said behind her. "I suppose you're right. It's an awkward business."

"I'm sorry."

"But I'd like to—it's difficult to suggest——"

"I'll be perfectly all right," she said with savage brightness. "Please don't give it another thought."

"Why, by the way, are you still in the theatre?"

"I was going to sleep here," Martyn said loudly. "I did last night. The night-watchman knows."

"You would be paid on Friday."

"Like the actors?"

"Certainly. How much is there in the exchequer between now and Friday?" Martyn was silent and he said with a complete change of voice: "My manners, you will already have been told, are notoriously offensive but I don't believe I was going to say anything that would have offended you."

"I've got two and fourpence."

He opened the door and shouted: "Jacko!" into the echoing darkness. She heard the greenroom door creak and in a moment or two Jacko came in. He carried a board with a half-finished drawing pinned to it. This he exhibited to Poole. "Crazy, isn't it?" he said. "Helena's costume for the ball. What must I do but waste my beauty-sleep concocting it. Everybody will have to work very hard if it is to be made. I see you are in need of my counsel. What goes on?"

"Against my better judgment," Poole said, "I'm going to follow your advice. You always think you're indispensible at auditions. Give me some light out there and then sit in front."

"It is past midnight. This child has worked and worried herself into a complete *boulversement*. She is as pale as a pierrot."

Poole looked at her. "Are you all right?" he asked her. "It won't take ten minutes."

"I don't understand, but I'm all right."

"There you are, Jacko," Poole said and sounded pleased. "It's over to you."

Jacko took her by the shoulders and gently pushed her down on the chair. "Attention," he said. "We make a bargain. I live not so far from here in an apartment house kept by a well-disposed French couple. An entirely respectable house, you understand, with no funny business. At the top one finds an attic room as it might be in a tale for children, and so small, it is but twice the size of its nice little bed. The rental is low, within the compass of a silly girl who gets herself into equivocal situations. At my recommendation she will be accommodated in the attic which is included in my portion of the house and will pay me the rent at the end of a week. But in exchange for my good offices she does for us a little service. Again, no funny business."

"Oh, dear!" Martyn said. She leant towards the dressing-shelf and propped her face in her hands. "It sounds so wonderful," she said and tried to steady her voice, "a nice little bed."

"All right, Jacko," Poole said. She heard the door open and shut. "I want you to relax for a few minutes," his voice went on. "Relax all over like a cat. Don't think of anything in particular. You're going to sleep sound to-night. All will be well."

The gas fire hummed, the smell of roses and cosmetics filled the warm room. "Do you smoke?" Poole asked.

"Sometimes."

"Here you are."

She drew in the smoke gratefully. He went into the passage and she watched him light his own cigarette. Her thoughts drifted aimlessly about the bony structure of his head and face. Presently a stronger light streamed down the passage. Jacko's voice called something from a great distance.

Poole turned to her. "Come along," he said.

On the stage, dust-thickened rays from pageant-lamps settled in a pool of light about a desk and two chairs. It was like an island in a vague region of blueness. She found herself seated there at the desk, facing him across it. In response to a gesture of Poole's she rested her arms on the desk and her face in her arms.

"Listen," he said, "and don't move. You are in the hall of an old house, beautifully but decaying. You are the girl with the bad heredity. You are the creature who goes round and round in her great empty cage like a stoat filled with a wicked desire. The object of your desire is the man on the other side of the desk who is joined to you in blood and of whose face and mind you are the ill reflection. In a moment you will raise your face to his. He will make a gesture and you will make the same gesture. Then you will say: 'Don't you like what you see?' It must be horrible and real. Don't move. Think of it. Then raise your head and speak."

There was a kind of voluptuousness in Martyn's fatigue. Only the chair she sat on and the desk that propped her arms and head prevented her, she felt, from slipping to the floor. Into this defencelessness Poole's suggestion entered like those of a mesmerist, and that perfection of duality for which actors pray and which they are so rarely granted now fully invested her. She was herself and she was the girl in the play. She guided the girl and was aware of her and she governed the possession of the girl by the obverse of the man in the play. When at last she raised her face and looked at him and repeated his gesture it seemed to her that she looked into a glass and saw her own reflection and spoke to it.

"Don't you like what you see?" Martyn said.

In the pause that followed, the sound of her own breathing and Poole's returned. She could hear her heart beat.

"Can you do it again?" he said.

"I don't know," she said helplessly. "I don't know at all." She turned away and with a childish gesture hid her face in the crook of her arm. In dismay and shame she set loose the tears she had so long denied herself.

"There now!" he said, not so much as if to comfort her as to proclaim some private triumph of his own. Out in the dark auditorium Jacko struck his hands together once.

Poole touched her shoulder. "It's nothing," he said. "These are growing pains. They will pass." From the door in the set he said: "You can have the under-study. We'll make terms to-morrow. If you prefer it, the relationship can be forgotten. Good night."

He left her alone and presently Jacko returned to the stage carrying her suitcase.

"Now," he said, "we go home."

CHAPTER IV

SECOND DRESS-REHEARSAL

When Martyn opened her eyes on the second morning of her adventure it was with the sensation of having come to rest after a painful journey.

She lay quiet and looked about her. It was a bright morning and the sun came in at the attic window above her bed. The room had an air of great cleanliness and freshness. She remembered now that Jacko had told her he occasionally made use of it and indeed, tiny as it was it bore his eccentric imprint. A set of designs for *Twelfth Night* was pinned to a wall-board. Ranged along the shelf were a number of figures dressed in paper as the persons in this play and on the wall facing her bed hung a mask of the fool, Feste, looking very like Jacko himself.

"There never was such a little room," Martyn sighed and began to plan how she would collect and stow away her modest belongings. She was filled with gratitude and with astonished humility.

The bathroom was on the next floor and as she went downstairs she smelt coffee and fresh bread. A door on the landing opened and Jacko's clownish head looked out.

"Breakfast in ten minutes," he said. "Speed is essential."

Of all the amenities, it seemed to Martyn, a hot bath was the most beneficent and after that a shower under which one could wash one's hair quickly. "Lucky it's short," she thought and rubbed it dry with her towel.

She was out again in eight minutes to find Jacko on the landing.

"Good," he said. "In your wollen gown you are entirely respectable. A clean school child In."

He marshalled her into a largish room set out in an orderly

manner as a workshop. Martyn wondered why Jacko, who showed such exquisite neatness in his 'work, should in his person present such a wild front to the world. He was dressed now in faded cotton trousers, a paint-stained undervest and a tattered dressing-gown. He was unshaven and uncombed and his prominent eyes were slightly bloodshot. His manner, however, was as usual, amiable and disarming.

" I propose," he said, " that we breakfast together as a general rule. A light breakfast and supper are included in the arrangement. You will hand me your ration book and I shall shop with discretion. Undoubtedly I am a better cook than you and will therefore make myself responsible for supper. For luncheon you may return if you wish and forage ineffectually for yourself or make what other arrangement seems good to you. Approved?"

Martyn said carefully: " If you please, Jacko, I'm so grateful and so muddled I can't think at all sensibly. You see, I don't know what I shall be earning."

" For your dual and unusual role of understudy and dresser, I imagine about eight pounds a week. Your rental, *demi-pension,* here, is two."

" It seems so little," Martyn said timidly. " The rent, I mean."

Jacko tapped the side of the coffee-pot with a spoon. " *Attention,*" he said. " How often must I repeat. You will have the goodness to understand I am not a dirty old man. It is true that I am virile," he continued with some complacency, " but you are not my type. I prefer the more mature, the more *mondaine,* the——" He stopped short, the spoon with which he had been gesticulating, still held aloof. His eyes were fixed on the wall behind Martyn. She turned her head to see a sketch in water-colour of Helena Hamilton. When she faced Jacko again, he was grinning desperately.

" Believe me," he said, " you are in no danger of discomfort from the smallest whisper of scandal. I am notoriously pure. This morning there are eggs and therefore an omelette. Let us observe silence while I make it."

He was gay, in his outlandish fashion, from then onwards. When they had finished their admirable breakfast she helped him wash-up and he gave her what he called her orders for the day. She was to go down to the theatre with him, set about her work as a dresser and at three o'clock she would be given a formal rehearsal as understudy. At night, for the second dress-rehearsal, she would again take up her duties as Miss Hamilton's dresser.

"An eccentric arrangement," Jacko said. He groped in the bosom of his undervest and produced a somewhat tattered actor's "part," typewritten and bound in paper. "Only thirteen sides," he said. "A bit-part. You will study the lines while you press and stitch and by this afternoon you are word perfect, isn't it? You are, of course, delighted?"

"Delighted," Martyn said, "is not exactly the word. I'm flabbergasted and excited and grateful for everything and I just can't believe it's true. But it is a bit worrying to feel I've sort of got in on a fluke and that everybody's wondering what it's all about. They are, you know."

"All that," Jacko said with an ungainly sweep of his arm, "is of no importance. Gay Gainsford is still to play the part. She will not play it well but she is the niece of the leading lady's husband and she is therefore in a favourable position."

"Yes, but her uncle——"

He said quickly: "Clark Bennington was once a good actor. He is now a stencil. He drinks too much and when he is drunk he is offensive. Forget him." He turned away and with less than his usual deftness began to set him out his work-table. From an adjoining room he said indistinctly: "I advise that which I find difficult to perform. Do not allow yourself to become hag-ridden by this man. It is a great mistake. I myself——" His voice was lost in the spurt of running water. Martyn heard him shout: "Run off and learn your lines. I have a job in hand."

With a feeling of unease she returned to her room. But when she opened her part and began to read the lines this feeling retreated until it hung like a very small cloud over the hinterland of her mind. The foreground was occupied entirely by the exercise of memorising and in a few minutes she had almost, but not quite, forgotten her anxiety.

II

She was given her moves that afternoon by the stage-manager and, at three o'clock, rehearsed her scenes with the other two understudies. The remaining parts were read from the script. Jacko pottered about back-stage intent on one of his odd jobs; otherwise the theatre seemed to be deserted. Martyn had memorised her lines but inevitably lost them from time to time in her effort to associate them with physical movement. The uncompromising half-light of a working-stage, the mechanical pacing to and fro of understudies, the half-muted lines raised to concert pitch only for cues, and the dead sound of voices in an empty house: all these work-aday circumstances, though she was familiar enough with them, after all, laid a weight upon her: she lost her belief in the magic of the previous night. She was oppressed by this anti-climax, and could scarcely summon up the resources of her young experience to meet it.

The positions and moves had been planned with a vivid understanding of the text and seemed to spring out of it. She learnt them readily enough. Rather to her surprise, and, she thought, that of the other understudies, they were finally taken through her scenes at concert pitch so that by the end of the rehearsal the visual and aural aspects of her part had fused into a whole. She had got her routine. But it was no more than a routine: she spoke and paused and moved and spoke and there was no reality at all, she felt, in anything she did. Clem Smith, the stage-manager, said nothing about interpretation but, huddled in his overcoat, merely set the moves and then crouched over the script. She was not even a failure, she was just another colourless understudy and nothing had happened.

When it was over, Clem Smith shut the book and said: "Thank you, ladies and gentlemen. Eleven in the morning if you please." He lit a cigarette and went down into the auditorium and out through the front of the house.

Left alone on the stage, Martyn struggled with an acute attack of deflation. She tried to call herself to order. This in itself was a humiliating if salutary exercise. If, she thought savagely, she had been a Victorian young lady, she would at this juncture have locked herself away with a plush-bound journal and after shedding some mortified tears, forced a confession out of herself. As it was, she set her jaw and worked it out there and then. The truth was, she told herself, she had been at her old tricks again: she had indulged in the most blatant kind of day-dream. She had thought up a success story and dumped herself down in the middle of it with half a dozen pageant-lamps bathing her girlish form. Because she looked like Poole and because last night she had had a mild success with one line by playing it off her nerves she had actually had the gall to imagine:— Here Martyn felt her scalp creep and her face burn. "Come on," she thought, "out with it."

Very well, then. She had dreamed up a further rehearsal with Poole. She had seen herself responding eagerly to his

63

production, she had heard him say regretfully that if things had been different. . . . She had even . . . At this point overtaken with self-loathing Martyn performed the childish exercise of throwing her part across the stage, stamping violently and thrusting her fingers through her hair.

"*Damn and blast and hell,*" said Martyn, pitching her voice to the back row of the gallery.

"Not quite as bad as all that."

Adam Poole came out of the shadowed pit and down the centre aisle of the stalls. He rested his hands on the rail of the orchestral well. Martyn gaped at him.

"You've got the mechanics," he said. "Walk through it again by yourself before to-morrow. Then you can begin to think about the girl. Get the layout of the house into your head. Know your environment. What has she been doing all day before the play opens? What has she been thinking about? Why does she say the things she says and do the things she does? Listen to the other chaps' lines. Come down here for five minutes and we'll see what you think about acting."

Martyn went down into the house. Of all her experiences during these three days at the Vulcan Theatre, she was to remember this most vividly. It was a curious interview. They sat side by side as if waiting for the rise of curtain. Their voices were deadened by the plush stalls. Jacko could be heard moving about behind the set and in some distant room, back-stage, somebody in desultory fashion hammered and sawed. At first Martyn was ill at ease, unable to dismiss or to reconcile the jumble of distracted notions that beset her. But Poole was talking about theatre and about problems of the actor. He talked well, without particular emphasis but with penetration and authority. Soon she listened with single hearing and with all her attention to what he had to say. Her nervousness and uncertainty were gone and presently she was able to speak of matters that had exercised her in her own brief experience of the stage. Their conversation was adult and fruitful. It didn't even occur to her that they were getting on rather well together.

Jacko came out on the stage. He shielded his eyes with his hand and peered into the auditorium.

"Adam?" he said.

"Hallo? What is it?"

"It is Helena on the telephone to inquire why have you not rung her at four the time being now five-thirty. Will you take it in the office?"

64

"Good Lord!" he ejaculated and got up. Martyn moved into the aisle to let him out.

He said: "All right, Miss Tarne. Work along the lines we've been talking about and you should be able to cope with the job. We take our understudies seriously at the Vulcan and like to feel they're an integral part of the company. You'll . rehearse again to-morrow morning and——" He stopped unaccountably and after a moment said hurriedly: "You're all right, aren't you? I mean you feel quite happy about this arrangement?"

"Yes," she said. "Very happy."

"Good." He hesitated again for a second and then said: "I must go," and was off down the aisle to the front of the house. He called out: "I'll be in the office for some time, Jacko, if anyone wants me." A door banged. There was a long silence.

Jacko advanced to the footlights. "Where are you?" he asked.

"Here," said Martyn.

"I see you. Or a piece of you. Where is the rest? Re-assemble yourself. There is work to be done."

The work turned out to be the sewing together of a fantastic garment created and tacked up by Jacko himself. It had a flamboyant design, stencilled in black and yellow, of double-headed eagles and was made, in part, of scenic canvas. There was an electric sewing-machine in the ward-robe-room which was next to Mr. J. G. Darcey's at the end of the passage. Here Jacko sat Martyn down and here, for the next hour, she laboured under his exacting direction while he himself crawled about the floor cutting out further garments for the Combined Art Ball. At half-past six he went out, saying he would return with food.

Martyn laboured on. Sometimes she repeated the lines of the part, her voice drowned by the clatter of the machine. Sometimes, when engaged in hand-work it would seem, in the silent room, that she had entered into a new existence, as if she had at that moment been born and was a stranger to her former self. And since this was rather a frightening sensation, though not new to Martyn, she must rouse herself and make a conscious effort to dispel it. On one of these occasions, when she had just switched off the machine, she felt something of the impulse that had guided her first attempt at the scene with Poole. Wishing to retain and strengthen this experience she set aside her work and rested her head on her arms as the scene required. She waited in this posture, summoning her resources, and when she was ready, raised her head to confront her opposite.

Gay Gainsford stood on the other side of the table, watching her.

III

Martyn's flesh leapt on her bones. She cried out and made a sweeping gesture with her arms. A pair of scissors clattered to the floor.

"I'm sorry I startled you," said Miss Gainsford. "I came in quietly. I thought you were asleep but I realise now—you were doing that scene. Weren't you?"

"I've been given the understudy," Martyn said.

"You've had an audition and a rehearsal, haven't you?"

"Yes. I was so frightful at rehearsal, I thought I'd have another shot by myself."

"You needn't," Miss Gainsford said, "try to make it easy for me."

Martyn, still shaken and bewildered, looked at her visitor. She saw a pretty face that, under its make-up, was sodden with tears. Even as she looked the large photogenic eyes hooded and the small mouth quivered.

"I suppose," Miss Gainsford said, "you know what you're doing to me."

"Good Lord!" Martyn ejaculated, "what *is* all this? What have I done? I've got your understudy. I'm damn' thankful to have it and so far I've made a pretty poor showing."

"It's no good taking that line with me. I know what's happening."

"Nothing's happening. Oh, *please*," Martyn implored, torn between pity and a rising fear, "*please* don't cry. I'm nothing. I'm just any old understudy."

"That's pretty hot, I must say," Miss Gainsford said. Her voice wavered grotesquely between two registers like an adolescent boy's; "to talk about any old understudy when you've got that appearance. What's everyone saying about you when they think I'm not about? 'She's got the appearance!' It doesn't matter to them that I've had to dye my hair because they don't like wigs. I still haven't got the appearance. I'm a shoulder-length natural ash-blonde and I've had to have an urchin cut and go black and all I get is insults. In any other management," she continued

66

wildly, " the author wouldn't be allowed to speak to the artistes like that man speaks to me. In any other management an artiste would be protected against that kind of treatment. Adam's worse if anything. He's so bloody patient and persistent and half the time you don't know what he's talking about."

She drew breath, sobbed and hunted in her bag for her handkerchief.

Martyn said: "I'm so terribly sorry. It's awful when things go badly at rehearsals. But the worst kind of rehearsals *do* have a way of turning into the best kind of performances. And it's a grand play, isn't it?"

"I loathe the play. To me it's a lot of highbrow hokum and I don't care who knows it. Why the hell couldn't Uncle Ben leave me where I was, playing leads and second leads in fortnightly rep.? We were a happy family in fortnightly rep.; everyone had fun and games and there wasn't this ghastly graveyard atmosphere. I was miserable enough, God knows, before you came but now it's just *more* than I can stand."

"But I'm not going to play the part," Martyn said desperately. "You'll be all right. It's just got you down for the moment. I'd be no good, I expect, anyway."

"It's what they're all saying and thinking. It's a pity, they're saying, that you came too late."

"Nonsense. You only imagine that because of the likeness."

"Do I? Let me tell you I'm not imagining *all* the things they're saying about you. And about Adam. How you *can* stay here and take it! Unless it's true. *Is* it true?"

Martyn closed her hands on the material she had been sewing. "I don't want to know what they're saying. There's nothing unkind that's true for them to say."

"So the likeness is purely an accident? There's no relationship?"

Martyn said: "It seems that we are very distantly related: so distantly that the likeness is a freak. I didn't want to tell anyone about it. It's of no significance at all. I haven't used it to get into the theatre."

"I don't know how and why you got in but I wish to God you'd get out. How you *can* hang on knowing what they think, if it isn't true! You can't have any pride or decency. It's so cruel. It's so *damnably* cruel."

Martyn looked at the pretty tear-blubbered face and thought in terror that if it had been that of Atropos it could scarcely have offered a more dangerous threat. "Don't!" she cried out. "Please don't say that, I need this job so desperately. Honestly, *honestly* you're making a thing of all this. I'm not hurting you."

"Yes, you are. You're driving me completely frantic. I'm nervously and emotionally exhausted." Miss Gainsford sobbed with an air of quoting somebody else. "It just needed you to send me over the border-line. Uncle Ben keeps on and on and on about it until I think I'll go mad. This is a beastly unlucky theatre anyway. Everyone knows there's something wrong about it and then you come in like a Jonah and it's the rock *bottom*. If," Miss Gainsford went on, developing a command of histrionic climax of which Martyn would scarcely have suspected her capable, "if you have *any* pity at all, *any* humanity, you'll spare me this awful ordeal."

"But this is all nonsense. You're making a song about nothing. I won't be taken in by it," Martyn said and recognised defeat in her own voice.

Miss Gaisford stared at her with watery indignation and through trembling lips uttered her final cliché. "You can't," she said, "do this thing to me," and broke down completely.

It seemed to Martyn that beyond a façade of stock emotionalism she recognised a real and a profound distress. She thought confusedly that if they had met on some common and reasonable ground she would have been able to put up a better defence. As it was they merely floundered in a welter of unreason. It was intolerably distressing to her. Her precarious happiness died, she wanted to escape: she was lost. With a feeling of nightmarish detachment she heard herself say: "All right. I'll speak to Mr. Poole. I'll say I can't do the understudy."

Miss Gainsford had turned away. She held her handkerchief to her face. Her shoulders and head had been quivering but now they were still. There was a considerable pause. She blew her nose fussily, cleared her throat, and looked up at Martyn.

"But if you're Helena's dresser," she said, "you'll still be *about*."

"You can't mean you want to turn me out of the theatre altogether."

"There's no need," Miss Gainsford mumbled, "to put it like that."

Martyn heard a voice and footsteps in the passage. She didn't want to be confronted with Jacko. She said: "I'll see if Mr. Poole's still in the theatre. I'll speak to him now if he is."

As she made for the door Miss Gainsford snatched at her arm. "Please!" she said. "I *am* grateful. But you will be really generous won't you? Really big? You won't bring me into it, will you? With Adam I mean. Adam wouldn't underst——"

Her face set as if she had been held in suspension like a motion picture freezing into a still. She didn't even release her hold on Martyn's arm.

Martyn spun round and saw Poole, with Jacko behind him in the passage. To her own astonishment she burst out laughing.

"No really!" she stammered, "it's too much! This is the third time. Like the demon king in pantomime."

"What the devil do you mean?"

"I'm sorry. It's just your flair popping up in crises. Other people's crises. Mine in fact."

He grimaced as if he gave her up as a bad job. "What's the present crisis?" he said and looked at Miss Gainsford who had turned aside and was uneasily painting her mouth. "What is it, Gay?"

"Please!" she choked. "Please let me go. I'm all right, really. Quite all right. I just rather want to be alone."

She achieved a tearful smile at Poole and an imploring glance at Martyn. Poole stood away from the door and watched her go out with her chin up and with courageous suffering neatly portrayed in every inch of her body.

She disappeared into the passage and a moment later the door of the greenroom was heard to shut.

"It is a case of miscasting," said Jacko, coming into the room. "She should be in Hollywood. She has what it takes in Hollywood. What an exit! We have misjudged her."

"Go and see what's the matter."

"She wants," said Jacko, making a dolorous face, "to be alone."

"No, she doesn't. She wants an audience. You're it. Get along and do your stuff."

Jacko put several parcels on the table. "I am the dogsbody," he said, "to end all dogsbodies." And went out.

"Now, then," Poole said.

Martyn gathered up her work and was silent.

"What's the matter? You're as white as a sheet. Sit down. What is all this?"

She sat behind the machine.

" Come on," he said.

" I'm sorry if it's inconvenient for you but I'm afraid I've got to give notice."

" Indeed? As dresser or as understudy?"

" As both."

" It's extremely inconvenient and I don't accept it."

" But you must. Honestly, you must. I can't go on like this: it isn't fair."

" Do you mean because of that girl?"

" Because of her and because of everything. She'll have a breakdown. There'll be some disaster."

" She doesn't imagine you're going to be given the part over her head, does she?"

" No, no, of course not. It's just that she's finding it hard anyway and the—the sight of me sort of panics her."

" The likeness?"

" Yes."

" She needn't look at you. I'm afraid she's the most complete ass, that girl," he muttered. He picked up a fold of the material Martyn had been sewing, looked absently at it and pushed the whole thing across the table. " Understand," he said, " I won't for a second entertain the idea of your going. For one thing Helena can't do without you and for another I will not be dictated to by a minor actress in my own company. Nor," he added with a change of tone, " by anyone else."

" I'm so terribly sorry for her," Martyn said. " She feels there's some sort of underground movement against her. She really feels it."

" And you?"

" I must admit I don't much enjoy the sensation of being in the theatre on sufferance. But I was so thankful——" she caught her breath and stopped.

" Who makes you feel you're on sufferance? Gay? Bennington? Percival?"

" I used a silly phrase. Naturally, they all must think it a bit queer, my turning up. It *looks* queer."

" It'd look a damn' sight queerer if you faded out again. I can't think," he said impatiently, " how you could let yourself be bamboozled by that girl."

" But it's *not* all bamboozle. She really is at the end of her tether."

Martyn waited for a moment. She thought inconsequently how strange it was that she should talk like this to Adam Poole who two days ago, had been a celebrated name, a remote legend, seen and heard and felt through a veil of characterisation in his films.

"Oh, well," she thought and said aloud: "I'm thinking of the show. It's such a good play. She mustn't be allowed to fail. I'm thinking about that."

He came nearer and loked at her with a sort of incredulity. "Good Lord," he said, "I believe you are! Do you mean to say you haven't considered your own chance if she did crack up? Where's your wishful thinking?"

Martyn slapped her palm down on the table. "But of course I have. Of course I've done my bit of wishful thinking. But don't you see——"

He reached across the table and for a brief moment his hand closed over hers. "I think I do," he said. "I'm beginning it seems, to get a taste of your quality. How do you suppose the show would get on if you had to play?"

"That's unfair," Martyn cried.

"Well," he said, "don't run out on me. That'd be unfair, if you like. No dresser. No understudy. A damn' shabby trick. As for this background music, I know where it arises. It's a more complex business than you may suppose. I shall attend to it." He moved behind her chair, and rested his hands on its back. "Well," he said, "shall we 'clap hands and a bargain'? How say you?"

Martyn said slowly: "I don't see how I can do anything but say yes."

"There's my girl." His hand brushed across her head and he moved away.

"Though I must say," Martyn added, "you do well to quote Petruchio. And Henry V, if it comes to that."

"A brace of autocratic male animals? Therefore it must follow, you are 'Kate' in two places. And—shrewd Kate, French Kate, kind Kate but never curs't Kate—you will rehearse at eleven to-morrow, hold or cut bowstrings. Agreed?"

"I am content."

"Damned if you look it, however. All right. I'll have a word with that girl. Good day to you, Kate."

"Good day, sir," said Martyn.

That night the second dress-rehearsal went through as for performance, without, as far as Martyn knew, any interruption during the action.

She stayed throughout in one or the other of Miss Hamilton's dressing-rooms and, on the occasions when she was in transit, contrived to be out of the way of any players. In the second act, her duties kept her in the improvised dressing-room on the stage and she heard a good deal of the dialogue.

There is perhaps nothing that gives one so strong a sense of theatre from the inside as the sound of invisible players in action. The disembodied and remote voices, projected at an unseen mark, the uncanny quiet off-stage, the smells and the feeling that the walls and the dust listen, the sense of a simmering expectancy; all these together make a corporate life so that the theatre itself seems to breathe and pulse and give out a warmth. This warmth communicated itself to Martyn and, in spite of all her misgivings, she glowed and thought to herself. "This is my place. This is where I belong."

Much of the effect of the girl's part in this act depended, not so much on what she said, which was little, but on mime and on that integrity of approach, which is made manifest in the smallest gesture, the least movement. Listening to Miss Gainsford's slight uncoloured voice Martyn thought: "But perhaps if one watched her it would be better. Perhaps something is happening that cannot be heard; only seen."

Miss Hamilton, when she came off for her changes, spoke of nothing but the business in hand and said little enough about that. She was indrawn and formal in her dealings with her dresser. Martyn wondered uneasily how much Poole had told her of their interviews, whether she had any strong views or prejudices about her husband's niece or shared his resentment that Martyn herself had been cast as an understudy.

The heat radiated by the strong lights of the dressing-rooms intensified their characteristic smells. With business-like precision Miss Hamilton would aim an atomiser at her person and spray herself rhythmically with scent while Martyn, standing on a chair, waited to slip a dress over her head. After the end of the second act when she was about this business in the star-room, Poole came in: "That went very nicely, Ella," he said.

Martyn paused with the dress in her hands. Miss Hamilton

extended her whitened arms and, with a very beautiful movement, turned to him.

"Oh, darling," she said. "Did it? Did it really?"

Martyn thought she had never seen anyone more lovely than her employer was then. Hers was the kind of beauty that declared itself when most simply arrayed. The white cloth that protected her hair added a Holbein-like emphasis to the bones and subtly turning planes of her face. There was a sort of naïvety and warmth in her posture: a touching intimacy. Martyn saw Poole take the hands that were extended to him and she turned her head away, not liking, with the voluminous dress in her arms, to climb down from her station on the chair. She felt suddenly desolate and shrunken within herself.

"Was it *really* right?" Miss Hamilton said.

"You were, at least."

"But—otherwise?"

"Much as one would expect."

"Where's John?"

"In the circle, under oath not to come down until I say so."

"Pray God he keep his oath," she quoted sombrely.

"Hallo, Kate," Poole said.

"Kate?" Miss Hamilton asked. "Why, Kate?"

"I suspect her," said Poole, "of being a shrew. Get on with your job, Kate. What are you doing up there?"

Miss Hamilton said: "Really, darling!" and moved away to the chair. Martyn slipped the dress over her head, jumped down and began to fasten it. She did this to a running accompaniment from Poole. He whispered to himself anxiously as if he were Martyn, muttered and grunted as if Miss Hamilton complained that the dress was tight, and thus kept up a preposterous dialogue, matching his words to their actions. This was done so quaintly and with so little effort that Martyn had much ado to keep a straight face and Miss Hamilton was moved to exasperated laughter. When she was dressed she took him by the arms. "Since when, my sweet, have you become a dressing-room comedian?"

"Oh, God, your only jig-maker!"

"Last act, please, last act," said the call-boy in the passage.

"Come on," she said, and they went out together.

When the curtain was up, Martyn returned to the improvised dressing-room on the stage and there, having for the moment no duties, she listened to the invisible play and tried to discipline her most unruly heart.

Bennington's last exit was followed in the play by his suicide, off-stage. Jacko, who had, it seemed, a passion for even the simplest of off-stage stunts, had come round from the front of the house to supervise the gunshot. He stood near the entry into the dressing-room passage with a stage-hand who carried an effects-gun. This was fired at the appropriate moment and as they were stationed not far from Martyn in her canvas room, she leapt at the report which was nerve-shatteringly successful. The acrid smell of the discharge drifted into her roofless shelter.

Evidently Bennington was standing nearby. His voice, carefully lowered to a murmur, sounded just beyond the canvas wall. "And that," he said, "takes me *right* off, thank God. Give me a cigarette, Jacko, will you?" There was a pause. The stage-hand moved away. A match scraped and Bennington said: "Come to my room and have a drink."

"Thank you, Ben, not now," Jacko whispered. "The curtain comes down in five minutes."

"Followed by a delicious post-mortem conducted by the Great Producer and the Talented Author. Entrancing prospect! How did I go, Jacko?"

"No actor," Jacko returned, "cares to be told how he goes in anything but terms of extravagant praise. You know how clever you always are. You are quite as clever to-night as you have always been. Moreover you showed some discretion."

Martyn heard Bennington chuckle. "There's still to-morrow," he said. "I reserve my fire, old boy. I bide my time."

There was a pause. Martyn heard one of them fetch a long sigh: Jacko, evidently, because Bennington as if in answer to it said: "Oh, nonsense." After a moment he added: "The kid's all right," and when Jacko didn't answer: "Don't you think so?"

"Why, yes," said Jacko.

On the stage the voices of Helena Hamilton and Adam Poole built towards a climax. The call-boy came round behind the set and went down the passage chanting: "All on for the Curtain please. All on."

Martyn shifted the chair in the dressing-room and moved noisily. There was a brief silence.

"I don't give a damn if she can hear," Bennington said more loudly. "Wait a moment. Stay where you are. I was asking you what you thought of Gay's performance. She's all right. Isn't she?"

"Yes, yes. I must go."

"Wait a bit. If the fools left her alone she'd go tremendously. I tell you what, old boy. If our Eccentric Author exercises his talent for wisecracking on that kid to-night I'll damn' well take a hand."

"You will precipitate a further scene, and that is to be avoided."

"I'm not going to stand by and hear her bullied. By God, I'm not. I understand you've given harbourage, by the way, to the Mystery Maiden."

"I must get round to the side. By your leave, Ben."

"Plenty of time."

And Martyn knew that Bennington stood in the entry to the passage, barring the way.

"I'm talking," he said, "about this understudy-cum-dresser. Miss X."

"You are prolific in cryptic titles."

"Call her what you like, it's a peculiar business. What is she? You may as well tell me, you know. Some ancient indiscretion of Adam's adolescence come home to roost?"

"Be quiet, Ben."

"For twopence I'd ask Adam himself. And that's not the only question I'd like to ask him. Do you think I relish my position?"

"They are getting near the tag. It is almost over."

"Why do you suppose I drink a bit? What would you do in my place?"

"Think before I speak," said Jacko, "for one thing."

A buzzer sounded. "There's the curtain," said Jacko. "Look out."

Martyn heard a kind of scuffle followed by an oath from Bennington. There were steps in the passage. The curtain fell with a giant whisper. A gust of air swept through the region back-stage.

"All on," said the stage-manager distantly. Martyn heard the players go on and the curtain rise and fall again.

Poole, on the stage, said: "And that's all of that. All right, everyone. Settle down and I'll take the notes. John will be round in a moment. I'll wait for you, Ella."

Miss Hamilton came into the improvised room. Martyn removed her dress and put her into her gown.

"I'll take my make-up off out there," she said. "Bring the things, Martyn, will you? Grease, towels and my cigarettes?"

Martyn had them ready. She followed Miss Hamilton out and for the first time that night went on to the set.

Poole, wearing a dark dressing-gown, stood with his back

to the curtain. The other five members of the cast sat, relaxed but attentive, about the stage. Jacko and Clem Smith waited by the prompt corner with papers and pencils. Martyn held a looking-glass before Miss Hamilton who said: " Adam, darling, you don't mind, do you? I mustn't miss a word but I *do* rather want to get on," and began to remove her make-up.

Upon this scene Dr. John James Rutherford erupted. His arrival was prefaced in his usual manner by slammed doors, blundering footsteps and loud ejaculations. He then appeared in the central entrance, flame-headed, unshaven, overcoated, and grasping a sheaf of papers.

" Roast me," he said, " in sulphur. Wash me in steep-down gulfs of liquid fire 'ere I again endure the loathy torment of a dress-rehearsal. What have I done, ye gods, that I should——"

" All right, John," Poole said. " Not yet. Sit down. On some heavy piece of furniture and carefully."

Clem Smith shouted: " Alf! The doctor's chair."

A large chair with broken springs was brought on and placed with its back to the curtain. Dr. Rutherford hurled himself into it and produced his snuff-box. " I am a child to chiding," he said. " What goes on, chums?"

Poole said: " I'm going to take my stuff. If anything I have to say repeats exactly any of your own notes you might leave it out for the sake of saving time. If you've any objections, be a good chap and save them till I've finished. Agreed?"

" Can't we cut the flummery and get down to business."

" That's just what I'm suggesting."

" Is it? I wasn't listening. Press on then, my dear fellow. Press on."

They settled down. Jacko gave Poole a block of notes and he began to work through them. " Nothing much in Act I," he said, " until we get to——" His voice went on evenly. He spoke of details in timing, of orchestration and occasionally of stage-management. Sometimes a player would ask a question and there would be a brief discussion. Sometimes Clem Smith would make a note. For the scenes where Poole had been on, Jacko, it appeared, had taken separate notes. Martyn learnt for the first time that Jacko's official status was that of assistant to Poole and thought it characteristic of him that he made so little of his authority.

From where she stood, holding the glass for Helena Hamilton, she could see all the players. In the foreground was the alert and beautiful face of her employer, a little older now with its make-up gone, turning at times to the looking-glass and at times, when something in his notes concerned her, towards Poole. Beyond Miss Hamilton sat J. G. Darcey alone and thoughtfully filling his pipe. He glanced occasionally, with an air of anxious solicitude, at Miss Gainsford. At the far side Parry Percival lay in an arm-chair looking fretful. Bennington stood near the centre with a towel in his hands. At one moment he came behind his wife. Putting a hand on her shoulder he reached over it, helped himself to a dollop of grease from a jar in her case and slapped it on his face. She made a slight movement of distaste and immediately afterwards a little secret grimace as if she had caught herself out in a blunder. For a moment he retained his hold of her shoulder. Then he looked down at her, dragged his clean fingers across her neck and, smearing the grease over his face, returned to his former position and began to clean away his make-up.

Martyn didn't want to look at Gay Gainsford but was unable altogether to avoid doing so. Miss Gainsford sat, at first alone, on a smallish sofa. She seemed to have herself tolerably well in hand but her eyes were restless and her fingers plaited and replaited the folds of her dress. Bennington watched her from a distance until he had done with his towel. Then he crossed the stage and sat beside her, taking one of the restless hands in his. He looked hard at Martyn who was visited painfully by a feeling of great compassion for both of them and by a sensation of remorse. She had a notion, which she tried to dismiss as fantastic, that Poole sensed this reaction. His glance rested for a moment on her and she thought: " This is getting too complicated. It's going to be too much for me." She made an involuntary movement and at once Miss Hamilton put out a hand to the glass.

When Poole had dealt with the first act he turned to Dr. Rutherford who had sat throughout with his legs extended and his chin on his chest, directing from under his brows a glare of extreme malevolence at the entire cast.

" Anything to add to that, John?" Poole asked.

" Apart from a passing observation that I regard the whole thing as a *tour de force* of understatement and with reservations that I keep to myself——" Here Dr. Rutherford looked fixedly at Parry Percival. " I am mum. I reserve my fire."

" Act Two, then," said Poole and began again.

Martyn became aware after a few minutes that Dr. Rutherford, like Bennington, was staring at her. She was as horridly fascinated as birds are said to be by the un-winking gaze of a snake. Do what she could to look else-where about the stage, she must after a time steal a glance at him only to meet his speculative and bloodshot regard. This alarmed her profoundly. She was persuaded that a feeling of tension had been communicated to the others and that they, too, were aware of some kind of impending crisis. This feeling grew in intensity as Poole's voice went steadily on with his notes. He had got about half-way through the second act when Dr. Rutherford ejaculated " Hi! Wait a bit!" and began a frenzied search through his own notes which seemed to be in complete disorder. Finally he pounced on a sheet of paper, dragged out a pair of spectacles and, with a hand raised to enjoin silence, read it to himself with strange noises in his breathing. Having scattered the rest of his notes over his person and the floor he now folded this particular sheet and sat on it.

" Proceed," he said. The cast stirred uneasily. Poole continued. He had come to the scene between himself and Miss Gainsford and beyond a minor adjustment of position said nothing about it. Miss Hamilton, who had arrived at the final stage of her street make-up, dusted her face with powder, nodded good-humouredly at Martyn and turned to face Poole. Martyn thankfully shut the dressing-case and made for the nearest exit.

At the same moment Poole reached the end of his notes for the second act and Dr. Rutherford shouted: " Hold on! Stop that wench!"

Martyn, with a sensation of falling into chaos, turned in the doorway.

She saw nine faces lifted towards her own. They made a pattern against the smoke-thickened air. Her eyes travelled from one to the other and rested finally on Poole's.

" It's all right," he said. " Go home."

" No, you don't," Dr. Rutherford shouted excitedly.

" Indeed she does," said Poole. " Run away home, Kate. Good night to you."

Martyn heard the storm break as she fled down the passage.

CHAPTER V

OPENING NIGHT

From noon until half-past six on the opening night of Dr. Rutherford's new play, the persons most concerned in its birth were absent from their theatre. Left to itself the Vulcan was possessed only by an immense expectancy. It waited. In the auditorium, rows of seats, stripped of their dust-cloths, stared at the curtain. The curtain itself presented its reverse side to Jacko's set, closing it in with a stuffy air of secrecy. The stage was dark. Battalions of dead lamps, focused at crazy angles, overhung it with the promise of light. Cue-sheets fixed to the switchboard awaited the electrician, the prompt-script was on its shelf, the properties were ranged on trestle-tables. Everything abided its time in the dark theatre.

To enter into this silent house was to feel as if one surprised a poised and expectant presence. This air of suspense made itself felt to the occasional intruders: to the boy who from time to time came through from the office with telegrams for the dressing-rooms, to the girl from Florian's and the young man from the wigmakers, and to the piano-tuner who, for an hour, twanged and hammered in the covered well. And to Martyn Tarne who, alone in the ironing-room, set about the final pressing of the dresses under her care.

The offices were already active and behind their sand-blasted glass walls typewriters clattered and telephone bells rang incessantly. The blacked-out box-plan lay across Bob Grantley's desk and stacked along the wall were rectangular parcels of programmes, fresh from the printer.

And at two o'clock the queues for the early doors began to form up in Carpet Street.

II

It was at two o'clock that Helena Hamilton, after an hour's massage, went to bed. Her husband had telephoned, with a certain air of opulence which she had learnt to dread, that he would lunch at his club and return to their flat during the afternoon to rest.

In her darkened room she followed a practised routine and, relaxing one set of muscles after another, awaited sleep. This time, however, her self-discipline was unsuccessful. If only she could hear him come in it would be better: if only she could see into what sort of state he had got himself. She used all her formulae for repose but none of them worked. At three o'clock she was still awake and still miserably anxious.

It was no good trying to cheer herself up by telling over her rosary of romantic memories. Usually this was a successful exercise. She had conducted her affairs of the heart, she knew, with grace and civility. She had almost always managed to keep them on a level of enchantment. She had simply allowed them to occur with the inconsequence and charm of self-sown larkspurs in an otherwise correctly ordered border. They had hung out their gay little banners for a season and then been painlessly tweaked up. Except, perhaps, for Adam. With Adam, she remembered uneasily, it had been different. With Adam, so much her junior, it had been a more deeply-rooted affair. It had put an end, finally, to her living with Ben as his wife. It had made an enemy of Ben. And at once her thoughts were infested with worries about the contemporary scene at the theatre. " It's such a muddle!" she thought, " and I hate muddles." They had had nothing but trouble all through rehearsals. Ben fighting with everybody and jealous of Adam. The doctor bawling everybody out. And that wretchedly unhappy child Gay (who, God knew, would never be an actress as long as she lived) first pitchforked into the part by Ben and now almost bullied out of it by the doctor. And, last of all, Martyn Tarne.

She had touched the raw centre of her anxieties. Under any other conditions, she told herself, she would have welcomed the appearance out of a clear sky and, one had to face it, under very odd circumstances, of this little antipodean: this throw-back to some forebear that she and Adam were supposed to have in common. Helena would have been inclined to like Martyn for the resemblance instead of feeling so uncomfortably disturbed by it. Of course she accepted Adam's explanation but at the same time she thought it rather naïve of him to believe that the girl had actually kept away from the theatre because she didn't want to make capital out of the relationship. That, Helena thought, turning restlessly on her bed, was really too simple of Adam. Moreover he had stirred up the already exacerbated nerves of the company by giving this girl the understudy without, until last night, making public the relationship.

There she went, thinking about last night's scene: John Rutherford demanding that even at this stage Martyn should play the part, Gay imploring Adam to release her, Ben saying he would walk out on the show if Gay went, and Adam . . . Adam had done the right thing of course. He had come down strongly with one of his rare thrusts of anger and reduced them to complete silence. He had then described the circumstances of Martyn's arrival at the theatre and had added in a voice of ice that there was and could be no question of any change in the cast. He finished his notes and left the theatre, followed by Jacko.

This had been the signal for an extremely messy row in which everybody seemed to come to light with some deep-seated grudge. Ben had quarrelled almost simultaneously with Parry Percival (on the score of technique) with Dr. Rutherford (on the score of casting) with his niece (on the score of humanity) and, unexpectedly, with J. G. Darcey (on the score of Ben bullying Gay). Percival had responded to a witticism of the doctor's by a stream of shrill invective which astonished everybody, himself included, and Gay had knitted the whole scene into a major climax by having a fit of hysterics from which she was restored with brutal efficiency by Dr. Rutherford himself.

The party had then broken up. J. G. sustained his new role of knightly concern by taking Gay home. Parry Percival left in a recrudescence of fury occasioned by the doctor flinging after him a composite Shakesperian epithet: (" Get you gone, you dwarf ; your minimus of hind'ring knot-grass made ; you bead, you acorn.") She herself had retired into the wings. The stage-staff had already disappeared. The doctor and Ben finding themselves in undisputed possession of the stage had squared up to each with the resolution of all-in wrestlers and she, being desperately tired, had taken the car home and asked their man to return to the theatre for her husband. When she woke late in the morning she was told he had already gone out.

" I wish," a voice cried out in her mind, " I wish to God he'd never come back."

And at that moment she heard him stumble heavily upstairs.

She expected him to go straight to his room and was dismayed when he came to a halt outside her door and, with a clumsy sound that might have been intended for a knock, opened it and came in. The smell of brandy and cigars came in with him and invaded the whole room. It was more than a year since that had happened.

He walked uncertainly to the foot of the bed and leant on it—and she was frightened of him.

"Hallo," he said.

"What is it, Ben? I'm resting."

"I thought you might be interested. There'll be no more nonsense from John about Gay."

"Good," she said.

"He's calmed down. I got him to see reason."

"He's not so bad, really—old John."

"He's had some good news from abroad. About the play."

"Translation right?"

"Something like that." He was smiling at her, uncertainly. "You look comfy," he said. "All tucked up."

"Why don't you try and get some rest yourself?" He leant over the foot of the bed and said something under his breath. "What?" she said anxiously. "What did you say?"

"I said it's a pity Adam didn't appear a bit sooner, isn't it? I'm so extraneous."

Her heart thumped like a fist inside her ribs. "Ben, *please*," she said.

"And another thing. Do you both imagine I don't see through this dresser-cum-understudy racket? Darling, I don't much enjoy playing the cuckold in your restoration comedy but I'm just bloody well furious when you so grossly underestimate my intelligence. When was it? On his New Zealand tour in 1930?"

"What is this nonsense!" she said breathlessly.

"Sorry. How are you managing to-night? You and Adam?"

"My dear Ben!"

"I'll tell you. You're making shift with me for once in a blue moon. And I'm not talking about to-night."

She recognised this scene. She had dreamt it many times. His face had advanced upon her while she lay inert with terror, as one does in a nightmare. For an infinitesimal moment she was visited by the hope that perhaps after all she had slept and if she could only scream, would awaken. But she couldn't scream. She was quite helpless.

Adam Poole's telephone rang at half-past four. He had gone late to rest and was wakened from a deep sleep. For a second or two he didn't recognise her voice and she spoke so disjointedly that even when he was broad awake he couldn't make out what she was saying.

"What is it?" he said: "Ella, what's the matter? I can't hear you."

Then she spoke more clearly and he understood.

At six o'clock the persons in the play began to move towards the theatre. In their lodgings and flats they bestirred themselves after their several fashions: to drink tea or black coffee, choke down pieces of bread and butter that tasted like sawdust, or swallow aspirin and alcohol. This was their zero hour: the hour of low vitality when the stimulus of the theatre and the last assault of nerves was yet to come. By a quarter past six they were all on their way. Their dressers were already in their rooms and Jacko prowled restlessly about the darkened stage. Dr. John James Rutherford, clad in an evening-suit and a boiled shirt garnished with snuff, both of which dated from some distant period when he still attended the annual dinners of the B.M.A., plunged into the office and made such a nuisance of himself that Bob Grantley implored him to go away.

At twenty past six the taxi carrying Gay Gainsford and J. G. Darcey turned into Carpet Street. Darcey sat with his knees crossed elegantly and his hat perched on them. In the half light his head and profile looked like those of a much younger man.

"It *was* sweet of you to call for me, J. G.," Gay said unevenly.

He smiled, without looking at her, and patted her hand. "I'm always petrified myself," he said, "on first nights."

"Are you? I suppose a true artiste must be."

"Ah, youth, youth!" sighed J. G., a little stagily perhaps, but, if she hadn't been too preoccupied to notice it, with a certain overtone of genuine nostalgia.

"It's worse than the usual first-night horrors for *me*," she said. "I'm just boxing on in a private hell of my own."

" My poor child."

She turned a little towards him and leant her head into his shoulder. " Nice!" she murmured and after a moment: " I'm so frightened of him, J. G."

With the practised ease of a good actor, he slipped his arm round her. " I won't have it," he said. " By God, I won't! If he worries you again, author or no author——"

" It's not *him*," she said. " Not the doctor. Oh, I know he's simply filthy to work with and he does fuss me dreadfully but it's not the doctor *really* who's responsible for all my misery."

" No? Who is then?"

" Uncle Ben!" She made a small wailing noise that was muffled by his coat. He bent his head attentively to listen. " J. G., I'm just plain *terrified* of Uncle Ben."

v

Parry Percival always enjoyed his arrival at the theatre when there was a gallery queue to be penetrated. One raised one's hat and said: " Pardon me. Thanks so much," to the gratified ladies. One heard them murmur one's name. It was a heartening little fillip to one's self-esteem.

On this occasion the stimulant didn't work with its normal magic. He was too worried to relish it whole-heartedly.

Ben, he thought hotly, was insufferable. Every device by which a second-leading man could make a bit-part actor look foolish had been brought into play during rehearsals. Ben had up-staged him, had flurried him by introducing new business, had topped his lines and, even while he was seething with impotent fury, had reduced him to nervous giggles by looking sideways at him. It was the technique with which a schoolmaster could torture a small boy, and it revived in Parry hideous memories of his childhood.

Only partially restored by the evidence of prestige afforded by the gallery queue he walked down the stage-door alley and into the theatre. He was at once engulfed in its warmth and expectancy.

He passed into the dressing-room passage. Helena Hamilton's door was half-open and the lights were on. He tapped, looked in and was greeted by the smell of greasepaint, powder, wet-white and flowers. The gas-fire groaned comfortably. Martyn, who was spreading towels, turned and found herself confronted by his deceptively boyish face.

" Early at work?" he fluted.

Martyn wished him good evening.

" Helena not down yet?"

" Not yet."

He hung about the dressing-room, fingering photographs and eyeing Martyn.

" I hear you come from Down Under," he said. " I nearly accepted an engagement to go out there last year but I didn't really like the people so I turned it down. Adam played it in the year dot, I believe. Well, more years ago than he would care to remember, I dare say. Twenty, if we're going to let our back hair down. Before you were born, I dare say."

" Yes," Martyn agreed. " Just before."

Her answer appeared to give him extraordinary satisfaction. " Just before?" he repeated. " Really?" and Martyn thought: " I mustn't let myself be worried by this."

He seemed to hover on the edge of some further observation and pottered about the dressing-room examining the great mass of flowers. " I'll swear," he said crossly, " those aren't the roses I chose at Florian's. Honestly that female's an absolute menace."

Martyn, seeing how miserable he looked, felt sorry for him. He muttered: " I do so *abominate* first nights," and she rejoined: " They are pretty ghastly, aren't they?" Because he seemed unable to take himself off, she added with an air of finality: " Anyway, may I wish you luck for this one?"

" Sweet of you," he said. " I'll need it. I'm the stooge of this piece. Well, thanks, anyway."

He drifted into the passage, halted outside the open door of Poole's dressing-room and greeted Bob Cringle. " Governor not down yet?"

" We're on our way, Mr. Percival."

Parry inclined his head and strolled into the room. He stood close to Bob leaning his back against the dressing-shelf, his legs elegantly crossed.

" Our little stranger," he murmured, " seems to be new-brooming away next door."

" That's right, sir," said Bob. " Settled in very nice."

" Strong resemblance," Parry said invitingly.

" To the guvnor, sir?" Bob rejoined cheerfully. " That's right. Quite a coincidence."

" A coincidence!" Parry echoed. " Well, not precisely, Bob. I understand there's a distant relationship. It was

85

mentioned for the first time last night. Which accounts for the set-up, one supposes. Tell me, Bob, have you ever before heard of a dresser doubling an understudy?"

"Worked-out very convenient, hasn't it, sir?"

"Oh, very," said Parry discontentedly. "Look, Bob. You were with the governor on his New Zealand tour in '30, weren't you?"

Bob said woodenly: "That's correct, sir. 'E was just a boy in them days. Might I trouble you to move, Mr. Percival. I got my table to lay out."

"Oh, sorry. I'm in the way. As usual. Quite! Quite!" He waved his hand and walked jauntily into the passage.

"Good luck for to-night, sir," said Bob and shut the door after him.

Parry moved on to J. G. Darcey's room. He tapped, was answered, and went in. J. G. was already embarked on his make-up.

"Bob," said Parry, "refuses to be drawn."

"Good evening, dear boy. About what?"

"Oh, *you* know. The New Zealand tour and so on."

"Did you see her?"

"I happened to look in."

"What's she like?"

Parry lit a cigarette. "As you have seen," he said, "she's fantastically like *him*. Which is really the point at issue. But *fantastically* like."

"Can she give a show?"

"Oh *yes*," said Parry. He leaned forward and hugged his knees boyishly. "Oh, yes indeed. Indeed she can, my dear J. G. You'd be surprised."

J. G. made a non-committal sound and went on with his make-up.

"This morning," Parry continued, "the doctor was there. And Ben. Ben, quite obviously devoured with chagrin. I confess I couldn't help rather gloating. As I remarked, it's getting under his skin. Together, no doubt, with vast potations of brandy and soda."

"I hope to God he's all right to-night."

"It appears Gay was in the back of the house, poor thing, while it was going on."

"She didn't tell me that," J. G. said anxiously and, catching Parry's sharpened glance, he added: "I didn't really hear anything about it."

"It was a repetition of last night. Really, one feels quite dizzy. Gay rushed weeping to Adam and again implored him

86

to let her throw in the part. The doctor, of course, was all for it. Adam was charming but Uncle Ben produced another temperament. He and the doctor left simultaneously in a silence more ominous, I assure you, than last night's dog fight. Ben's not down, yet."

" Not yet," J. G. said and repeated: " I hope to God he's all right."

For a moment the two men were united in a common anxiety. J. G. said: " Christ, I wish I didn't get nervous on first nights."

VI

Clark Bennington's dresser, a thin melancholy man, put him into his gown and hovered, expressionless, behind him. " I shan't need you before the change," said Bennington. " See if you can help Mr. Darcey."

The man went out. Bennington knew he had guessed the reason for his dismissal. He wondered why he could never bring himself to have a drink in front of his dresser. After all there was nothing in taking a nip before the show. Adam, of course, chose to make a great thing of never touching it. And at the thought of Adam Poole he felt resentment and fear stir at the back of his mind. He got his flask out of his overcoat pocket and poured a stiff shot of brandy.

" The thing to do," he told himself, " is to wipe this afternoon clean out. Forget it. Forget everything except my work." But he remembered, unexpectedly, the way, fifteen years ago, he used to prepare himself for a first night. He used to make a difficult and intensive approach to his initial entrance so that when he walked out on the stage he was already possessed by a life that had been created in the dressing-room. Took a lot of concentration: Stanislavsky and all that. Hard going: but in those days it had seemed worth the effort. Helena had encouraged him. He had a notion she and Adam still went in for it. But now he had mastered the easier way: the repeated mannerism, the trick of pause and the unexpected flattening of the voice: the technical box of tricks.

He finished his drink quickly and began to grease his face. He noticed how the flesh had dropped into sad folds under the eyes, had blurred the jaw-line and had sunk into grooves about the nostrils and the corners of the mouth. All right for this part, of course, where he had to make a sight of

87

himself, but he had been a fine-looking man. Helena had fallen for him in a big way until Adam cut him out. At the thought of Adam he experienced a sort of regurgitation of misery and anger. " I'm a haunted man," he thought suddenly.

He had let himself get into a state, he knew, because of this afternoon. Helena's face, gaping with terror, like a fish, almost, kept rising up in his mind and wouldn't be dismissed. Things always worked like that with him: remorse always turned into nightmare.

It had been a bad week altogether. Rows with everybody: with John Rutherford in particular and with Adam over that blasted little dresser. He felt he was the victim of some elaborate plot. He was fond of Gay: she was a nice friendly little thing: his own flesh and blood. Until he had brought her into this piece she had seemed to like him. Not a bad little artiste either and good enough, by God, for the artsy-craftsy part they had thrown at her. He thought of her scene with Poole and of her unhappiness in her failure and how, in some damned cock-eyed way, they all, including Gay, seemed to blame him for it. He supposed she thought he had bullied her into hanging on. Perhaps in a way he had, but he felt so much that he was the victim of a combined assault. " Alone," he thought, " I'm so desperately *alone*," and he could almost hear the word as one would say it on the stage, making it echo, forlorn and hopeless and extremely effective.

" I'm giving myself the jim-jams," he thought. He wondered if Helena had told Adam about this afternoon. By God, that would rock Adam, if she had. And at once a picture rose up to torture him, a picture of Helena weeping in Adam's arms and taking solace there. He saw his forehead grow red in the looking-glass and told himself he had better steady-up. No good getting into one of his tempers with a first performance ahead of him and everything so tricky with young Gay. There he was, coming back to that girl, that phoney dresser. He poured out another drink and began his make-up.

He recognised with satisfaction a familiar change of mood and he now indulged himself with a sort of treat. He brought out a little piece of secret knowledge he had stored away. Among this company of enemies there was one over whom he exercised almost complete power. Over one, at least, he had, overwhelmingly, the whip-hand and the knowledge of his sovereignty warmed him almost as comfortably as the brandy. He began to think about his part. Ideas, brand new and as clever as paint, crowded each other in his imagination. He anticipated his coming mastery.

His left hand slid towards the flask. " One more," he said, " and I'll be fine."

VII

In her room across the passage, Gay Gainsford faced her own reflection and watched Jacko's hands pass across it. He dabbed with his fingertips under the cheekbones and made a droning sound behind his closed lips. He was a very good make-up; it was one of his many talents. At the dress-rehearsals the touch of his fingers had soothed rather than exacerbated her nerves but to-night, evidently, she found it almost intolerable.

" Haven't you finished?" she asked.

" Patience, patience. We do not catch a train. Have you never observed the triangular shadows under Adam's cheek-bones? They are yet to be created."

" Poor Jacko!" Gay said breathlessly, " this must be such a bore for you. Considering everything."

" Quiet, now. How can I work?"

" No, but I mean it must be so exasperating to think that two doors away there's somebody who wouldn't need your help. Just a straight make-up, wouldn't it be? No trouble."

" I adore making-up. It is my most brilliant gift."

" But she's your find in a way, isn't she? You'd like her to have the part, wouldn't you?"

He rested his hands on her shoulders. " Ne vous dérangez pas," he said. " Shut up, in fact. Tranquillise yourself, idiot-girl."

" But I want you to tell me."

" Then I tell you. Yes, I would like to see this little freak play your part because she is in fact a little freak. She has dropped into this theatre like an accident in somebody else's dream and the effect is fantastic. But she is well content to remain off-stage and it is you who play and we have faith in you and wish you well with all our hearts."

" That's very nice of you," Gay said.

" What a sour voice! It is true. And now reflect. Reflect upon the minuteness of Edmund Kean, upon Sarah's one leg and upon Irving's two, upon ugly actresses who convince
89

their audiences they are beautiful and old actors who persuade them they are young. It is all in the mind, the spirit
and the preparation. What does Adam say? Think in, and
then play out. Do so."

"I can't," Gay said between her teeth. "I can't." She
twisted in her chair. He lifted his fingers away from her face
quickly, with a wide gesture. "Jacko," she said. "There's
a jinx on this night. Jacko, did you know? It was on the
night of the Combined Arts Ball that it happened."

"What is this foolishness?"

"You know. Five years ago. The stage-hands were talking
about it. I heard them. The gas-fire case. The night that
man was murdered. Everyone knows."

"Be silent!" Jacko said loudly. "This is idiocy. I forbid
you to speak of it. The chatter of morons. The Combined
Arts Ball has no fixed date and if it had, shall an assembly
of British bourgeoisie in bad fancy-dress control our destiny?
I am ashamed of you. You are altogether too stupid.
Master yourself."

"It's not only that. It's everything. I can't face it."

His fingers closed down on her shoulders. "Master yourself," he said. "You must. If you cry I shall beat you and
wipe your make-up across your face. I defy you to cry."

He cleaned his hands, tipped her head forward and began
to massage the nape of her neck. "There are all sorts of
things," he said, "that you must remember and as many more
to forget. Forget the little freak and the troubles of to-day.
Remember to relax all your muscles and also your nerves and
your thoughts. Remember the girl in the play and the faith
I have in you, and Adam and also your Uncle Bennington."

"Spare me my Uncle Bennington, Jacko. If my Uncle
Bennington had left me where I belong, in fortnightly rep.,
I wouldn't be facing this hell. I know what everyone thinks
of Uncle Ben and I agree with them. I never want to see
him again. I hate him. He's made me go on with this. I
wanted to throw the part in. It's not my part. I loathe it. No,
I don't loathe it, that's not true. I loathe myself for letting
everybody down. Oh, God, Jacko, what am I going to do."

Across the bowed head Jacko looked at his own reflection
and poked a face at it.

"You shall play this part," he said through his teeth,
"Mouse-heart, skunk-girl. You shall play. Think of nothing.
Unbridle your infinite capacity for inertia and be dumb."

Watching himself, he arranged his face in an unconvincing
glower and fetched up a Shakespearian belly-voice.

" *The devil damn thee black thou creamfaced loon. Where gottest thou that goose-look?*"

He caught his breath. Beneath his fingers, Gay's neck stiffened. He began to swear elaborately, in French and in a whisper.

" Jacko. *Jacko.* Where does that line come?"

" I invented it."

" You didn't. You *didn't.* It's Macbeth," she wailed. " *You've quoted from Macbeth!*" and burst into a flurry of terrified weeping.

" Great suffering and all-enduring Saints of God," apostrophised Jacko, " give me some patience with this Quaking Thing."

But Gay's cries mounted in a sharp crescendo. She flung out her arms and beat with her fists on the dressing-table. A bottle of wet-white rocked to and fro, over-balanced, rapped smartly against the looking-glass and fell over. A neatly splintered star frosted the surface of the glass.

Gay pointed to it with an air of crazy triumph, snatched up her towel, and scrubbed it across her make-up. She thrust her face, blotched and streaked with black cosmetic, at Jacko.

" *Don't you like what you see?*" she quoted, and rocketed into genuine hysteria.

Five minutes later Jacko walked down the passage towards Adam Poole's room leaving J. G., who had rushed to the rescue in his shirtsleeves, in helpless contemplation of the screaming Gay. Jacko disregarded the open doors and the anxious painted faces that looked out at him.

Bennington shouted from his room:

" What the hell goes on? Who *is* that?"

" Listen," Jacko began, thrusting his head in at the door. He looked at Bennington and stopped short. " Stay where you are," he said and crossed the passage to Poole's room.

Poole had swung round in his chair to face the door. Bob Cringle stood beside him twisting a towel in his hands.

" Well?" Poole said. " What is it? Is it Gay?"

" She's gone up. Sky high. I can't do anything nor can J. G. and I don't believe anyone can. She refuses to go on."

" Where's John. Is this his doing?"

" God knows. I don't think so. He came in an hour ago and said he'd be back at five-to-seven."

" Has Ben tried?"

" She does nothing but scream that she never wants to see him again. In my opinion, Ben would be fatal."

"He must be able to hear all this."

"I told him to stay where he is."

Poole looked sharply at Jacko and went out. Gay's laughter had broken down in a storm of irregular sobbing that could be heard quite clearly. Helena Hamilton called out, "Adam, shall I go to her?" and he answered from the passage, "Better not I think."

He was some time with Gay. They heard her shouting. "No. No. I won't go on. No," over and over again like an automaton.

When he came out he went to Helena Hamilton's room. She was dressed and made-up. Martyn, with an ashen face, stood inside the doorway.

"I'm sorry, darling," Poole said, "but you'll have to do without a dresser."

The call-boy came down the passage chanting:

"Half-hour. Half-hour, please."

Poole and Martyn looked at each other.

"You'll be all right," he said.

CHAPTER VI

PERFORMANCE

At ten-to-eight Martyn stood by the entrance.

She was dressed in Gay's clothes and Jacko had made her up very lightly. They had all wished her luck: J. G., Parry Percival, Helena Hamilton, Adam Poole, Clem Smith and even the dressers and stage-hands.

There had been something real and touching in their way of doing this so that, even in her terror, she had felt they were good and very kind. Bennington alone had not wished her well but he had kept right away and this abstention, she thought, showed a certain generosity.

She no longer felt sick but the lining of her mouth and throat was harsh as if, in fact, she had actually vomited. She thought her sense of hearing must have become distorted. The actors' voices on the other side of the canvas wall had the remote quality of voices in a nightmare whereas the hammer-blows of her heart and the rustle of her dress that accompanied them sounded exceeding loud.

She saw the frames of the set, their lashings and painted legends, "Act I, P. 2" and the door which she was to open.

She could look into the prompt corner where the A.S.M. followed the lighted script with his finger and where, high above him, the electrician leaned over his perch, watching the play. The stage-lights were reflected into his face. Everything was monstrous in its preoccupation. Martyn was alone.

She tried to command the upsurge of panic in her heart, to practise an approach to her ordeal, to create, in place of these implacable realities, the reality of the house in the play and that part of it in which now, out of sight of the audience, she must already have her being. This attempt went down before the clamour of her nerves. " I'm going to fail," she thought.

Jacko came round the set. She hoped he wouldn't speak to her and as if he sensed this wish, he stopped at a distance and waited.

" I must listen," she thought. " I'm not listening. I don't know where they've got to. I've forgotten which way the door opens. I've missed my cue." Her inside deflated and despair griped it like a colic.

She turned and found Poole beside her.

" You're all right," he said. " The door opens on. You can do it. Now, my girl. On you go."

Martyn didn't hear the round of applause with which a London audience greets a player who appears at short notice.

She was on. She had made her entry and was engulfed in the play.

II

Dr. Rutherford sat in the O.P. box with his massive shoulder turned to the house and his gloved hands folded together on the balustrade. His face was in shadow but the stage-lights just touched the bulging curve of his old-fashioned shirt-front. He was monumentally still. One of the critics, an elderly man, said in an aside to a colleague, that Rutherford reminded him of Watt's picture of the Minotaur.

For the greater part of the first act he was alone, having, as he had explained in the office, no masochistic itch to invite a guest to a Roman holiday where he himself was the major sacrifice. Towards the end of the act, however, Bob Grantley came into the box and stood behind him. Grantley's attention was divided. Sometimes he looked down through beams of spot-lights at the stalls, cobbled with heads, sometimes at the stage and sometimes, sideways and with caution, at the doctor himself. Really, Grantley thought, he was quite uncomfortably motionless. One couldn't tell what he was thinking and one hesitated, the Lord knew, to ask him.

Down on the stage Clark Bennington and Parry Percival and J. G. Darcey had opened the long crescendo leading to Helena's entrance. Grantley thought suddenly how vividly an actor's nature could be exposed on the stage: there was for instance a kind of bed-rock niceness about old J. G., a youthfulness of spirit that declaimed itself through the superimposed make-up, the characterisation and J. G.'s indisputable middle-age. And Bennington? And Percival? Grantley had begun to consider them in these terms when Percival, speaking one of his colourless lines, turned downstage. Bennington moved centre, looked at Darcey and neatly sketched a parody of Percival's somewhat finicking movement. The theatre was filled with laughter. Percival turned quickly, Bennington smiled innocently at him, prolonging the laugh.

Grantley looked apprehensively at the doctor.

" Is that new?" he ventured in a whisper. "That business?"

The doctor didn't answer and Grantley wondered if he only imagined that the great hands on the balustrade had closed more tightly over each other.

Helena Hamilton came on to a storm of applause and with her entrance the action was roused to a new excitement and was intensified with every word she uttered. The theatre grew warm with her presence and with a sense of heightened suspense.

" Now they're all on," Grantley thought, " except Adam and the girl."

He drew a chair forward stealthily and sat behind Rutherford.

" It's going enormously," he murmured to the massive shoulder. " Terrific, old boy." And because he was nervous he added : " This brings the girl on, doesn't it?"

For the first time, the doctor spoke. His lips scarcely moved. A submerged voice uttered within him. "Hence," it said, " heap of wrath, foul indigested lump."

" Sorry, old boy," whispered Grantley and began to wonder what hope in hell there was of persuading the d'stinguished author to have a drink in the office during the interval with a hand-picked number of important persons.

He was still preoccupied with this problem when a side door in the set opened and a dark girl with short hair walked out on the stage.

Grantley joined in the kindly applause. The doctor remained immovable.

The players swept up to their major climax, Adam came on and five minutes later the curtain fell on the first act. The hands of the audience filled the house with a storm of rain. The storm swelled prodigiously and persisted even after the lights had come up.

"Ah, good girl," Bob Grantley stammered, filled with the sudden and excessive emotion of the theatre. "Good old Adam. Jolly good show!"

Greatly daring, he clapped the doctor on the shoulders. The doctor remained immovable.

Grantley edged away to the back of the box. "I must get back," he said. "Look, John, there are one or two people coming to the office for a drink who would be——"

The doctor turned massively in his seat and faced him.

"No," he said, "thank you."

"Well, but look, dear boy, it's just one of those things. You know how it is, John, you know how——"

"Shut up," said the doctor, without any particular malice. "I'm going back-stage," he added. He rose and turned away from the audience. "I have no desire to swill tepid spirits with minor celebrities among the backsides of sandblasted gods. Thank you, however. See you later."

He opened the pass-door at the back of the box.

"You're pleased, aren't you?" Grantley said. "You *must* be pleased."

"Must I? Must I indeed?"

"With the girl, at least? So far?"

"The wench is a good wench. So far. I go to tell her so. By your leave, Robert."

He lumbered through the pass-door and Grantley heard him plunge dangerously down the narrow stairway to the stage.

III

Dr. Rutherford emerged in a kaleidoscopic world: a world where walls fell softly apart, landscapes ascended into darkness and stairways turned and moved aside. A blue haze rose from the stage which was itself in motion. Jacko's first set revolved bodily, giving way to a new and more distorted version of itself which came to rest, facing the curtain. Masking pieces were run forward to frame it in. The doctor started off for the dressing-room passage and was at once involved with moving flats. "If you please, sir." "Stand aside, there, *please*." "Clear stage, *by* your leave." His bulky shape was screened and exposed again and again plunged forward confusedly. Warning bells rang, the call-boy began to chant: "Second Act beginners, please. Second Act."

"Lights," Clem Smith said.

The shifting world stood still. Circuit by circuit the lights came on and bore down on the acting area. The last toggle-line slapped home and was made fast and the sweating stage-hands walked disinterestedly off the set. Clem Smith, with his back to the curtain, made a final check. "Clear Stage," he said and looked at his watch. The curtain-hand climbed an iron ladder.

"Six minutes," said the A.S.M. He wrote it on his chart. Clem moved into the promt corner. "Right," he said. "Actors, please."

J. G. Darcey and Parry Percival walked on to the set and took up their positions. Helena Hamilton came out of her dressing-room. She stood with her hands clasped lightly at her waist at a little distance from the door by which she must enter. A figure emerged from the shadows near the passage and went up to her.

"Miss Hamilton," Martyn said nervously, "I'm not on for your quick change. I can do it."

Helena turned. She looked at Martyn for a moment with an odd fixedness. Then a smile of extraordinary charm broke across her face and she took Martyn's head lightly between her hands.

"My dear child," she murmured, "my ridiculous child." She hesitated for a moment and then said briskly: "I've got a new dresser."

"A new dresser?"

"Jacko. He's most efficient."

Poole came down the passage. She turned to him and linked her arm through his. "She's going to be splendid in her scene," she said. "Isn't she?"

Poole said: "Keep it up, Kate. All's well." And in the look he gave Helena Hamilton there was something of comradeship, something of compassion and something, perhaps, of gratitude.

Dr. Rutherford emerged from the passage and addressed himself to Martyn: "Here!" he said, "I've been looking for you, my pretty. You might be a lot worse, considering, but you haven't done anything yet. When you play this next scene, my poppet, these few precepts in thy——"

"No, John," Poole and Helena Hamilton said together. "Not now."

He glowered at them. Poole nodded to Martyn who began to move away but had not got far before she heard Rutherford say: "Have you tackled that fellow? Did you see it? Where is he? By God, when I get at him——"

"Stand by," said Clem Smith.

"Quiet, John," said Poole imperatively. "Back to your box, sir."

The curtain rose on the second act.

For the rest of her life the physical events that were encompassed by the actual performance of the play were to be almost lost for Martyn: indeed she could not be perfectly certain that they had happened at all. She might have been under hypnosis or some partial anæsthesia for all the reality they afterwards retained.

This odd condition which was perhaps the result of some kind of physical compensation for the extreme assault on her nerves and emotion, persisted until she made her final exit in the last act. It happened some time before the curtain. The character she played was the first to relinquish its hold and to fade out of the picture. She came off and returned to her corner near the entry into the passage. The others were all on, the dressers and stage-staff, drawn by the hazards of a first night watched from the side and Jacko was near the prompt corner. The passage and dressing-rooms seemed deserted and Martyn was quit alone. She began to emerge from her trance-like suspension. Parry Percival and J. G. Darcey came off and, in turn, spoke to her.

Parry said incoherently: "Darling, you were perfectly splendid. I'm just *so* angry at the moment I can't *speak* but I do congratulate you."

Martyn saw that he actually trembled with an emotion that was, she must suppose, fury. Out of the dream from which she was not yet fully awakened there came a memory of gargantuan laughter and she thought she associated it with Bennington and with Percival. He said: "This settles it. I'm taking action. God, this settles it!" and darted down the passage.

Martyn thought, still confusedly, that she should go to the dressing-room and tidy her make-up for the curtain call. But it was not her dressing-room, it was Gay's and she felt uneasy about it. While she hesitated J. G. Darcey came off.

He put his hand on Martyn's shoulder. "Well done, child," he said. "A very creditable performance."

Martyn thanked him and, on an impulse, added: "Mr. Darcey, is Gay still here? Should I say something to her? I'd like to but I know how she must feel and I don't want to be clumsy."

He waited for a moment, looking at her. "She's in the greenroom," he said. "Perhaps later. Not now, I think. Nice of you."

"I won't unless you say so, then."

He made her a little bow. "I am at your service," he said and followed Percival down the passage.

Jacko came round the set with the stage-hand who was to fire the effects gun. When he saw Martyn his whole face split in a grin. He took her hands in his and kissed them and she was overwhelmed with shyness.

"But your face," he said, wrinkling his own into a monkey's grimace. "It shines like a good deed in a naughty world. Do not touch it yourself. To your dressing-room. I come in two minutes. Away, before your ears are blasted."

He moved down-stage, applied his eye to a secret hole in the set through which he could watch the action and held out his arm in warning to the stage-hand who then lifted the effects gun. Martyn went down the passage as Bennington came off. He caught her up: "Miss Tarne. Wait a moment, will you?"

Dreading another intolerable encounter Martyn faced him. His make-up had been designed to exhibit the brutality of the character and did so all too successfully. The lips were painted a florid red, the pouches under the eyes and the sensual drag from the nostrils to the mouth had been carefully emphasised. He was sweating heavily through the greasepaint and his face glistened in the dull light of the passage.

"I just wanted to say"—he began and at that moment the gun was fired and Martyn gave an involuntary cry; he went on talking—"when I see it," he was saying, "I suppose you aren't to be blamed for that. You saw your chance and took it. Gay and Adam tell me you offered to get out and were not allowed to go. That may be fair enough: I wouldn't know. But I'm not worrying about that." He spoke disjointedly. It was as if his thoughts were too disordered for any coherent expression. "I just wanted to tell you that you needn't suppose what I'm going to do—you needn't think—I mean——"

He touched his shining face with the palm of his hand. Jacko came down the passage and took Martyn by the elbow. "Quick," he said, "into your room. You want powdering, Ben. Excuse me."

Bennington went into his own room. Jacko thrust Martyn into hers, and leaving the door open followed Bennington. She heard him say: "Take care with your upper lip. It is dripping with sweat." He darted back to Martyn, stood her near the dressing-shelf and, with an expression of the utmost concentration effected a number of what he called running repairs to her make-up and her hair. They heard Percival and Darcey go past on their way to the stage. A humming noise caused by some distant dynamo made itself heard, the tap in the wash-basin dripped, the voices on the stage sounded intermittently. Martyn looked at Gay's make-up box, at her dressing-gown and at the array of mascots on the shelf and wished very heartily that Jacko would have done. Presently the call-boy came down the passage with his summons for the final curtain. "Come," said Jacko.

He took her round to the prompt side.

Here she found a group already waiting: Darcey and Percival, Clem Smith, the two dressers and, at a distance, one or two stage-hands. They all watched the final scene between Helena Hamilton and Adam Poole. In this scene Rutherford tied up and stated finally the whole thesis of his play. The man was faced with his ultimate decision. Would he stay and attempt, with the woman, to establish a sane and enlightened formula for living in place of the one he himself had destroyed or would he go back to his island community and attempt a further development within himself and in a less complex environment? As throughout the play, the conflict was set out in terms of human and personal relationships. It could be played like many another love scene, purely on those terms. Or it could be so handled that the wider implictions could be felt by the audience and in the hands of these two players that was what happened. The play ended with them pledging themselves to each other and to an incredible task. As Poole spoke the last lines the electrician, with one eye on Clem below, played madly over his switchboard. The entire set changed its aspect, seemed to dissolve, turned threadbare, a skeleton, a wraith, while

99

beyond it a wide stylised landscape was flooded with light and became as Poole spoke the tag, the background upon which the curtain fell.

"Might as well be back in panto," said the electrician leaning on his dimmers, "we got the transformation scene. All we want's the bloody fairy queen."

It was at this moment, when the applause seemed to surge forward and beat against the curtains, when Clem shouted: "All on." And Dr. Rutherford plunged out of the O.P. pass-door, when the players walked on and linked hands, that Poole, looking hurriedly along the line said: "Where's Ben!"

One of those panic-stricken crises peculiar to the theatre boiled up on the instant. From her position between Darcey and Percival on the stage Martyn saw the call-boy make some kind of protest to Clem Smith and disappear. Above the applause they heard him hare down the passage, yelling: "Mr. Bennington! Mr. Bennington! Please! You're on!"

"We can't wait," Poole shouted. "Take it up, Clem."

The curtain rose and Martyn looked into a sea of faces and hands. She felt herself led forward into the roaring swell, bowed with the others, felt Darcey's and Percival's hands tighten on hers, bowed again and with them retreated a few steps up-stage as the first curtain fell.

"Well?" Poole shouted into the wings. The call-boy could be heard beating on the dressing-room door.

Percival said: "What's the betting he comes on for a star call?"

"He's passed out," said Darcey. "Had one or two more since he came off."

"By God, I wouldn't cry if he never came to."

"Go on, Clem," said Poole.

The curtain rose and fell again, twice. Percival and Darcey took Martyn off and it went up again on Poole and Helena Hamilton, this time to those cries of "bravo" that reach the actors as a long open sound like the voice of a singing wind. In the wings, Clem Smith with his eyes on the stage was saying repeatedly: "He doesn't answer. He's locked in. The b—— doesn't answer."

Martyn saw Poole coming towards her and stood aside. He seemed to tower over her as he took her hand. "Come along," he said. Darcey and Percival and the group off-stage began to clap.

Poole led her on. She felt herself resisting and heard him say: "Yes, it's all right."

So bereft was Martyn of her normal stage-wiseness that

100

he had to tell her to bow. She did so and wondered why there was a warm sound of laughter in the applause. She looked at Poole, found he was bowing to her and bent her head under his smile. He returned her to the wings.

They were all on again. Dr. Rutherford came out from the O.P. corner. The cast joined in the applause. Martyn's heart had begun to sing so loudly that it was like to deafen every emotion but a universal gratitude. She thought Rutherford looked like an old lion standing there in his out-of-date evening-dress, his hair ruffled, his gloved hand touching his bulging shirt, bowing in an unwieldy manner to the audience and to the cast. He moved forward and the theatre was abruptly silent: silent, but for an obscure and intermittent thudding in the dressing-room passage. Clem Smith said something to the A.S.M. and rushed away, jingling keys.

"Hah," said Dr. Rutherford with a preliminary bellow. "Hah—thankee. I'm much obliged to you, ladies and gentlemen and to the actors. The actors are much obliged, no doubt, to you but not necessarily to me." Here the audience laughed and the actors smiled. "I am not able to judge," the doctor continued with a rich roll in his voice, "whether you have extracted from this play the substance of its argument. If you have done so we may all felicitate each other with the indiscriminate enthusiasm characteristic of these occasions: if you have not, I for my part am not prepared to say where the blame should rest."

A solitary man laughed in the audience. The doctor rolled an eye at him and, with this clownish trick, brought the house down. "The prettiest epilogue to a play that I am acquainted with," he went on, "is (as I need perhaps hardly mention to so intelligent an audience), that written for a boy-actor by William Shakespeare. I am neither a boy nor an actor but I beg leave to end by quoting to you. 'If it be true that good wine needs no bush——'"

"Gas!" Parry Percival said under his breath. Martyn, who thought the doctor was going well, glanced indignantly at Parry and was astonished to see that he looked frightened.

"'——therefore,'" the doctor was saying arrogantly, "'to beg will not become me——'"

"Gas!" said an imperative voice off-stage and someone else ran noisily round the back of the set.

And then Martyn smelt it. Gas.

To the actors it seemed afterwards as if they had been fantastically slow to understand that disaster had come upon the theatre. The curtain went down on Dr. Rutherford's last word. There was a further outbreak of applause. Someone off-stage shouted: "The King, for God's sake," and at once the anthem rolled out disinterestedly in the well. Poole ran off the stage and was met by Clem Smith who had a bunch of keys in his hand. The rest followed him.

The area back-stage reeked of gas.

It was extraordinary how little was said. The players stood together and looked about them with the question in their faces that they were unable to ask.

Poole said: "Keep all visitors out, Clem. Send them to the foyer." And at once the A.S.M. spoke into the prompt telephone. Bob Grantley burst through the pass-door, beaming from ear to ear.

"*Stupendous!*" he shouted. "John! Ella! Adam! My God, chaps, you've done it——"

He stood, stock-still, his arms extended, the smile dying on his face.

"Go back, Bob," Poole said. "Cope with the people. Ask our guests to go on and not wait for us. Ben's ill. Clem: get all available doors open. We want air."

Grantley said: "Gas?"

"Quick," Poole said. "Take them with you. Settle them down and explain. He's ill. Then ring me here. But quickly, Bob. Quickly."

Grantley went out without another word.

"Where is he?" Dr. Rutherford demanded.

Helena Hamilton suddenly said: "Adam?"

"Go on to the stage, Ella. It's better you shouldn't be here, believe me. Kate will stay with you. I'll come in a moment."

"Here you are, Doctor," said Clem Smith.

There was a blundering sound in the direction of the passage. Rutherford said, "Open the dock doors," and went behind the set.

Poole thrust Helena through the prompt entry and shut the door behind her. Draughts of cold air came through the side entrances.

"Kate," Poole said, "go in and keep her there if you can. Will you? And, Kate——"

Rutherford reappeared and with him four stage-hands bearing with difficulty the inert body of Clark Bennington. the head swinging upside down between the two leaders, its mouth wide open.

Poole moved quickly but he was too late to shield Martyn. "Never mind," he said. "Go in with Helena."

"Anyone here done respiration for gassed cases?" Dr. Rutherford demanded. "I can start but I'm not good for long."

"I can," said the A.S.M. "I was a warden."

"I can," said Jacko.

"And I," said Poole.

"In the dock then. Shut these doors and open the outer ones."

Kneeling by Helena Hamilton and holding her hand, Martyn heard the doors roll back and the shambling steps go into the dock. The doors crashed behind them.

Martyn said: "They're giving him respiration, Dr. Rutherford's there."

Helena nodded with an air of sagacity. Her face was quite without expression, and she was shivering.

"I'll get your coat," Martyn said. It was in the improvised dressing-room on the O.P. side. She was back in a moment and put Helena into it as if she was a child, guiding her arms and wrapping the fur about her.

A voice off-stage—J. G. Darcey's—said: "Where's Gay? Is Gay still in the greenroom?"

Martyn was astonished when Helena, behind the mask that had become her face, said loudly: "Yes. She's there. In the greenroom."

There was a moment's silence and then J.G. said: "She mustn't stay there. Good God——"

They heard him go away.

Parry Percival's voice announced abruptly that he was going to be sick. "But where?" he cried distractedly. "Where?"

"In your dressing-room for Pete's sake," Clem Smith said.

"It'll be full of gas. Oh, *really*!" There was an agonised and not quite silent interval. "I couldn't be more sorry," Percival said weakly.

"I want," Helena said, "to know what happened. I want to see Adam. Ask him to come, please."

Martyn made for the door but before she reached it Dr. Rutherford came in, followed by Poole. Rutherford had taken off his coat and was a fantastic sight in boiled shirt, black trousers and red braces.

"Well, Ella," he said, "this is not a nice business. We're doing everything that can be done. I'm getting a new oxygen thing in as quickly as possible. There have been some remarkable saves in these cases. But I think you ought to know it's a thinnish chance. There's no pulse and so on."

"I want," she said, holding out her hand to Poole, "to know what happened."

Poole said gently: "All right, Ella, you shall. It looks as if Ben locked himself in after his exit and then turned the gas-fire off—and on again. When Clem unlocked the door and went in he found Ben on the floor. His head was near the fire and a coat over both. He could only have been like that for quite a short time."

"This theatre," she said. "This awful theatre."

Poole looked as if he would make some kind of protest but after a moment's hesitation he said: "All right, Ella. Perhaps it did suggest the means but if he had made up his mind he would, in any case, have found the means."

"Why?" she said. "Why has he done it?"

Dr. Rutherford growled inarticulately and went out. They heard him open and shut the dock doors. Poole sat down by Helena and took her hands in his. Martyn was going but he looked up at her and said: "No, don't. Don't go, Kate," and she waited near the door.

"This is no time," Poole said, "to speculate. He may be saved. If he isn't, then we shall of course ask ourselves just why. But he was in a bad way, Ella. He'd gone to pieces and he knew it."

"I wasn't much help," she said, "was I? Though it's true to say I did try for quite a long time."

"Indeed you did. There's one thing you must be told. If it's no go with Ben, we'll have to inform the police."

She put her hand to her forehead as if she was puzzled. "The police?" she repeated and stared at him. "No, darling, no!" she cried and after a moment whispered, "They might think—oh, darling, darling, darling, the Lord knows what they think!"

The door up-stage opened and Gay Gainsford came in, followed by Darcey.

She was in her street clothes and at some time during the evening had made extensive repairs to her face which were, at the moment, an expression oddly compounded of triumph and distraction. Before she could speak she was seized with a paroxism of coughing.

Darcey said: " Is it all right for Gay to wait here?"

" Yes, of course," said Helena.

He went out and Poole followed him saying he would return.

" Darling," Miss Gainsford gasped, " I knew. I knew as soon as I smelt it. There's a Thing in this theatre. Everything pointed to it. I just sat there and *knew*." She coughed again. " Oh I do feel so sick," she said.

" Gay for pity's sake what are you talking about?" Helena said.

" It was Fate, I felt. I wasn't a bit surprised. I just knew something had to happen to-night."

" Do you mean to say," Helena murmured, and the wraith of her gift for irony was on her mouth, " that you just sat in the greenroom with your finger raised, telling yourself it was Fate?"

" Darling Aunty—I'm sorry. I forgot—darling, Ella, wasn't it amazing?"

Helena made a little gesture of defeat. Miss Gainsford looked at her for a moment and then, with the prettiest air of compassion, knelt at her feet. " Sweet," she said, " I'm so terribly, terribly sorry. We're together in this, aren't we? He was my uncle and your husband."

" True enough," said Helena. She looked at Martyn over the head bent in devoted commiseration, and shook her own helplessly. Gay Gainsford sank into a sitting posture and leant her cheek against Helena's hand. The hand, after a courteous interval, was withdrawn.

There followed a very long silence. Martyn sat at a distance and wondered if there was anything in the world she could do to help. There was an intermittent murmur of voices somewhere off-stage. Gay Gainsford, feeling perhaps that she had sustained her position long enough, moved by gradual degrees away from her aunt by marriage, rose and, sighing heavily, transferred herself to the sofa.

Time dragged on, mostly in silence. Helena lit one cigarette from the butt of another, Gay sighed with infuriating punctuality and Martyn's thoughts drifted sadly about the evaporation of her small triumph.

Presently there were sounds of arrival. One or two persons walked round the set from the outside entry to the dock and were evidently admitted into it.

105

"Who can that be, I wonder?" Helena Hamilton asked idly, and after a moment, "Is Jacko about?"

"I'll see," said Martyn.

She found Jacko off-stage with Darcey and Parry Percival. Percival was saying: "Well, naturally, nobody wants to go to the party but I must say that as one is quite evidently useless here I don't see why one can't go home."

Jacko said: "You would be recalled by the police, I dare say, if you went."

He caught sight of Martyn who went up to him. His face was beaded with sweat. "What is it, my small?" He asked. "This is a sad epilogue to your success story. Never mind. What is it?"

"I think Miss Hamilton would like to see you."

"Then, I come. It is time, in any case."

He took her by the elbow and they went in together. When Helena saw him she seemed to rouse herself. "Jacko?" she said.

He didn't answer and she got up quickly and went to him. "Jacko! What is it? Has it happened?"

Jacko's hands, so refined and delicate that they seemed like those of another man, touched her hair and her face.

"It has happened," he said. "We have tried very hard but nothing is any good at all and there is no more to be done. He has taken wing."

Gay Gainsford broke into a fit of sobbing but Helena stooped her head to Jacko's shoulder and when his arms had closed about her said: "Help me to feel something, Jacko. I'm quite empty of feeling. Help me to be sorry."

Above her head, Jacko's face, glistening with sweat, grotesque and primitive, had the fixed inscrutability of a classic mask.

CHAPTER VII

DISASTER

Clem Smith rang up the police as soon as Dr. Rutherford said that Bennington was beyond recovery and within five minutes a constable and sergeant had appeared at the stage-door. They went into the dock with Rutherford and then to Bennington's dressing-room where they remained alone for some time. During this period an aimless discussion developed among the members of the company about where they should go. Clem Smith suggested the greenroom as the warmest place and added, tactlessly, that the fumes had probably dispersed and if so there was no reason why they shouldn't light the fire. Both Parry Percival and Gay Gainsford had made an outcry against this suggestion on the grounds of delicacy and susceptibility. Darcey supported Gay, the A.S.M. suggested the offices and Jacko the auditorium. Doctor Rutherford, who appeared to be less upset than anyone else, merely remarked that "all places that the eye of Heaven visits, are to a wise man, ports and happy havens," which, as Percival said acidly, got them nowhere.

Finally Poole asked if the central-heating couldn't be stoked up and a stage-hand was dispatched to the underworld to find out. Evidently he met with success as presently the air became less chilled. With only a spatter of desultory conversation, the players sat about the stage and cleaned their faces. And they listened.

They heard the two men come back along the passage and separate. Then the central door opened and the young constable came in.

He was a tall good-looking youth with a charming smile.

"The sergeant," he said, "has asked me to explain that he's telephoning Scotland Yard. He couldn't be more sorry but he's afraid he'll have to ask everybody to wait until he gets his instructions. He's sure you'll understand that it's just a matter of routine."

He might have been apologising for his mother's late arrival at her own dinner-party.

He was about to withdraw when Dr. Rutherford said: "Hi! Sonny!"

"Yes, sir?" said the young constable obligingly.

"You intrigue me. You talk, as they say, like a book. *Non sine dis animosus infans.* You swear with a good grace and wear your boots very smooth, do you not?"

The young constable was, it seemed, only momentarily taken aback. He said: "Well, sir, for my boots they are after the Dogberry fashion and for my swearing, sir, it goes by the book."

The doctor who until now, had seemed to share the general feeling of oppression and shock, appeared to cheer up with indecent haste. He was, in fact, clearly enchanted: "Definite, definite, well-educated infant," he quoted exultantly.

"I mean that in court, sir, we swear by the Book. But I'm afraid, sir," added the young constable apologetically,

" that I'm not much of a hand at 'Bardinage.' My purse is empty already. If you'll excuse me," he concluded, with a civil glance round the company, " I'll just——"

He was again about to withdraw when his sergeant came in at the O.P. entrance.

" Good evening, ladies and gentlemen," the sergeant said in what Martyn, for one, felt was the regulation manner. " Very sorry to keep you, I'm sure. Sad business. In these cases we have to do a routine check-up as you might say. My superior officers will be here in a moment and then, I hope, we shan't be long. Thank you."

He tramped across the stage, said something inaudible to the constable and was heard to go into the dock. The constable took a chair from the prompt corner, placed it in the proscenium entrance and, with a modest air, sat on it. His glance fell upon Martyn and he smiled at her. They were the youngest persons there and it was as if they signalled in a friendly manner to each other. In turning away from this pleasant exchange, Martyn found that Poole was watching her with fixed and it seemed, angry glare. To her fury she found that she was very much disturbed by this circumstance.

They had by this time all cleaned their faces. Helena Hamilton with an unsteady hand put on a light street make-up. The men looked ghastly in the cold working lights that bleakly illuminated the stage.

Parry Percival said fretfully: " Well, I must say I do *not* see the smallest point in our hanging about like this."

The constable was about to answer when they all heard sounds of arrival at the stage-door. He said: " This will be the party from the Yard, sir," and crossed to the far exit. The sergeant was heard to join him there.

There was a brief conversation off-stage. A voice said: " You two go round with Gibson then, will you? I'll join you in a moment."

The young constable reappeared to usher in a tall man in plain clothes.

" Chief Detective-Inspector Alleyn," he said.

II

Martyn, in her weary pilgrimage round the West End, had seen men of whom Alleyn at first reminded her. In the neighbourhood of the St. James's Theatre, they had emerged

108

from clubs, from restaurants and from enchanting and preposterous shops. There had been something in their bearing
and their clothes that gave them a precise definition. But
when she looked more closely at Inspector Alleyn's face, this
association became modified. It was a spare and scholarly
face with a monkish look about it.

Martyn had formed the habit of thinking of people's voices
in terms of colour. Helena Hamilton's voice, for instance,
was for Martyn golden, Gay Gainsford's pink, Darcey's
brown and Adam Poole's violet. When Alleyn spoke she
decided that his voice was a royal blue of the clearest sort.

Reminding herself that this was no time to indulge this
freakish habit of classification she gave him her full attention.

"You will, I'm sure," he was saying, "realise that in
these cases, our job is simply to determine that they are,
on the face of it, what they appear to be. In order to do this
effectively we are obliged to make a fairly thorough examination of the scene as we find it. This takes a little time always
but if everything's quite straightforward, as I expect it will
be, we won't keep you very long. Is that clear?"

He looked round his small audience. Poole said at once:
"Yes, of course. We all understand. At the same time,
if it's a matter of taking statements, I'd be grateful if you'd
see Miss Hamilton first."

"Miss Hamilton?" Alleyn said and after a moment's
hesitation, looked at her.

"I'm his wife," she said. "I'm Helena Bennington."

"I'm so sorry. I didn't know. Yes, I'm sure that can be
managed. Probably the best way will be for me to see you
all together. If everything seems quite clear there may
be no excuse for further interviews. And now, if you'll excuse
me, I'll have a look round and then rejoin you. There is
a doctor among you, isn't there? Dr. Rutherford?" Dr.
Rutherford cleared his throat portentously. "Are you he, sir?
Perhaps you'll join us."

"Indubitably," said the doctor. "I had so concluded."

"Good," Alleyn said and looked faintly amused. "Will
you lead the way?"

They were at the door when Jacko suddenly said: "A
moment, if you please, Chief Inspector."

"Yes?"

"I would like permission to make soup. There is a filthy
small kitchen-place inhabited only by the night-watchman
where I have waiting a can of prepared soup. Everyone is

very cold and fatigued and entirely empty. My name is
Jacques Doré. I am dogsbody-in-waiting in this theatre and
there is much virtue in my soup."

Alleyn said: " By all means. Is the kitchen-place that
small sink-room near the dock with the gas-jet in it?"

" But you haven't looked at the place yet!" Parry Percival
ejaculated.

" I've been here before," said Alleyn. " I remember the
theatre. Shall we get on, Dr. Rutherford?"

They went out. Gay Gainsford, whose particular talent,
from now onwards, was to lie in the voicing of disquieting
thoughts which her companions shared but decided to leave
unspoken, said in a distracted manner: " *When* was he here
before?" And when nobody answered she said dramatically:
" I can see it all! He must be the man they sent that other
time." She paused and collected their reluctant attention. She
laid her hand on J. G.'s arm and raised her voice: " That's
why he's come again," she announced.

" Come now, dear," J. G. murmured inadequately and
Poole said quickly: " My *dear* Gay!"

" But I'm all right!" she persisted. " I'm sure I'm right.
Why else should he know about the sink-room?" She looked
about her with an air of terrified complacency.

" *And last time*," she pointed out, " *it was Murder.*"

" Climax," said Jacko. " Picture and Slow Curtain! Put
your hands together, ladies and gentlemen, for this clever
little artiste."

He went out with his eyes turned up.

" Jacko's terribly hard, isn't he?" Gay said to Darcey.
" After all Uncle Ben *was* my uncle." She caught sight of
Helena Hamilton. " And your husband," she said hurriedly,
" of course, darling."

III

The stage-hands had set up in the dock one of the trestle
tables used for properties. They had laid Clark Bennington's
body on it and had covered it with a sheet from the ward-
robe-room. The dock was a tall echoing place, concrete
floored, with stacks of old flats leaning against the walls. A
solitary unprotected lamp bulb, dust-encrusted, hung above
the table.

A group of four men in dark overcoats and hats stood
beside this improvised bier and it so chanced they had taken

up their places at the four corners and looked therefore as if they kept guard over it. Their hats shadowed their faces and they stood in pools of shadow. A fifth man, bareheaded, stood at the foot of the bier and a little removed from it. When the tallest of the men reached out to the margin of the sheet, his arm cast a black bar over its white and eloquent form. His gloved hand dragged down the sheet and exposed a rigid gaping face encrusted with greasepaint. He uncovered his head and the other three, a little awkwardly, followed his example.

"Well, Curtis?" he said.

Dr. Curtis, the police-surgeon, bent over the head, blotting it out with his shadow. He took a flashlamp from his pocket and the face, in this changed light, started out with an altered look as if it had secretly rearranged its expression.

"God!" Curtis muttered. "He looks pretty ghastly doesn't he. What an atrocious make-up."

From his removed position Dr. Rutherford said loudly: "My dear man, the make-up was required for My Play. It should, in point of fact, be a damn' sight more repellent. But *vanitas vanitatum*. Also: *Mit der Dummheit kämpfen Götter selbst vergebens*. I didn't let them fix him up at all. Thought you'd prefer not." His voice echoed coldly round the dock.

"Quite so," Curtis murmered. "Much better not."

"Smell very noticeable still," a thick-set grizzled man observed. "Always hangs about in these cases," rejoined the sergeant, "doesn't it, Mr. Fox?"

"We worked damn' hard on him," Dr. Rutherford said. "It never looked like it from the start. Not a hope."

"Well," said Curtis, drawing back, "it all seems straightforward enough, Alleyn. It doesn't call for a very extensive autopsy but of course we'll do the usual things."

"Lend me your torch a moment," Alleyn said, and after a moment: "Very heavy make-up, isn't it? He's so thickly powdered."

"He needed it. He sweated," Dr. Rutherford said, "like a pig. Alcohol and a dicky heart."

"Did you look after him, sir?"

"Not I. I don't practise nowadays. The alcohol declared itself and he used to talk about a heart condition. Valvula trouble, I should imagine. I don't know who his medical man was. His wife can tell you."

Dr. Curtis replaced the sheet. "That," he said to Rutherford, "might account for him going quickly."

"Certainly."

"There's a mark under the jaw," Alleyn said. "Did either of you notice it. The make-up is thinner there. Is it a bruise?"

Curtis said: "I saw it, yes. It might be a bruise. We'll see better when we clean him up."

"Right. I'll look at the room," Alleyn said. "Who found him?"

"The stage-manager," said Rutherford.

"Then perhaps you wouldn't mind asking him to come along when you rejoin the others. Thank you, so much, Dr. Rutherford. We're glad to have had your report. You'll be called for the inquest, I'm afraid."

"Hell's teeth, I suppose I shall. So be it." He moved to the doors. The sergeant obligingly rolled them open and he muttered: "Thankee," and with an air of dissatisfaction went out.

Dr. Curtis said: "I'd better go and make professional noises at him."

"Yes, do," Alleyn said.

On their way to Bennington's room they passed Jacko and a stage-hand bearing a fragrant steaming can and a number of cups to the stage. In his cubby-hole, Fred Badger was entertaining a group of stage-hands and dressers. They had steaming pannikins in their hands and they eyed the police party in silence.

"Smells very tasty, doesn't it?" Detective-Inspector Fox observed rather wistfully.

The young constable, who was stationed by the door through which Martyn had made her entrance, opened it for the soup-party and shut it after them.

Fox growled: "Keep your wits about you."

"Yes, sir," said the young constable and exhibited his note-book.

Clem Smith was waiting for them in Bennington's room. The lights were full on and a white glare beat on the dressing-shelf and walls. Bennington's street clothes and his suit for the first act hung on coat-hangers along the walls. His make-up was laid out on a towel and the shelf was littered with small objects that in their casual air of usage suggested that he had merely left the room for a moment and would return to take them up again. On the floor, hard by the dead gas-fire, lay an overcoat from which the reek of gas, which still hung about the room, seemed to arise. The worn rug was drawn up into wrinkles.

Clem Smith's face was white and anxious under his shock of dark hair. He shook hands jerkily with Alleyn and then looked as if he wondered if he ought to have done so. " This a pretty ghastly sort of party," he muttered, " isn't it?"

Alleyn said: " It seems that you came in for the worst part of it. Do you mind telling us what happened?"

Fox moved behind Clem and produced his note-book. Sergeant Gibson began to make a list of the objects in the room. Clem watched him with an air of distaste.

" Easy enough to tell you," he said. " He came off about eight minutes before the final curtain and I suppose went straight to this room. When the boy came round for the curtain-call, Ben didn't appear with the others. I didn't notice. There's an important light-cue at the end and I was watching for it. Then, when they all went on, he just wasn't there. We couldn't hold the curtain for long. I sent it up for the first call and the boy went back and hammered on this door. It was locked. He smelt gas and began to yell for Ben and then ran back to tell me what was wrong. I'd got the doctor on for his speech by that time. I left my A.S.M. in charge, took the bunch of extra keys from the prompt corner and tore round here."

He wetted his lips and fumbled in his pocket. " Is it safe to smoke," he asked.

" I'm afraid we'd better wait a little longer," Alleyn said. " Sorry."

" O.K. Well, I unlocked the door. As soon as it opened the stink hit me in the face. I don't know why but I expected him to be sitting at the shelf. I don't suppose, really, it was long before I saw him but it seemed fantastically long. He was lying there, by the heater. I could only see his legs and the lower half of his body. The rest was hidden by that coat. It was tucked in behind the heater, and over his head and shoulders. It looked like a tent. I heard the hiss going on underneath it." Clem rubbed his mouth. " I don't think," he said, " I was as idiotically slow as all this makes me out to be. I don't think honestly, it was more than seconds before I went in. Honestly, I don't think so."

" I expect you're right about that. Time goes all relative in a crisis."

" Does it? Good. Well, then: I ran in and hauled the coat away. He was on his left side—his mouth—it was—— The lead-in had been disconnected and it was by his mouth, hissing. I turned it off and dragged him by the heels. He sort of stuck on the carpet. Jacko—Jacques Doré bolted in and helped."

" One moment," Alleyn said. " Did you knock over that box of powder on the dressing-table? Either of you?"

Clem Smith stared at it. " That? No, I didn't go near it and I'd got him half-way to the door when Jacko came in. He must have done it himself."

" Right. Sorry. Go on."

" We lifted Ben into the passage and shut his door. At the far end of the passage there's a window, the only one near. We got it open and carried him to it. I think he was dead even then. I'm sure he was. I've seen gassed cases before; in the blitz."

Alleyn said: " You seem to have tackled this one like an old hand, at all events."

" I'm damn' glad you think so," said Clem, and sounded it.

Alleyn looked at the Yale lock on the door. " This seems in good enough shape," he said absently.

" It's new," Clem said. " There were pretty extensive reno-vations and a sort of general clean up when Mr. Poole took the theatre over. It's useful for the artistes to be able to lock up valuables in their rooms and the old locks were clumsy and rusted up. In any case——" He stopped and then said uncomfortably: " The whole place has been re-painted and modernised."

" Including the gas installations?"

" Yes," said Clem, not looking at Alleyn. " That's all new too."

" Two of the old dressing-rooms have been knocked together to form the greenroom?"

" Yes."

" And there are new dividing walls? And ventilators, now, in the dressing-rooms?"

" Yes," said Clem unhappily and added: " I suppose that's why he used his coat."

" It does look," Alleyn said without stressing it, " as if the general idea was to speed things up, doesn't it? All right, Mr. Smith, thank you. Would you explain to the people on the stage that I'll come as soon as we've finished our job here? It won't be very long. We'll probably ask you to sign a statement of the actual discovery as you've described it to us. You'll be glad to get away from this room, I expect."

Inspector Fox had secreted his note-book and now ushered Clem Smith out. Clem appeared to go thankfully.

" Plain sailing, wouldn't you say, Mr. Alleyn," said Fox,

looking along the passage; "nobody about," he added. "I'll leave the door open."

Alleyn rubbed his nose. "It looks like plain sailing, Fox, certainly. But in view of the other blasted affair we can't take a damn' thing for granted. You weren't on the Jupiter case, were you, Gibson?"

"No, sir," said Gibson looking up from his note-book. "Homicide dressed up to look like suicide, wasn't it?"

"It was, indeed. The place has been pretty extensively chopped up and rehashed but the victim was on this side of the passage and in what must have been the room now taken in to make the greenroom. Next door there was a gas-fire backing on to his own. The job was done by blowing down the tube next door. This put out the fire in this room and left the gas on, of course. The one next door was then relit. The victim was pretty well dead-drunk and the trick worked. We got the bloke on the traces of crêpe-hair and greasepaint he left on the tube."

"Very careless," Fox said. "Silly chap, really."

"The theatre," Alleyn said, "was shut up for a long time. Three or four years at least. Then Adam Poole took it, renamed it the Vulcan and got a permit for renovation. I fancy this is only his second production here."

"Perhaps," Fox speculated, "the past history of the place played on deceased's mind and led him to do away with himself after the same fashion."

"Sort of superstitious?" Gibson ventured.

"Not precisely," said Fox majestically. "And yet something after that style of thing. They're a very superstitious mob, actors, Fred. Very. And if he had reason, in any case, to entertain the notion of suicide——"

"He must," Alleyn interjected, "have also entertained the very nasty notion of throwing suspicion of foul play on his fellow-actors. If there's a gas-fire back to back with this——"

"And there is," Fox said.

"The devil there is! So what does Bennington do? He re-creates as far as possible the whole set-up, leaves no note, no indication, as far as we can see, of his intention to gas himself, and—who's next door, Fox?"

"A Mr. Parry Percival."

"All right. Bennington pushes off, leaving Mr. Parry Percival ostensibly in the position of the Jupiter murderer. Rotten sort of suicide that'd be, Br'er Fox."

"We don't know anything yet, of course," said Fox.

"We don't and the crashing hellish bore about the whole business lies in the all too obvious fact that we'll have to find out. What's on your inventory, Gibson?"

Sergeant Gibson opened his note-book and adopted his official manner.

"Dressing-table or shelf," he said. "One standing mirror. One cardboard box containing false hair, rouge, substance labelled 'nose-paste,' seven fragments of greasepaint and one unopened box of powder. Shelf. Towel spread out to serve as table-cloth. On towel—one tray containing six sticks of greasepaint. To right of tray, bottle of spirit-adhesive. Bottle containing what appears to be substance known as liquid powder. Open box of powder overturned. Behind box of powder, pile of six pieces of cotton-wool and a roll from which these pieces have been removed." He looked up at Alleyn. "Intended to be used for powdering purposes, Mr. Alleyn."

"That's it," Alleyn said. He was doubled up, peering at the floor under the dressing-shelf. "Nothing there," he grunted. "Go on."

"To left of tray: cigarette-case with three cigarettes and open box of fifty. Box of matches. Ash-tray. Towel, stained with greasepaint. Behind mirror: Flask: one-sixth full; and used tumbler smelling of spirits."

Alleyn looked behind the standing glass. "Furtive sort of cache," he said. "Go on."

"Considerable quantity of powder spilt on shelf and on adjacent floor area. Considerable quantity of ash. Left wall. Clothes. I haven't been through the pockets yet, Mr. Alleyn. There's nothing on the floor but powder and some paper ash, original form undistinguishable. Stain as of something burnt on hearth."

"Go ahead with it then. I wanted," Alleyn said with a discontented air, "to *hear* whether I was wrong."

Fox and Gibson looked placidly at him. "All right," he said, "don't mind me. I'm broody."

He squatted down by the overcoat. "It really is the most obscene smell, gas," he muttered. "How anybody *can* always passes my comprehension." He poked in a gingerly manner at the coat. "Powder over everything," he grumbled. "Where had this coat been? On the empty hanger near the door presumably. That's damned rum. Check it with his dresser. We'll have to get Bailey along, Fox. And Thompson. Blast!"

"I'll ring the Yard," said Fox and went out.
116

Alleyn squinted through a lens at the wing-taps of the gas-fire. "I can see prints clearly enough," he said, "on both. We can check with Bennington's. There's even a speck or two of powder settled on the taps."

"In the air, I dare say," said Gibson.

"I dare say it *was*. Like the gas. We can't go any further here until the dabs and flash party has done its stuff. Finished, Gibson?"

"Finished, Mr. Alleyn. Nothing much in the pockets. Bills. Old racing card. Cheque-book and so on. Nothing on the body, by the way, but a handkerchief."

"Come on, then. I've had my bellyful of gas."

But he stood in the doorway eyeing the room and whistling softly.

"I wish I could believe in you," he apostrophised it, "but split me and sink me if I can. No, by all that's phoney, not for one credulous second. Come on, Gibson. Let's talk to these experts."

IV

They all felt a little better for Jacko's soup which had been laced with something that as J. G. Darcey said (and looked uncomfortable as soon as he had said it) went straight to the spot marked X.

Whether it was this potent soup or whether extreme emotional and physical fatigue had induced in Martyn its familiar compliment, an uncanny sharpening of the mind, she began to consider for the first time the general reaction of the company to Bennington's death. She thought: "I don't believe there's one of us who really minds very much. How lonely for him! Perhaps he felt the awful isolation of a child that knows itself unwanted and thought he'd put himself out of the way of caring."

It was a shock to Martyn when Helena Hamilton suddenly gave voice to her own thoughts. Helena had sat with her chin in her hand, looking at the floor. There was an unerring grace about her and this fireside posture had the beauty of complete relaxation. Without raising her eyes she said: "My dears, my dears, for pity's sake don't let's pretend. Don't let me pretend. I didn't love him. Isn't that sad? We all know and we try to patch up a decorous scene but it won't do. We're shocked and uneasy and dreadfully tired. Don't let's put ourselves to the trouble of pretending. It's so useless."

Gay said: "But I *did* love him!" and J. G. put his arm about her.

"Did you?" Helena murmured. "Perhaps you did, darling. Then you must hug your sorrow to yourself. Because I'm afraid nobody really shares it."

Poole said: "We understand, Ella."

With that familiar gesture, not looking at him, she reached out her hand. When he had taken it in his, she said: "When one is dreadfully tired, one talks. I do, at all events. I talk much too easily. Perhaps that's a sign of a shallow woman. You know, my dears, I begin to think I'm only capable of affection. I have a great capacity for affection but as for my loves, they have no real permanency. None."

Jacko said gently: "Perhaps your talent for affection is equal to other women's knack of loving."

Gay and Parry Percival looked at him in astonishment but Poole said: "That may well be."

"What I meant to say," Helena went on, "only I do side-track myself so awfully, is this. Hadn't we better stop being muted and mournful and talk about what may happen and what we ought to do? Adam, darling, I thought perhaps they might all be respecting my sorrow or something. What should we be talking about? What's the situation?"

Poole moved one of the chairs with its back to the curtain and sat in it. Dr. Rutherford returned and lumped himself down in the corner. "They're talking," he said, "to Clem Smith in the—they're talking to Clem. I've seen the police-surgeon, a subfusc exhibit but one that can tell a hawk from a hernshaw if they're held under his nose. He agrees that there was nothing else I could have done which is no doubt immensely gratifying to me. What are you all talking about? You look like a dress-rehearsal."

"We were about to discuss the whole situation," said Poole. "Helena feels it should be discussed and I think we all agree with her."

"What situation pray? Ben's? Or ours? There is no more to be said about Ben's situation. As far as we know, my dear Ella, he has administered to himself a not too uncomfortable and effective anæsthetic which, after he had become entirely unconscious, brought about the end he had in mind. For a man who had decided to shuffle off this mortal coil he behaved very sensibly."

"Oh, *please*," Gay whispered. "*Please!*"

Dr. Rutherford contemplated her in silence for a moment and then said: "What's up, Misery?" Helena, Darcey and

Parry Percival made expostulatory noises. Poole said: " See here, John, you'll either pipe down or preserve the decencies."

Gay, fortified perhaps by this common reaction said loudly: " You might at least have the grace to remember he was my uncle."

. " Grace me no grace," Dr. Rutherford quoted inevitably. " And uncle me no uncles." After a moment's reflection, he added: " All right, Thalia, have a good cry. But you must know, if the rudiments of seasoned thinking are within your command, that your Uncle Ben did you a damn' shabby turn. A scurvy trick, by God. However, I digress. Get on with the post-mortem, Chorus. I am dumb."

" You'll be good enough to remain so," said Poole warmly. " Very well, then. It seems to me, Ella, that Ben took this —this way out—for a number of reasons. I know you want me to speak plainly and I'm going to speak very plainly indeed, my dear."

" Oh, yes," she said. " Please, but——" For a moment they looked at each other. Martyn wondered if she imagined that Poole's head moved in the faintest possible negative. " Yes," Helena said, " very plainly, please."

" Well, then," Poole said, " we know that for the last year Ben, never a very temperate man, has been a desperately intemperate one. We know his habits undermined his health, his character and his integrity as an actor. I think he realised this very thoroughly. He was an unhappy man who looked back at what he had once been and was appalled. We all know he did things in performance to-night that, from an actor of his standing, were quite beyond the pale."

Parry Percival ejaculated: " Well, I mean to say—oh, well. Never mind."

" Exactly," Poole said. " He had reached a sort of chronic state of instability. We all know he was subject to fits of depression. I believe he did what he did when he was at a low ebb. I believe he would have done it sooner or later by one means or another. And, in my view for what it's worth, that's the whole story. Tragic enough, God knows, but, in its tragedy, simple. I don't know if you agree."

Darcey said: " If there's nothing else. I mean," he said diffidently, glancing at Helena, " if nothing has happened that would seem like a further motive."

Helena's gaze rested for a moment on Poole and then on Darcey. " I think Adam's right," she said. " I'm afraid he was appalled by a sudden realisation of himself. I'm afraid he was insufferably lonely."

"Oh, my God!" Gay ejaculated and having by this means, collected their unwilling attenion, she added: "I shall never forgive myself: never."

Dr. Rutherford groaned loudly.

"I failed him," Gay announced. "I was a bitter, bitter disappointment to him. I dare say I turned the scale."

"*Now in the name of all the gods at once,*" Dr. Rutherford began and was brought to a stop by the entry of Clem Smith.

Clem looked uneasily at Helena Hamilton and said: "They're in the dressing-room. He says they won't keep you waiting much longer."

"It's all right, then?" Parry Percival blurted out and added in a flurry: "I mean there won't be a whole lot of formalities. I mean we'll be able to get away. I mean——"

"I've no idea about that," Clem said. "Alleyn just said they'd be here soon." He had brought a cup of soup with him and he withdrew into a corner and began to drink it. The others watched him anxiously but said nothing.

"What did he ask you about?" Jacko demanded suddenly.

"About what we did at the time."

"Anything else?"

"Well, yes. He—well in point of fact, he seemed to be interested in the alterations to the theatre."

"To the dressing-rooms in particular?" Poole asked quickly.

"Yes," Clem said unhappily. "To them."

There was a long silence broken by Jacko.

"I find nothing remarkable in this," he said. "Ella has shown us the way with great courage and Adam has spoken his mind. Let us all speak ours. I may resemble an ostrich but I do not propose to imitate its behaviour. Of what do we all think? There is the unpleasing little circumstance of the Jupiter case and we think of that. When Gay mentions it she does so with the air of one who opens a closet and out tumbles a skeleton. But why? It is inevitable that these gentlemen, who also remember the Jupiter case, should wish to inspect the dressing-rooms. They wish, in fact, to make very sure indeed that this is a case of suicide and not of murder. And since we are all quite certain that it is suicide we should not disturb ourselves that they do their duty."

"Exactly," Poole said.

"It's going," Darcey muttered, "to be damn' bad publicity."

"Merciful Heavens!" Parry Percival exclaimed. "The Publicity! None of us thought of that!"

"Did we not?" said Poole.

"I must say," Parry complained, "I *would* like to know what's going to happen, Adam. I mean—darling Ella, I know you'll understand—but I mean, about the piece. Do we go on? Or what?"

"Yes," Helena said. "We go on. Please, Adam."

"Ella, I've got to think. There are so many——"

"We go on. Indeed, indeed we do."

Martyn felt rather than saw the sense of relief in Darcey and Percival.

Darcey said, "I'm the understudy, Lord help me," and Percival made a tiny ambiguous sound that might have been one of satisfaction or of chagrin.

"How are you for it, J. G.?" Helena asked.

"I *know* it," he said heavily.

"I'll work whenever you like. We've got the week-end."

"Thank you, Ella."

"Your own understudy's all right," said Clem.

"Good."

It was clear to Martyn that this retreat into professionalism was a great relief to them and it was clear also that Poole didn't share in their comfort. Watching him, she was reminded of his portrait in the greenroom: he looked withdrawn and troubled.

A lively and almost cosy discussion about recasting had developed. Clem Smith, Jacko and Percival were all talking at once when, with her infallible talent for scenes, Gay exclaimed passionately:

"I can't bear it! I think you're all awful!"

They broke off. Having collected their attention she built rapidly to her climax. "To sit round and talk about the show as if nothing had happened! How you can! When beyond those doors, he's lying there forgotten. Cold and forgotten! It's the most brutal thing I've ever heard of and if you think I'm coming near this horrible fated, *haunted* place again, I'm telling you, here and now, that wild horses wouldn't drag me inside the theatre once I'm away from it. I suppose someone will find time to tell me when the funeral is going to be. I happen to be just about his only relation."

They all began to expostulate at once but she topped their lines with the determination of a robust star. "You needn't bother to explain," she shouted. "I understand only too well, thank you." She caught sight of Martyn and pointed wildly at her. "You've angled for this miserable part, and now you've got it. I think it's extremely likely you're responsible for what's happened."

121

Poole said: "You'll stop at once, Gay. Stop."

"I won't! I won't be gagged! It drove my Uncle Ben to despair and I don't care who knows it."

It was upon this line that Alleyn, as if he had mastered one of the major points of stage technique, made his entrance up-stage and centre.

v

Although he must have heard every word of Gay's final outburst, Alleyn gave no sign of having done so.

"Well, now," he said, "I'm afraid the first thing I have to say to you all won't be very pleasant news. We don't look like getting through with our side of this unhappy business as quickly as I hoped. I know you are all desperately tired and very shocked and I'm sorry. But the general circumstances aren't quite as straightforward as, on the face of it, you have probably supposed them to be."

A trickle of ice moved under Martyn's diaphragm. She thought: "No, it's not fair. I can't be made to have two goes of the jim-jams in one night."

Alleyn addressed himself specifically to Helena Hamilton.

"You'll have guessed—of course you will—that one can't overlook the other case of gas-poisoning that is associated with this theatre. It must have jumped to everybody's mind, almost at once."

"Yes, of course," she said. "We've been talking about it."

The men looked uneasily at her but Alleyn said at once: "I'm sure you have. So have we. And I expect you've wondered, as we have, if the memory of that former case could have influenced your husband."

"I'm certain it did," she said quickly. "We all are."

The others made small affirmative noises. Only Dr. Rutherford was silent. Martyn saw with amazement that his chin had sunk on his rhythmically heaving bosom, his eyes were shut and his lips pursed in the manner of a sleeper who is just not snoring. He was at the back of the group and, she hoped, concealed from Alleyn.

"Have you," Alleyn asked, "any specific argument to support this theory?"

"No *specific* reason. But I know he thought a lot of that other dreadful business. He didn't *like* this theatre. Mr. Alleyn, actors are sensitive to atmosphere. We talk a lot about the theatres we play in and we get very vivid—

you would probably think absurdly vivid—impressions of their 'personalities.' My husband felt there was a—an unpleasant atmosphere in this place. He often said so. In a way I think it had a rather horrible fascination for him. We'd a sort of tacit understanding in the Vulcan that its past history wouldn't be discussed among us but I know he did talk about it. Not to us but to people who had been concerned in the other affair."

"Yes, I see." Alleyn waited for a moment. The young constable completed a note. His back was now turned to the company. "Did anyone else notice this preoccupation of Mr. Bennington's?"

"Oh, yes!" Gay said with mournful emphasis. "*I* did. He talked to me about it, but when he saw how much it upset me—because I'm so stupidly sensitive to atmosphere —I just can't help it—it's one of those things—but I *am* —because when I first came—into the theatre I just knew —you may laugh at me but these things can't be denied——"

"When," Alleyn prompted, "he saw that it upset you?"

"He stopped. I was his niece. It was rather a marvellous relationship."

"He stopped," Alleyn said. "Right." He had a programme in his hand and now glanced at it. "You must be Miss Gainsford I think. Is that right?"

"Yes, I am. But my name's really Bennington. I'm his only brother's daughter. My father died in the war and Uncle Ben really felt we were awfully *near* to each other, do you know? That's why it's so devastating for me because I sensed how wretchedly unhappy he was."

"Do you mind telling us why you thought him so unhappy?"

J. G. Darcey interposed quickly: "I don't think it was more than a general intuitive sort of thing, was it, Gay? Nothing special."

"Well——" Gay said reluctantly and Helena intervened.

"I don't think any of us have any doubt about my husband's unhappiness, Mr. Alleyn. Before you came in I was saying how most *most* anxious I am that we should be very frank with each other and of course with you. My husband drank so heavily that he had ruined his health and his work quite completely. I wasn't able to help him and we were not——" The colour died out of her face and she hesitated. "Our life together wasn't true," she said, "it had no reality at all. To-night he behaved very badly on the stage. He coloured his part at the expense of the

123

other actors and I think he was horrified at what he'd done. He was very drunk indeed to-night. I feel he suddenly looked at himself and couldn't face what he saw. I feel that very strongly."

"One *does* sense these things," Gay interjected eagerly, "or I do at any rate."

"I'm sure you do," Alleyn agreed politely. Gay drew breath and was about to go on when he said: "Of course, if any of you can tell us any happenings or remarks or so on, that seem to prove that he had this thing in mind, it will be a very great help."

Martyn heard her voice, acting, it seemed, of its own volition: "I think, perhaps——"

Alleyn turned to her and his smile reassured her. "Yes," he said. "Forgive me, but I don't yet know all your names." He looked again at his programme and then at her. Gay gave a small laugh. Darcey put his hand over hers and said something undistinguishable.

Poole said quickly: "Miss Martyn Tarne. She is, or should be, our heroine to-night. Miss Gainsford was ill and Miss Tarne, who was the understudy, took her part at half an hour's notice. We'd all be extremely proud of her if we had the wits to be anything but worried and exhausted."

Martyn's heart seemed to perform some eccentric gyration in the direction of her throat and she thought: "That's done it. Now my voice is going to be ungainly with emotion."

Alleyn said: "That must have been a most terrifying and exciting adventure," and she gulped and nodded. "What had you remembered," he went on after a moment, "that might help us?"

"It was something he said when he came off in the last act."

"For his final exit in the play?"

"Yes."

"I'll be very glad to hear it."

"I'll try to remember exactly what it was," Martyn said carefully. "I was in the dressing-room passage on my way to my—to Miss Gainsford's room and he caught me up. He spoke very disjointedly and strangely, not finishing his sentences. But one thing he said—I think it was the last—I do remember quite distinctly because it puzzled me very much. He said: 'I just wanted to tell you that you needn't suppose what I'm going to do——' and then he stopped as if he was confused and added, I think: 'you needn't suppose——' and broke off again. And then Jacko—Mr. Doré—came and told

124

me to go into the dressing-room to have my make-up attended to and, I think, said something to Mr. Bennington about his."

" I told him he was shining with sweat," said Jacko. " And he went into his room."

" Alone?" Alleyn asked.

" I just looked in to make sure he had heard me. I told him again he needed powder and then went at once to this infant."

" Miss Tarne, can you remember anything else Mr. Bennington said?"

" Not really. I'm afraid I was rather in a haze myself just then."

" The great adventure?"

" Yes," said Martyn gratefully. " I've an idea he said something about my performance. Perhaps I should explain that I knew he must be very disappointed and upset about my going on instead of Miss Gainsford but his manner was not unfriendly and I have the impression that he meant to say he didn't bear for me, personally, any kind of resentment. But that's putting it too definitely. I'm not at all sure what he said, except for that one sentence. Of that I'm quite positive."

" Good," Alleyn said. " Thank you. Did you hear this remark, Mr. Doré?"

Jacko said promptly : " But certainly. I was already in the passage and he spoke loudly as I came up."

" Did you form any opinion as to what he meant?"

" I was busy and very pleased with this infant and I did not concern myself. If I thought at all it was to wonder if he was going to make a scene because the niece had not played. He had a talent for scenes. It appears to be a family trait. I thought perhaps he meant that this infant would not be included in some scene he planned to make or be scolded for her success."

" Did he seem to you to be upset?"

" Oh, yes. Yes. Upset. Yes."

" Very much distressed, would you say?"

" *All his visage wanned?*" inquired a voice in the background. " *Tears in his eyes. Distraction in's aspect?*"

Alleyn moved his position until he could look past Gay and Darcy at the recumbent doctor. " Or even," he said, " *his whole function suiting with forms to his conceit?*"

" Hah!" the doctor ejaculated and sat up. " Upon my soul the whirligig of time brings in his revenges. Even to the point where dull detection apes at artifice, inspectors echo with informéd breath their pasteboard prototypes of fancy wrought. I am amazed and know not what to say." He helped himself to snuff and fell back into a recumbent position.

"Please don't mind him," Helena said, smiling at Alleyn. "He is a very foolish vain old man and has read somewhere that it's clever to quote in a muddled sort of way from the better known bits of the Bard."

"We encourage him too much," Jacko added gloomily.

"We have become too friendly with him," said Poole.

"A figo for your friendship," said Dr. Rutherford.

Parry Percival sighed ostentatiously and Darcey said: "Couldn't we get on?" Alleyn looked good-humouredly at Jacko and said: "Yes, Mr. Doré?"

"I wouldn't agree," Jacko said, "that Ben was very much upset but that was an almost chronic condition of late with poor Ben. I believe now with Miss Hamilton that he had decided there was little further enjoyment to be found in observing the dissolution of his own character and was about to take the foolproof way of ending it. He wished to assure Martyn that the decision had nothing to do with chagrin over Martyn's success or the failure of his niece. And that, if I am right, was nice of Ben."

"I don't think we need use the word 'failure,' " J. G. objected. "Gay was quite unable to go on."

"I hope you are better now, Miss Gainsford," Alleyn said.

Gay made an eloquent gesture with both hands and let them fall in her lap. "What does it matter?" she said. "Better? Oh, yes, I'm better." And with the closest possible imitation of Helena Hamilton's familiar gesture she extended her hand, without looking at him to J. G. Darcey. He took it anxiously. "Much better," he said, patting it.

Martyn thought: "Oh, dear, he *is* in love with her. *Poor J. G.!*"

Alleyn looked thoughtfully at them for a moment and then turned to the others.

"There's a general suggestion," he said, "that none of you was very surprised by this event. May I just—sort of tally-up —the general opinion as far as I've heard it? It helps to keep things tidy, I find. Miss Hamilton, you tell us that your husband had a curious, an almost morbid interest in the Jupiter case. You and Mr. Doré agree that Mr. Bennington had decided to take his life because he couldn't face the 'dissolution of his character.' Miss Gainsford if I understand her, believes he was deeply disturbed by the *mise en scène* and also by her inability to go on to-night for this part. Miss Tarne's account of what was probably the last statement he made suggests that he wanted her to understand that some action he had in mind had nothing to do with her. Mr. Doré supports this interpretation and confirms the actual words that were used. This, as far as it goes, is the only tangible bit of evidence as to intention that we have."

Poole lifted his head. His face was very white and a lock of black hair had fallen over his forehead turning him momentarily into the likeness, Martyn thought inconsequently, of Michaelangelo's " Adam." He said: " There's the fact itself, Alleyn. There's what he did."

Alleyn said carefully: " There's an interval of perhaps eight minutes between what he said and when he was found."

" Look here——" Parry Percival began and then relapsed. " Let it pass," he said. " *I* wouldn't know."

" Pipe up, Narcissus," Dr. Rutherford adjured him, " the inspector won't bite you."

" Oh, shut up!" Parry shouted and was awarded a complete and astonished silence. He rose and addressed himself to the players. " You're all being *so* bloody frank and sensible about this suicide," he said. " You're *so* anxious to show everybody how honest you are. The doctor's *so* unconcerned he can even spare a moment to indulge in his favourite pastime of me-baiting. I know what the doctor thinks of me and it doesn't say much for his talents as a diagnostician. But if it's Queer to feel desperately sorry for a man who was miserable enough to choke himself to death at a gas-jet, if it's Queer to be physically and mentally sick at the thought of it then, by God, I'd rather be Queer than normal. Now!"

There followed a silence broken only by the faint whisper of the young constable's pencil.

Doctor Rutherford struggled to his feet and lumbered down to Parry.

" Your argument, my young coxcomb," he said thoughtfully, " is as seaworthy as a sieve. As for my diagnosis, if you're the normal man you'd have me believe, why the hell don't you show like one? You exhibit the stigmata of that water-fly whom it is a vice to know, and fly into a fit when the inevitable conclusion is drawn." He took Parry by the elbow and addressed himself to the company in the manner of a lecturer. " A phenomenon," he said, " that is not without its dim interest. I invite your attention. Here is an alleged

127

actor who, an hour or two since, was made a public and egregious figure of fun by the deceased. Who was roasted by the deceased before an audience of a thousand whinnying nincompoops? Who allowed his performance to be prostituted by the deceased before this audience? Who before his final and most welcome exit suffered himself to be tripped up contemptuously by the deceased, and who fell on his painted face before this audience? Here is this phenomenon, ladies and gents, who now proposes himself as Exhibit A in the Compassion Stakes. I invite your——"

Poole said: " *Quiet!*" and when Dr. Rutherford grinned at him added: " I meant it, John. You will be quiet if you please."

Parry wrenched himself free from the doctor and turned on Alleyn. " You're supposed to be in charge here——" he began and Poole said quickly: " Yes, Alleyn, I really do think that this discussion is getting quite fantastically out of hand. If we're all satisfied that this is a case of suicide——"

" Which," Alleyn said, " we are not."

They were all talking at once: Helena, the doctor, Parry, Gay and Darcey. They were like a disorderly chorus in a verse play. Martyn, who had been watching Alleyn, was terrified. She saw him glance at the constable. Then he stood up.

" One moment," he said. The chorus broke off inconsequently as it had begun.

" We've reached a point," Alleyn said, " where it's my duty to tell you I'm by no means satisfied that this is, in fact, a case of suicide."

Martyn was actually conscious, in some kind, of a sense of relief. She could find no look either of surprise or anger in any of her fellow-players. Their faces were so many white discs and they were motionless and silent. At last Clem Smith said with an indecent lack of conviction: " He was horribly careless about things like that—taps—I mean——" His voice sank to a murmur. They heard the word " accident."

" Is it not strange," Jacko said loudly, " how loath one is to pronounce the word that is in all our minds. And truth to tell, it has a soft and ugly character." His lips closed over his fantastic teeth. He used the exaggerated articulation of an old actor. " Murder," he said. " So beastly, isn't it? "

It was at this point that one of the stage-hands, following, no doubt, his routine for the night, pulled up the curtain and exhibited the scene of climax to the deserted auditorium.

CHAPTER VIII

AFTER-PIECE

When Martyn considered the company as they sat about their own working stage, bruised by anxiety and fatigue, Jacko's ugly word sounded not so much frightening as preposterous. It was unthinkable that it could kindle even a bat-light of fear in any of their hearts. " And yet," thought Martyn, " it has done so. There are little points of terror, burning in all of us like match-flames."

After Jacko had spoken there was a long silence broken at last by Adam Poole who asked temperately: " Are we to understand, Alleyn, that you have quite ruled out the possibility of suicide?"

" By no means," Alleyn rejoined. " I still hope you may be able, among you, to show that there is at least a clear enough probability of suicide for us to leave the case as it stands until the inquest. But where there are strong indications that it may *not* be suicide we can't risk waiting as long as that without a pretty exhaustive look round."

" And there are such indications?"

" There are indeed."

" Strong?"

Alleyn waited a moment. " Sufficiently strong," he said.

" What are they?" Dr. Rutherford demanded.

" It must suffice," Alleyn quibbled politely, " that they are sufficient."

" An elegant sufficiency, by God!"

" But, Mr. Alleyn," Helena cried out, " what can we tell you? Except that we all most sincerely believe that Ben did this himself. Because we know him to have been bitterly unhappy. What else is there for us to say?"

" It will help, you know, when we get a clear picture of what you were all doing and where you were between the time he left the stage and the time he was found. Inspector Fox is checking now with the stage-staff. I propose to do so with the players."

" I see," she said. She leant forward and her air of reasonableness and attention was beautifully executed. " You want to find out which of us had the opportunity to murder Ben?"

Gay Gainsford and Parry began an outcry but Helena raised her hand and they were quiet. "That's it, isn't it?" she said.

"Yes," Alleyn said, "that really is it. I fancy you would rather be spared the stock evasions about routine inquiries and all the rest of it."

"Much rather."

"I was sure of it," Alleyn said. "Then shall we start with you, if you please?"

"I was on the stage for the whole of that time, Mr. Alleyn. There's a scene, before Ben's exit between J. G. —that's Mr. Darcey, over there—Parry, Adam, Ben and myself. Then J. G. and Parry go off and Ben follows a moment later. Adam and I finish the play."

"So you, too," Alleyn said to Poole, "were here, on the stage, for the whole of this period?"

"I go off for a moment after his exit. It's a strange, rather horridly strange, coincidence that in the play he—the character he played, I mean—does commit suicide off-stage. He shoots himself. When I hear the shot I go off. The two other men have already made their exits. They remain off but I come on again almost immediately. I wait outside the door on the left from a position where I could watch Miss Hamilton and I re-enter on a 'business' cue from her."

"How long would this take?"

"Shall we show you?" Helena suggested. She got up and moved to the centre of the stage. She raised her clasped hands to her mouth and stood motionless. She was another woman.

As if Clem had called: "Clear stage," and indeed he looked about him with an air of authority, Martyn, Jacko and Gay moved into the wings. Parry and J. G. went to the foot of the stairs and Poole crossed to above Helena. They placed themselves thus in the business-like manner of a rehearsal. The doctor however remained prone on his sofa breathing deeply and completely disregarded by everybody. Helena glanced at Clem Smith who went to the book.

"From Ben's exit, Clem," Poole said and after a moment Helena turned and addressed herself to the empty stage on her left.

"*I've only one thing to say, but it's between the three of us.*" She turned to Parry and Darcey. "*Do you mind?*" she asked them.

Parry said: "*I don't understand and I'm past minding.*"

130

Darcey said: "*My head is buzzing with a sense of my own inadequacy. I shall be glad to be alone.*"

They went out, each on his own line, leaving Helena, Adam, and the ghost of Bennington, on the stage.

Helena spoke again to vacancy. "*It must be clear to you, now. It's the end, isn't it?*"

"*Yes,*" Clem's voice said. "*I understand you perfectly. Good-bye, my dear.*"

They looked at the door on the left. Alleyn took out his watch. Helena made a quick movement as if to prevent the departure of an unseen person and Poole laid his hand on her arm. They brought dead Ben back to the stage by their mime and dismissed him as vividly. It seemed that the door must open and shut for him as he went out.

Poole said: "*And now I must speak to you alone.*" There followed a short passage of dialogue which he and Helena played *a tempo* but with muted voices. Jacko, in the wings, clapped his hands and the report was as startling as a gun shot. Poole ran out through the left-hand door.

Helena traced a series of movements about the stage. Her gestures were made in the manner of an exercise but the shadow of their significance was reflected in her face. Finally she moved into the window and seemed to compel herself to look out. Poole re-entered.

"Thank you," Alleyn said, shutting his watch. "Fifty seconds. Will you all come on again, if you please?"

When they had assembled in their old positions, he said: "Did anyone notice Mr. Poole as he waited by the door for his re-entry?"

"The door's recessed," Poole said. "I was more or less screened."

"Someone off-stage may have noticed, however." He looked from Darcey to Percival.

"We went straight to our rooms," said Parry.

"Together?"

"I was first. Miss Tarne was in the entrance to the passage and I spoke to her for a moment. J. G. followed me, I think."

"Do you remember this, Miss Tarne?"

It had been at the time when Martyn had begun to come back to earth. It was like a recollection from a dream. "Yes," she said. "I remember. They both spoke to me."

"And went on down the passage?"

"Yes."

"To be followed in a short time by yourself and Mr. Bennington?"

" Yes."

" And then Mr. Doré joined you and you went to your rooms?"

" Yes."

" So that after Mr. Bennington had gone to his room, you, Mr. Percival, were in your dressing-room which is next door to his, Mr. Darcey was in his room which is on the far side of Mr. Percival's and Miss Tarne was in her room —or more correctly, perhaps, Miss Gainsford's—with Mr. Doré, who joined her there after looking in on Mr. Bennington. Right?"

They murmured an uneasy assent.

" How long were you all in these rooms?"

Jacko said: " I believe I have said I adjusted this infant's make-up and returned with her to the stage."

" I think," said Martyn, " that the other two went out to the stage before we did. I remember hearing them go up the passage together. That was before the call for the final curtain. We went out after the call, didn't we Jacko?"

" Certainly, my infant. And by that time you were a little more awake, isn't it? The pink clouds had receded a certain distance?"

Martyn nodded, feeling foolish. Poole came behind her and rested his hands on her shoulders. " So there would appear at least to be an alibi for the Infant Phenomenon," he said. It was the most natural and inevitable thing in the world for her to lean back. His hands moved to her arms and he held her to him for an uncharted second while a spring of well-being broke over her astounded heart.

Alleyn looked from her face to Poole's and she guessed that he wondered about their likeness to each other. Poole, answering her thoughts and Alleyn's unspoken question, said: " We are remotely related, but I am not allowed to mention it. She's ashamed of the connection."

" That's unlucky," Alleyn said with a smile, " since it declares itself so unequivocally."

Gay Gainsford said loudly to Darcey: " Do you suppose, darling, they'd let me get my cigarettes?"

Helena said: " Here you are, Gay." Darcey had already opened his case and held it out to her in his right hand. His left hand was in his trousers pocket. His posture was elegant and modish, out of keeping with his look of anxiety and watchfulness.

" Where are your cigarettes?" Alleyn asked and Gay said

quickly: " It doesn't matter, thank you. I've got one. I won't bother. I'm sorry I interrupted."

" But where are they?"

" I don't really know what I've done with them."

" Where were you during the performance?"

She said impatiently: " It *really* doesn't matter. I'll look for them later or something."

" Gay," said Jacko, " was in the greenroom throughout the show.

" Lamprey will see if he can find them."

The young constable said: " Yes, of course, sir," and went out.

" In the greenroom?" Alleyn said. " Were you there all the time, Miss Gainsford?"

Standing in front of her with his back to Alleyn, Darcey held a light to her cigarette. She inhaled and coughed violently. He said: " Gay didn't feel fit enough to move. She curled up in a chair in the greenroom. I was to take her home after the show."

" When did you leave the greenroom, Miss Gainsford?"

But it seemed that Gay had half-asphyxiated herself with her cigarette. She handed it wildly to Darcey, buried her face in her handkerchief and was madly convulsed. P.C. Lamprey returned with a packet of cigarettes, was waved away with vehemence, gave them to Darcey and on his own initiative fetched a cup of water.

" If the face is congested," Dr. Rutherford advised from the sofa, " hold her up by the heels." His eyes remained closed.

Whether it was the possibility of being subjected to this treatment or the sip of water that Darcey persuaded her to take or the generous thumps on her back, administered by Jacko, that effected a cure, the paroxysm abated. Alleyn, who had watched this scene thoughtfully, said: " If you are quite yourself again. Miss Gainsford, will you try to remember when you left the greenroom?"

She shook her head weakly and said in an invalid's voice: " Please, I honestly don't remember. Is it very important?"

" Oh, for pity's sake, Gay!" cried Helena with every sign of the liveliest irritation. " Do stop being such an unmitigated ass. You're not choking: if you were your eyes would water and you'd probably dribble. Of course it's important. You were in the greenroom and next door to Ben. Think!"

" But you can't imagine——" Gay said wildly. " Oh,

133

Aunty—I'm sorry, I mean, Ella—I do think that's a frightful thing to suggest."

" My dear Gay," Poole said, " I don't suppose Ella or Mr. Alleyn or any of us imagines you went into Ben's room, knocked him senseless with a straight left to the jaw and then turned the gas on. We merely want to know what you did do."

J. G. who had given a sharp ejaculation and, half-risen from his chair, now sank back.

Alleyn said: " It would also be interesting Mr. Poole, to hear how you knew about the straight left to the jaw."

II

Poole was behind Martyn and a little removed from her. She felt his stillness in her own bones. When he spoke it was a shock rather than a relief to hear how easy and relaxed his voice sounded,

" Do you realise, Alleyn," he said, " you've given me an opportunity to use, in reverse, a really smashing detective's cliché. I didn't know. You have just told me!"

" And that," Alleyn said with some relish, " as I believe you would say in the profession, takes me off with a hollow laugh and a faint hiss. So you merely guessed at the straight left?"

" If Ben was killed, and I don't believe he was, it seemed to me to be the only way this murder could be brought about."

" Surely not," Alleyn said without emphasis. " There is the method that was used before in this theatre with complete success."

" I don't know that I would describe as completely successful, a method that ended with the arrest of its employer."

" Oh," Alleyn said lightly, " that's another story. He underestimated our methods."

" A good enough warning to anyone else not to follow his plan of action."

" Or perhaps merely a hint that it could be improved upon," Alleyn said. " What do you think, Mr. Darcey?"

" I?" J. G. sounded bewildered. " I don't know. I'm afraid I haven't followed the argument."

" You were still thinking about the straight-left theory perhaps?"

134

"I believe with the others that it was suicide," said J. G. He had sat down again beside Gay. His legs were stretched out before him and crossed at the ankles, his hands were in his trousers pockets and his chin on his chest. It was the attitude of a distinguished M.P. during a damaging speech from the opposite side of the House.

Alleyn said: "And we still don't know when Miss Gainsford left the greenroom."

"Oh, *lawks*!" Parry ejaculated. "This is *too* tiresome, J. G., you looked in at the greenroom door when we came back for the curtain call, don't you remember? Was she there then? Were you there, then, Gay darling?"

Gay opened her mouth to speak but J. G. said quickly: "Yes, of course I did. Stupid of me to forget. Gay was sound asleep in the arm-chair, Mr. Alleyn. I didn't disturb her." He passed his right hand over his beautifully groomed head. "It's a most extraordinary thing," he said vexedly, "that I should have forgotten this. Of course she was asleep. Because later, when—well, when, in point of fact the discovery had been made—I asked where Gay was and someone said she was still in the greenroom and I was naturally worried and went to fetch her. She was still asleep and the greenroom, by that time, reeking with gas. I brought her back here."

"Have you any idea, Miss Gainsford," Alleyn asked, "about when you dropped off?"

"I was exhausted, Mr. Alleyn. Physically and emotionally exhausted. I still am."

"Was it, for instance, before the beginning of the last act?"

"N-n-no. No. Because J. G. came in to see how I was in the second interval. Didn't you, darling? And I was exhausted wasn't I?"

"Yes, dear."

"And he gave me some aspirins and I took two. And I suppose, in that state of utter exhaustion, they work. So I fell into a sleep—an exhausted sleep, it was."

"Naturally," Helena murmured with a glance at Alleyn. "It would be exhausted."

"Undoubtedly," said Jacko, "it was exhausted."

"Well, it was," said Gay crossly. "Because I was. Utterly."

"Did anyone else beside Mr. Darcey go into the greenroom during the second interval?"

Gay looked quickly at J. G. "Honestly," she said, "I'm *so* muddled about times it really isn't safe to ask me. I'm sure to be wrong."

135

" Mr. Darcey?"

" No," J. G. said.

" Well, my dearest J. G.," Parry said, " I couldn't be more reluctant to keep popping in like one of the Eumenides in that utterly incomprehensible play but I do assure you that you're at fault here. Ben went into the greenroom in the second interval."

" Dear Heaven!" Helena said, on a note of desperation. " What has happened to us all!"

" I'm terribly sorry, Ella darling," Parry said and sounded it.

" But why should you be sorry? Why shouldn't Ben go and see his niece in the interval? He played the whole of the third act afterwards. Of course you should say so Parry, if you know what you're talking about. Shouldn't he, Adam? Shouldn't he, Mr. Alleyn?"

Poole was looking with a sort of incredulous astonishment at Darcey. " I think he should," he said slowly.

" And you, Mr. Darcey?" asked Alleyn.

" All right, Parry," said J. G., " go on."

" There's not much more to be said and anyway I don't suppose it matters. It was before they'd called the third act. Helena and Adam and Martyn had gone out. They begin the act. I come on a bit later and Ben after me and J. G. later still. I wanted to see how the show was going and I was on my way in the passage when Ben came out of his room and went into the greenroom next door. The act was called soon after that."

" Did you speak to him?" Alleyn asked.

" I did not," said Parry with some emphasis. " I merely went out to the stage and joined Jacko and the two dressers and the call-boy who were watching from the prompt side, and Clem."

" That's right," Clem said. " I remember telling you all to keep away from the bunches. The boy called J. G. and Ben about five minutes later."

" Were you still in the greenroom when you were called, Mr. Darcey?"

" Yes."

" With Mr. Bennington?"

" He'd gone to his room."

" Not for the life of me," Helena said, wearily, " can I see why you had to be so mysterious, J. G."

" Perhaps," Alleyn said, " the reason is in your left trousers pocket, Mr. Darcey."

136

J. G. didn't take his hand out of his pocket. He stood up and addressed himself directly to Alleyn.

" May I speak to you privately? " he asked.

" Of course," Alleyn said. " Shall we go to the greenroom?"

III

In the greenroom and in the presence of Alleyn and of Fox who had joined them there, J. G. Darcey took his left hand out of his trousers pocket and extended it palm downwards for their inspection. It was a well-shaped and well-kept hand but the knuckles were grazed. A trace of blood had seeped out round the greasepaint and powder which had been daubed over the raw skin.

" I suppose I've behaved very stupidly," he said. " But I hoped there would be no need to come out. It has no bearing whatever on his death."

" In that case," Alleyn said, " it will not be brought out. But you'll do well to be frank."

" I dare say," said J. G. wryly.

" There's a bruise under the deceased's jaw on the right side that could well have been caused by that straight left Mr. Poole talked about. Now, we could ask you to hold your left fist to this bruise and see if there's any correspondence. If you tell me you didn't let drive at him we'll ask you if you are willing to make this experiment."

" I assure you that rather than do any such thing I'd willingly admit that I hit him," J. G. said with a shudder.

" And also why you hit him?"

" Oh, yes, if I can. If I can," he repeated and pressed his hand to his eyes. " D'you mind if we sit down, Alleyn? I'm a bit tired."

" Do."

J. G. sat in the leather arm-chair where Martyn, and in her turn, Gay Gainsford had slept. In the dim light of the greenroom his face looked wan and shadowed. " Not the chicken I was," he said and it was an admission actors do not love to make.

Alleyn faced him. Fox sat down behind him, flattened his note-book on the table and placed his spectacles across his nose. There was something cosy about Fox when he took notes. Alleyn remembered absently that his wife had once observed that Mr. Fox was a cross between a bear and a baby and exhibited the most pleasing traits of both creatures.

The masked light above Jacko's sketch of Adam Poole shone down upon it and it thus was given considerable emphasis in an otherwise shadowed room.

"If you want a short statement," J. G. said, "I can give it to you in a sentence. I hit Ben under the jaw in this room during the second act wait. I didn't knock him out but he was so astonished he took himself off. I was a handy amateur welter-weight in my young days but it must be twenty years or more since I put up my hands. I must say I rather enjoyed it."

"What sort of condition was he in?"

"Damned unpleasant. Oh, you mean drunk or sober? I should say ugly-drunk. Ben was a soak. I've never seen him incapacitated but really I've hardly ever seen him stone-cold either. He was in his second degree of drunkenness: offensive, outrageous and incalculable. He'd behaved atrociously throughout the first and second acts."

"In what way?"

"As only a clever actor with too much drink in him can behave. Scoring off other people. Playing for cheap laughs. Doing unrehearsed bits of business that made nonsense of the production. Upon my word," said J. G. thoughtfully, "I wonder Adam or the doctor or poor little Parry, if he'd had the guts, didn't get in first and give him what he deserved. A perfectly bloody fellow."

"Was it because of his performance that you hit him?"

J. G. looked at his fingernails and seemed to ponder. "No," he said at last. "Or not directly. If I thought you'd believe me I'd say yes, but no doubt you'll talk to her and she's so upset anyway——"

"You mean Miss Gainsford?"

"Yes," said J. G. with the oddest air of pride and embarrassment. "I mean Gay."

"Was it on her account you dotted him one?"

"It was. He was damned offensive."

"I'm sorry," Alleyn said, "but you'll realise that we do want to be told a little more than that about it."

"I suppose so." He clasped his hands and examined his bruised knuckles. "Although I find it extremely difficult and unpleasant to go into the wretched business. It's only because I hope you'll let Gay off, as far as possible, if you know the whole story. That's why I asked to see you alone." He slewed round and looked discontentedly at Fox.

"Inspector Fox," Alleyn said, "is almost pathologically discreet."

"Glad to hear it. Well, as you've heard, I'd managed to get hold of a bottle of aspirins and I brought them to her, here, in the second interval. Gay was sitting in his chair. She was still terribly upset. Crying. I don't know if you've realised why she didn't go on for the part?"

"No. I'd be glad to have the whole story."

J. G. embarked on it with obvious reluctance but as he talked his hesitancy lessened and he even seemed to find some kind of ease in speaking. He described Gay's part and her struggle at rehearsals. It was clear that, however unwillingly, he shared the general opinion of her limited talent. "She'd have given a reasonable show," he said, " if she'd been given a reasonable chance but from the beginning the part got her down. She's a natural ingénue and this thing's really ' character.' It was bad casting. Adam kept the doctor at bay as much as possible but she knew what he thought. She didn't *want* the part. She was happy where she was in repertory but Ben dragged her in. He saw himself as a sort of fairy-godfather-uncle and when she found the part difficult he turned obstinate and wouldn't let her throw it in. Out of vanity really. He was very vain. She's a frail little thing, you know, all heart and sensitivity, and between them they've brought her to the edge of a breakdown. It didn't help matters when Miss Martyn Tarne appeared out of a clear sky, first as Helena Hamilton's dresser and then as Gay's understudy and then—mysteriously as some of the cast, Ben in particular, thought—as Adam's distant cousin. You noticed the uncanny resemblance but you may not know the part in the play requires it. That was the last straw for Gay. She'd been ill with nerves and fright and to-night she cracked up completely and wouldn't—couldn't go on. When I saw her in the first interval she was a bit quieter but in the second act little Miss Tarne did very well indeed. Quite startling, it was. Incidentally, I suppose her success infuriated Ben. And Gay heard everybody raving about her as they came off. Naturally that upset her again. So she was in tears when I came in."

He leant forward and rested his head in his hands. His voice was less distinct. "I'm fond of her," he said. "She's got used to me being about. When I came in she ran to me and—— I needn't go into the way I felt. There's no explaining these things. She was sobbing in my arms, poor bird, and God knows my heart had turned over. Ben came in. He went for her like a pick-pocket. He was crazy. I tried to shut him up. He didn't make a noise—I don't mean

139

that—matter of fact what he said streamed out of him in a whisper. He was quite off his head and began talking about Helena—about his wife. He used straight out obscenities. There'd been an episode that afternoon and—well he used the sort of generalisation that Lear and Othello and Leontes use, if you remember your Shakespeare."

"Yes."

"Gay was still clinging to me and he began to talk the same sort of stuff about her. I'm not going into details. I put her away from me and quite deliberately gave him what was coming to him. I don't remember what I said. I don't think any of us said anything. So he went out nursing his jaw and they called me for the last act and I went out too. During this last act, when we were on together, I could see the bruise coming out under his make-up."

"What was his general behaviour like during the final act?"

"As far as I was concerned he behaved in the way people do when they play opposite someone they've had a row with off-stage. He didn't look me in the eye. He looked at my forehead or ears. It doesn't show from the front. He played fairly soundly until poor Parry got out of position. Parry is his butt in the piece but of course what Ben did was outrageous. He stuck out his foot as Parry moved and brought him down. That was not long before his own exit. I never saw him again after that until he was carried out. That's all. I don't know if you've believed me but I hope you'll let Gay off any more of this stuff."

Alleyn didn't answer. He looked at the young-old actor for a moment. J. G. was lighting a cigarette with that trained economy and grace of movement that were part of his stock-in-trade. His head was stooped and Alleyn saw how carefully the silver hair had been distributed over the scalp. The hands were slightly tremulous. How old was J. G. Fifty? Fifty-five? Sixty? Was he the victim of that Indian Summer that can so unmercifully visit an ageing man?

"It's the very devil, in these cases," Alleyn said, "how one has to plug away at everyone in turn. Not that it helps to say so. There's one more question that I'm afraid you won't enjoy at all. Can you tell me more specifically what Bennington said about—I think you called it an episode—of the afternoon, in which his wife was concerned?"

"No, by God I can't," said J. G. hotly.

"He spoke about it in front of Miss Gainsford didn't he?"

"You can't possibly ask Gay about it. It's out of the question."

140

"Not, I'm afraid, for an investigating officer," said Alleyn who thought that J. G.'s sense of delicacy, if delicacy was in question, was possibly a good deal more sensitive than Miss Gainsford's. "Do you suppose Bennington talked about this episode to other people?"

"In the condition he was in I should think it possible."

"Well," Alleyn said, "we shall have to find out."

"See here, Alleyn. What happened, if he spoke the truth, was something entirely between himself and his wife and it's on her account that I can't repeat what he said. You know she and Poole were on-stage at the crucial time and that there's no sense in thinking of motive if that's what you're after, where they are concerned."

Alleyn said: "This episode might constitute a motive for suicide, however."

J. G. looked up quickly. "Suicide? But—why?"

"Shame?" Alleyn suggested. "Self-loathing if he sobered up after you hit him and took stock of himself? I imagine they've been virtually separated for some time."

"I see you have a talent," said J. G., "for reading between the lines."

"Let us rather call it an ugly little knack. Thank you, Mr. Darcey, I don't think I need bother you any more for the moment."

J. G. went slowly to the door. He hesitated for a moment and then said: "If you're looking for a motive, Alleyn, you'll find it in a sort of way all over the place. He wasn't a likable chap and he'd antagonised everyone. Even poor little Parry came off breathing revenge after the way he'd been handled but, my God, actors do that kind of thing only too often. Feeling runs high, you know, on first nights."

"So it would seem."

"Can I take that child home?"

"I'm sorry," Alleyn said, "not yet. Not just yet."

IV

"Well," Alleyn said when J. G. had gone. "What have you got at your end of the table, Br'er Fox?"

Fox turned back the pages of his note-book.

"What you might call negative evidence on the whole, Mr. Alleyn. Clearance for the understudies who watched the show from the back of the circle and then went home. Clearance for the two dressers (male), the stage-manager and his

141

assistant and the stage-hands. They were all watching the play or on their jobs. On statements taken independently, they clear each other."

" That's something."

" No female dresser," Mr. Fox observed. " Which seems odd."

" Miss Tarne was the sole female dresser and she'd been promoted overnight to what I believe I should call starletdom. Which in itself seems to me to be a rum go. I've always imagined female dressers to be cups-of-tea in alpaca aprons and not embryo actresses. I don't think Miss Tarne could have done the job but she comes into the picture as the supplanter of Uncle Ben's dear little niece whom I find an extremely irritating ass with a certain amount of low cunning. Miss Tarne, on the other hand, seems pleasant and intelligent and looks nice. You must allow me my prejudices, Br'er Fox."

" She's Mr. Poole's third cousin or something."

" The case reeks with obscure relationships—blood, marital and illicit, as far as one can see. Did you get anything from Bennington's dresser?"

" Nothing much," said Fox, sighing. " It seems the deceased didn't like him to hang about on account of being a silent drinker. He was in the dressing-room up to about 7 p.m. and was then told to go and see if he could be of any use to the other gentlemen and not to come back till the first interval when the deceased changed his clothes. I must say that chap earns his wages pretty easily. As far as I could make out the rest of his duties for the night consisted in tearing off chunks of cotton-wool for the deceased to do up his face with. I checked his visits to the dressing-room by that. The last time he looked in was after the deceased went on the stage in the third act. He cleared away the used cotton-wool and powdered a clean bit. In the normal course of events I suppose he'd have put Mr. Bennington into the fancy-dress he was going to wear to the ball and then gone home quite worn out."

" Was he at all talkative?"

" Not got enough energy, Mr. Alleyn. Nothing to say for himself barring the opinion that deceased was almost on the D.T. mark. The other dresser, Cringle, seems a bright little chap. He just works for Mr. Poole."

" Have you let them go?"

" Yes, sir, I have. And the stage-hands. We can look them out again if we want them but for the moment I think we've just about cleaned them up. I've let the assistant stage-manager—A.S.M. they call him—get away, too. Wife's expecting any time and he never left the prompting book."

" That reduces the mixed bag a bit. You've been through all the rooms of course, but before we do anything else, Br'er Fox, let's have a prowl."

They went into the passage. Fox jerked his thumb at Bennington's room. " Gibson's doing a fly-crawl in there," he said. " If there's anything, he'll find it. That dresser-chap didn't clear anything up except his used powder-puffs."

They passed Bennington's room and went into Parry Percival's next door. Here they found Detective-Sergeants Thompson and Bailey, the one a photographic and the other a fingerprint expert. They were packing up their gear.

" Well, Bailey?" Alleyn asked.

Bailey looked morosely at his superior. " It's there all right, sir," he said grudgingly. " Complete prints, very near, and a check-up all over the shop."

" What about next door?"

" Deceased's room, sir? His prints on the wing-tap and the tube. Trace of red greasepaint on the rubber connection at the end of the tube. Matches paint on deceased's lips."

" Very painstaking," said Alleyn. " Have you tried the experiment?"

" Seeing the fires are back to back, sir," Fox said, " we have. Sergeant Gibson blew down this tube and deceased's fire went out. As in former case."

" Well," Alleyn said, " there you are. Personally I don't believe a word of it, either way." He looked, without interest, at the telegrams stuck round the frame of Parry's looking-glass and at his costume for the ball. " *Very* fancy," he muttered. " Who's in the next room?"

" Mr. J. G. Darcey," said Thompson.

They went into J. G.'s room which was neat and impersonal in character and contained nothing, it seemed, of interest, unless a photograph of Miss Gainsford looking *insouciante* could be so regarded.

In the last room on this side of the passage they saw the electric-machine, some rough sketches, scraps of material and other evidences of Martyn's sewing-party for Jacko. Alleyn glanced round it, crossed the passage and looked into the empty room opposite. " Dismal little cells when they're unoccupied, aren't they?" he said and moved on to Gay Gainsford's room.

He stood there, his hands in his pockets, with Fox at his

elbow. "This one suffers from the fashionable complaint, Fox," he said. "Schizophrenia. It's got a split personality. On my left a rather too smart overcoat, a frisky hat, chi-chi gloves, a pansy purse-bag, a large bottle of one of the less reputable scents, a gaggle of mascots, a bouquet from the management and orchids from—who do you suppose?" He turned over the card. "Yes. Alas, yes, with love and a thousand good wishes from her devoted J. G. On my right a well-worn and modest little topcoat, a pair of carefully tended shoes and gloves that remind one of the White Rabbit, a grey skirt and beret and a yellow jumper. A hand-bag that contains, I'm sure, one of those rather heart-rending little purses and—what else?" He explored the bag. "A New Zealand passport issued this year in which one finds Miss Tarne is twenty years old and an actress. So the dresser's job was—what? The result of an appeal to the celebrated third cousin? But why not give her the understudy at once? She's fantastically like him and I'll be sworn he's mightily catched with her. What's more, even old Darcey says she's a damn' good actress." He turned the leaves of the passport. "She only arrived in England seventeen days ago. Can that account for the oddness of the set-up? Anyway, I don't suppose it matters. Let's go next door, shall we?"

Cringle had left Poole's room in exquisite order. Telegrams were pinned in rows on the wall. A towel was spread over the make-up. A cigarette had been half-extracted from a packet and a match left ready on the top of its box. A framed photograph of Helena Hamilton stood near the glass. Beside it a tiny clock with a gay face ticked feverishly. It stood on a card. Alleyn moved it delicately and read the inscription. "From Helena. To-night and to-morrow and always: bless you."

"The standard for first night keepsakes seems to be set at a high level," Alleyn muttered. "This is a French clock, Fox, with a Sèvres face encircled with garnets. What do you suppose the gentleman gave the lady?"

"Would a tiara be common?" asked Fox.

"Let's go next door and see."

Helena's room smelt and looked like a conservatory. A table had been brought in to carry the flowers. Jacko had set out the inevitable telegrams and had hung up the dresses under their dust sheets. "Here we are," Alleyn said. "A sort of jeroboam of the most expensive scent on the market. Price, I should say, round about thirty pounds. 'From Adam.' Why don't you give me presents when we solve a petty larceny,

Foxkin? Now, I may be fanciful but this looks to me like the gift of a man who's at his wits' end and plumps for the expensive, the easy and the obvious. Here's something entirely different. Look at this, Fox."

It was a necklace of six wooden medallions strung between jade rings. Each plaque was most delicately carved in the likeness of a head in profile and each head was a portrait of one of the company of players. The card bore the date and the inscription: " From J."

" Must have taken a long time to do," observed Fox. " That'll be the foreign gentleman's work, no doubt, Mr. Doré."

" No doubt. I wonder if love's labour has been altogether lost," said Alleyn. " I hope she appreciates it."

He took up the leather-case with its two photographs of Poole. " He's a remarkable looking chap," he said. " If there's anything to be made of faces in terms of character, and I still like to pretend there is, what's to be made of this one? It's what they call a heart-shaped face, broad across the eyes with a firmly moulded chin and a generous but delicate mouth. Reminds one of a Holbein drawing. Doré's sketch in the greenroom is damn' good. Doré crops up all over the place doesn't he? Designs their fancy dresses. Paints their faces, in a double sense. Does their décor and with complete self-effacement, loves their leading lady."

" Do you reckon?"

" I do indeed, Br'er Fox," Alleyn said and rubbed his nose vexedly. " However. Gibson's done all the usual things in these rooms, I suppose?"

" Yes, Mr. Alleyn. Pockets, suitcases and boxes. Nothing to show for it."

" We may as well let them come home to roost, then. We'll see them separately. They can change into their day clothes. The Gainsford has already, of course, done so. Blast! I suppose I'll have to check Darcey's statement with the Gainsford. She gives me the horrors, that young woman."

" Shall I see her, Mr. Alleyn?"

" You can stay and take your notes. I'll see her in the greenroom. No, wait a bit. You stay with the others, Fox, and send young Lamprey along with her. Tell them they can change in their rooms, fan them before they go, and make sure they go singly. I don't want them talking together. And you might try again if you can dig up anything that sounds at all off-key with Bennington over the last few days. Anything that distressed or excited him."

145

" He seems to have been rather easily excited."

" He does, doesn't he, but you never know. I don't believe it was suicide, Fox, and I'm not yet satisfied that we've unearthed anything that's good enough for a motive for murder. Trip away, Foxkin. Ply your craft."

Fox went out sedately. Alleyn crossed the passage and opened the door of Bennington's room. Sergeant Gibson was discovered, squatting on his haunches before the dead gas-fire.

" Anything?" Alleyn asked.

" There's this bit of a stain that looks like a scorch on the hearth, sir."

" Yes, I saw that. Any deposit?"

" We-ll."

" We may have to try."

" The powder pads deceased's dresser cleared away were in the rubbish bin on the stage where he said he put them. Nothing else in the bin. There's this burnt paper on the floor but it's in small flakes—powder almost."

" All right. Seal the room when you've finished. And Gibson, don't let the mortuary van go without telling me."

" Very good, sir."

Alleyn returned to the greenroom. He heard Miss Gains-ford approaching under the wing of P.C. Lamprey. She spoke in a high grand voice that seemed to come out of a drawing-room comedy of the twenties.

" I think you're *too* intrepid," she was saying, " to start from rock bottom like this. It must be so devastatingly boring for you, though I will say it's rather a comfort to think one is in the hands of, to coin a phrase, a gent. Two gents in fact."

" Chief Inspector Alleyn " said P.C. Lamprey, " is in the greenroom I think, Miss."

" My dear, you do it quite marvellously. You ought, again to coin a phrase, to go on the stage."

Evidently Miss Gainsford lingered in the passage. Alleyn heard his subordinate murmur: " Shall I go first?" His regulation boots clumped firmly to the door which he now opened.

" Will you see Miss Gainsford, sir?" asked P.C. Lamprey, who was pink in the face.

" All right, Mike," Alleyn said. " Show her in and take notes."

" Will you come this way, Miss?"

Miss Gainsford made her entrance with a Mayfairish

gallantry that was singularly dated. Alleyn wondered if she had decided that her first reading of her new role was mistaken. "She's abandoned the brave little woman for the suffering mondaine who goes down with an epigram," he thought and sure enough Miss Gainsford addressed herself to him with staccato utterance and brittle high-handedness.

"Ought one to be terribly flattered because one is the first to be grilled?" she asked. "Or is it a sinister little hint that one is top of the suspect list?"

"As you don't have to change," Alleyn said, "I thought it would be convenient to see you first. Will you sit down, Miss Gainsford?"

She did so elaborately, gave herself a cigarette, and turned to P.C. Lamprey: "May one ask The Force for a light?" she asked. "Or would that be against the rules?"

Alleyn lit her cigarette while his unhappy subordinate retired to the table. She turned in her chair to watch him. "Is he going to take me down and use it all in evidence against me?" she asked. Her nostrils dilated, she raised her chin and added jerkily: "That's what's called the Usual Warning, isn't it?"

"A warning is given in police practice," Alleyn said as woodenly as possible, "if there is any chance that the person under interrogation will make a statement that is damaging to himself. Lamprey will note down this interview and if it seems advisable you will be asked, later on, to give a signed statement."

"If that was meant to be reassuring," said Miss Gainsford, "I can't have heard it properly. Could we get cracking?"

"Certainly. Miss Gainsford, you were in the greenroom throughout the performance. During the last interval you were visited by Mr. J. G. Darcey and by your uncle. Do you agree that as the result of something the deceased said, Mr. Darcey hit him on the jaw?"

She said: "Wasn't it too embarrassing! I mean the Gorgeous Primitive Beast is one thing but one old gentleman banging another about is so utterly another. I'm afraid I didn't put that very clearly."

"You agree that Mr. Darcey hit Mr. Bennington?"

"But madly. Like a sledge-hammer. I found it so difficult to know what to say, There just seemed to be no clue to further conversation."

"It is the conversation before rather than after the blow that I should like to hear about, if you please."

Alleyn had turned away from her and was looking at

147

Jacko's portrait of Poole. He waited for some moments before she said sharply. " I suppose you think because I talk like this about it I've got no feeling. You couldn't be more at fault." It was as if she called his attention to her performance.

He said, without turning: " I assure you I hadn't given it a thought. What did your uncle say that angered Mr. Darcey?"

" He was upset," she said sulkily, " because I was ill and couldn't play."

" Hardly an occasion for hitting him."

" J. G. is very sensitive about me. He treats me like a piece of china."

" This is more than he did for your uncle, it seems."

" Uncle Ben talked rather wildly." Miss Gainsford seemed to grope for her poise and made a half-hearted return to her brittle manner. " Let's face it," she said, " he was stinking, poor pet."

" You mean he was drunk?"

" Yes, I do."

" And abusive?"

" I didn't care. I understood him."

" Did he talk about Miss Hamilton?"

" Obviously J. G.'s already told you he did, so why ask me?"

" We like to get confirmation of statements."

" Well, you tell me what he said and I'll see about confirming it."

For the first time Alleyn looked at her. She wore an expression of rather frightened impertinence. " I'm afraid," he said, " that won't quite do. I'm sure you're very anxious to get away from the theatre, Miss Gainsford, and we've still a lot of work before us. If you will give me your account of this conversation I shall be glad to hear it ; if you prefer so to do so I'll take note of your refusal and keep you no longer."

She gaped slightly, attempted a laugh and seemed to gather up the rags of her impersonation.

" Oh, but I'll tell you," she said. " Why not? It's only that there's so pathetically little to tell. I can't help feeling darling auntie—she likes me to call her Ellen—was *too* Pinero and Galsworthy about it. It appears that poorest Uncle Ben came in from his club and found her in a suitable setting and—well, there you are, and—well, really even after all these years of segregation you couldn't call it a

148

seduction. Or could you? Anyway she chose to treat it as such and raised the most piercing hue and cry and he went all primitive and when he came in here he was ev'dently in the throes of a sort of hangover and seeing J. G. was being rather sweet to me put a sinister interpretation on it and described the whole incident and was rather rude about women generally and me and auntie in particular. And J. G. took a gloomy view of his attitude and hit him. And, I mean, taking it by and large, one couldn't help feeling: *what* a song and dance about nothing in particular. Is that all you wanted to know?"

"Do you think any other members of the company know of all this?"

She looked genuinely surprised. "Oh yes," she said. "Adam and Jacko, anyway. I mean Uncle Ben appeared to have a sort of nation-wide hook-up idea about it but even if *he* didn't mention it, *she'd* naturally tell Adam wouldn't you think? And Jacko, because everybody tells Jacko everything. And he was doing dresser for her. Yes, I'd certainly think she'd tell Jacko."

"I see. Thank you, Miss Gainsford. That's all."

"Really?" She was on her feet. "I can go home?"

Alleyn answered her as he had answered J. G. "I'm sorry: not yet. Not just yet."

P.C. Lamprey opened the door. Inevitably, she paused on the threshold. "Never tell *me* there's nothing in atmosphere," she said. "I *knew* when I came into this theatre. As if the very walls screamed it at me. I *knew*."

She went out.

"Tell me, Mike," Alleyn said, "are many young women of your generation like that?"

"Well, no sir. She's what one might call a composite picture, don't you think?"

"I do, indeed. And I fancy she's got her genres a bit confused."

"She tells me she's been playing in *Private Lives, The Second Mrs. Tanqueray* and *Sleeping Partners* in the provinces."

"That may account for it," said Alleyn.

An agitated voice—Parry Percival's—was raised in the passage to be answered in a more subdued manner by Sergeant Gibson's.

"Go and see what it is, Mike," Alleyn said.

But before Lamprey could reach the door it was flung open and Parry burst in, slamming it in Gibson's affronted face. He addressed himself instantly and breathlessly to Alleyn.

"I'm sorry," he said, "but I've just remembered something. I've been so *hideously* upset, I just simply never gave it a thought. It was when I smelt gas. When I went back to my room I smelt gas and I turned off my fire. I ought to have told you. I've just realised."

"I think perhaps what you have just realised," Alleyn said, "is the probability of our testing your gas-fire for fingerprints and finding your own."

CHAPTER IX

THE SHADOW OF OTTO BROD

Parry stood inside the door and pinched his lips as if he realised they were white and hoped to restore their colour.

"I don't know anything about fingerprints," he said. "I never read about crime. I don't know anything about it. When I came off after my final exit I went to my room. I was just going back for the call when I smelt gas. We're all nervous about gas in this theatre and anyway the room was frightfully hot. I turned the thing off. That's all."

"This was after Bennington tripped you up?"

"I've told you. It was after my last exit and before the call. It wasn't——"

He walked forward very slowly and sat down in front of Alleyn. "You can't think that sort of thing about me," he said and sounded as if he was moved more by astonishment than by any other emotion. "My God, *look* at me. I'm so hopelessly harmless. I'm not vicious. I'm not even odd. I'm just harmless."

"Why didn't you tell me at once that you noticed the smell of gas?"

"Because, as I've tried to suggest, I'm no good at this sort of thing. The doctor got me all upset and in any case the whole show was so unspeakable." He stared at Alleyn and, as if that explained everything, said: "I saw him. I saw him when they carried him out. I've never been much good about dead people. In the blitz I sort of managed but I never got used to it."

"Was the smell of gas very strong in your room?"

"No. Not strong at all. But in this theatre—we were

all thinking about that other time and I just thought it was too bad of the management to have anything faulty in the system considering the history of the place. I don't know that I thought anything more than that: I smelt it and remembered, and got a spasm of the horrors. Then I felt angry at being given a shock and then I turned my fire off and went out. It was rather like not looking at the new moon through glass. You don't really believe it can do anything but you avoid it. I forgot all about the gas as soon as I got on-stage. I didn't give it another thought until I smelt it again during the doctor's speech."

"Yes, I see."

"You do, really, don't you? After all, suppose I—suppose I had thought I'd copy that other awful thing: well, I'd scarcely be fool enough to leave my fingerprints on the tap, would I?"

"But you tell me," Alleyn said, not making too much of it, "that you don't know anything about fingerprints."

"God!" Parry whispered, staring at him, "you do frighten me. It's not fair. You frighten me."

"Believe me, there's no need for an innocent man to be frightened."

"How can you be so sure of yourselves? Do you never make mistakes?"

"We do indeed. But not," Alleyn said, "in the end. Not nowadays on these sorts of cases."

"What do you mean these sorts of cases!"

"Why, I mean on what may turn out to be a capital charge."

"I can't believe it!" Parry cried out. "I shall never believe it. We're not like that. We're kind, rather simple people. We wear our hearts on our sleeves. We're not complicated enough to kill each other."

Alleyn said with a smile: "You're quite complicated enough for us at the moment. Is there anything else you've remembered that you think perhaps you ought to tell me about?"

Parry shook his head and dragged himself to his feet. Alleyn saw, as Martyn had seen before him, that he was not an exceedingly young man. "No," he said. "There's nothing I can think of."

"You may go to your dressing-room now, if you'd like to change into—what should I say?—into plain clothes?"

"Thank you. I simply loathe the thought of my room after all this but I shall be glad to change."

" Do you mind if Lamprey does a routine search before you go? We'll ask this of all of you."

Parry showed the whites of his eyes but said at once: " Why should I mind?"

Alleyn nodded to young Lamprey who advanced upon Parry with an apologetic smile.

" It's a painless extraction, sir," he said.

Parry raised his arms in a curve with his white hands held like a dancer's above his head. There was a silence and a swift efficient exploration. " Thank you so much, sir," said Mike Lamprey. " Cigarette-case, lighter, and handkerchief, Mr. Alleyn."

" Right. Take Mr. Percival along to his room, will you?"

Parry said: " There couldn't be a more fruitless question but it would be nice to know, one way or the other, if you have believed me."

" There couldn't be a more unorthodox answer," Alleyn rejoined, " but at the moment I see no reason to disbelieve you, Mr. Percival."

When Lamprey came back he found his senior officer looking wistfully at his pipe and whistling under his breath.

" Mike," Alleyn said. " The nastiest cases in our game are very often the simplest. There's something sticking out under my nose in this theatre and I can't see it. I know it's there because of another thing that, Lord pity us all, Fox and I *can* see."

" Really, sir? Am I allowed to ask what it is?"

" You're getting on in the service, now. What have you spotted on your own account?"

" Is it something to do with Bennington's behaviour, sir?"

" It is indeed. If a man's going to commit suicide, Mike, and his face is made-up to look loathesome, what does he do about it? If he's a vain man (and Bennington appears to have had his share of professional vanity), if he minds about the appearance of his own corpse, he cleans off the greasepaint. If he doesn't give a damn, he leaves it as it is. But with time running short he does *not* carefully and heavily powder his unbecoming make-up for all the world as if he meant to go on and take his curtain-call with the rest of them. Now, does he?"

" Well, no sir," said Mike. " If you put it like that, I don't believe he does."

By half-past twelve most of the company on the stage seemed to be asleep or dozing. Dr. Rutherford on his couch occasionally lapsed into bouts of snoring from which he would rouse a little, groan, take snuff and then settle down again. Helena lay in a deep chair with her feet on a stool. Her eyes were closed but Martyn thought that if she slept it was but lightly. Clem had made himself a bed of some old curtains and was curled up on it beyond the twisting stairway. Jacko, having tucked Helena up in her fur coat, settled himself on the stage beside her, dozing, Martyn thought, like some eccentric watch-dog at his post. J. G. and Gay Gainsford were summoned in turn and in turn came back, J. G. silently, Gay with some attempt at conversation. In the presence of the watchful Mr. Fox this soon petered out. Presently she too, fell to nodding. Immediately after her return Parry Percival suddenly made an inarticulate ejaculation and, before Fox could move, darted off the stage. Sergeant Gibson was heard to accost him in the passage. Fox remained where he was and there was another long silence.

Adam Poole and Martyn looked into each other's faces. He crossed the stage to where she sat, on the left side which was the farthest removed from Fox. He pulled up a small chair and sat facing her.

"Kate," he muttered, "I'm so sorry about all this. There are hares-foot shadows under your eyes, your mouth droops, your hands are anxious and your hair is limp though not at all unbecoming. You should be sound asleep in Jacko's garret under the stars and there should be the sound of applause in your dreams. Really, it's too bad."

Martyn said: "It's nice of you to think so but you have other things to consider."

"I'm glad to have my thoughts interrupted."

"Then I still have my uses."

"You can see that chunk of a man over there. Is he watching us?"

"Yes. With an air of absent-mindedness which I'm not at all inclined to misunderstand."

"I don't think he can hear us though it's a pity my diction is so good. If I take your hand perhaps he'll suppose I'm making love to you and feel some slight constabular delicacy."

"I hardly think so," Martyn whispered and tried to make nothing of his lips against her palm.

"Will you believe, Kate, that I am not in the habit of making passes at young ladies in my company?"

Martyn found herself looking at the back of Helena's chair.

"Oh, yes," Poole said. "There's that, too. I make no bones about that. It's another and a long and a fading story. On both parts. Fading, on both parts, Kate. I have been very much honoured."

"I can't help feeling this scene is being played at the wrong time, in the wrong place and before the wrong audience. And I doubt," Martyn said, not looking at him, "if it should be played at all."

"But I can't be mistaken. It has happened for us, Martyn. Hasn't it? Suddenly, preposterously, almost at first sight we blinked and looked again and there we were. Tell me it's happened. The bird under your wrist is so wildly agitated. Is that only because you are frightened?"

"I am frightened. I wanted to ask your advice and now you make it impossible."

"I'll give you my advice. There. Now you are alone again. But for the sake of the law's peace of mind as well as my own you must take a firm line about your blushing."

"It was something he said to me that morning," she murmured in the lowest voice she could command.

"Do you mean the morning when I first saw you?"

"I mean," Martyn said desperately, "the morning the photographs were taken. I had to go to his dressing-room."

"I remember very well. You came to mine too."

"He said something, then. He was very odd in his manner. They've asked us to try and remember anything at all unusual."

"Are you going to tell me what it was?"

In a few words and under her breath she did so.

Poole said: "Perhaps you should tell them. Yes, I think you should. In a moment I'll do something about it but there's one thing more I must say to you. Do you know I'm glad this scene has been played so awkwardly—inaudible, huddled up, inauspicious and uneffective. Technically altogether bad. It gives it a kind of authority, I hope. Martyn, are you very much surprised? Please look at me."

She did as he asked and discovered an expression of such doubt and anxiety in his face that to her own astonishment she put her hand against his cheek and he held it there for a second. "God!" he said, "what a thing to happen!" He got up abruptly and crossed the stage.

" Inspector," he said, " Miss Tarne has remembered an incident three days old which we both think might possibly be of some help. What should we do about it?"

The others stirred a little. J. G. opened his eyes.

Fox got up. " Thank you very much, sir," he said. " When Mr. Alleyn is disengaged I'm sure he'll—— Yes? What is it?"

P.C. Lamprey had come in. He delivered his message about the dressing-rooms being open for the use of their occupants. At the sound of his brisk and loudish voice they all stirred. Helena and Darcey got to their feet. Jacko sat up. Clem, Gray and Dr. Rutherford opened their eyes, listened to the announcement and went to sleep again.

Fox said: " You can take this young lady along to the chief in three minutes, Lamprey. Now, ladies and gentlemen, if you'd care to go to your rooms."

He shepherded Helena and the two men through the door and looked back at Poole. " What about you, sir?"

Poole with his eyes on Martyn, said: " Yes, I'm coming." Fox waited stolidly at the door for him and after a moment's hesitation Poole followed the others. Fox went with them.

Mike Lamprey said: " We'll let them get settled, Miss Tarne, and then I'll take you along to Mr. Alleyn. You must be getting very bored with all this hanging about."

Martyn, whose emotional processes were in a state of chaos, replied with a vague smile. She wondered disjointedly if constables of P.C. Lamprey's class were a commonplace in the English Force. He glanced good-humouredly at Gay and the three dozing men and evidently felt obliged to make further conversation.

" I heard someone say," he began, " that you are a New Zealander. I was out there as a small boy."

" Were you, really?" Martyn said and wondered confusedly if he could have been the son of a former governor-general.

" We had a place out there on a mountain. Mount Silver it was. Would that be anywhere near your part of the world?"

Something clicked in Martyn's memory. " Oh, *yes*!" she said. " I've heard about the Lampreys of Mount Silver, I'm sure and——" Her recollections clarified a little. " Yes, indeed," she added lamely.

" No doubt," said Mike with a cheerful laugh, " a legend of lunacy has survived us. We came home when I was about

155

eight and soon afterwards my uncle happened to get murdered in our flat and Mr. Alleyn handled the case. I thought at the time I'd like to go into the Force and the idea sort of persisted. And there you are, you know. Potted autobiography. Shall we go along and see if he's free?"

He escorted her down the passage to the greenroom door past Sergeant Gibson who seemed to be on guard there. Mike chatted freely as they went, rather as if he was taking her into supper after a successful dance. The star-bemused Martyn found herself brightly chatting back at him.

This social atmosphere was not entirely dispelled, she felt, by Alleyn himself, who received her rather as a distinguished surgeon might greet a patient.

"Come in, Miss Tarne," he said cordially. "I hear you've thought of something to tell us about this wretched business. Do sit down."

She sat in her old chair, facing the gas-fire and with her back to the table. Only when she looked up involuntarily at the sketch of Adam Poole did she realise that young Lamprey had settled himself at the table and taken out a note-book. She could see his image reflected in the glass.

Inspector Fox came in and went quietly to the far end of the room where he sat in a shadowed corner and appeared to consult his own note-book.

"Well," Alleyn said, "what's it all about?"

"You'll probably think it's about nothing," Martyn began, "and if you do I shall be sorry I've bothered you with it. But I thought—just in case——"

"You were perfectly right. Believe me, we are 'conditioned' if that's the beastly word, to blind alleys. Let's have it."

"On my first morning in this theatre," Martyn said. "which was the day before yesterday . . . no, if it's past midnight, the day before that."

"Tuesday?"

"Yes. On that morning I went to Mr. Bennington's room to fetch Miss Hamilton's cigarette-case. He was rather strange in his manner but at first I thought that was because—I thought he'd noticed my likeness to Mr. Poole. He couldn't find the case and in hunting through the pockets of a jacket, a letter dropped to the floor. I picked it up and he drew my attention to it in the oddest sort of way. I'd describe his manner almost as triumphant. He said something about autographs. I think he asked me if I collected autographs

156

or autographed letters. He pointed to the envelope which I still had in my hand and said there was somebody who'd give a hell of a lot for that one. Those, I'm almost sure, were his exact words."

"Did you look at the letter?"

"Yes, I did, because of what he said. It was addressed to him and it had a foreign stamp on it. The writing was very bold and it seemed to me foreign looking. I put it on the shelf face downwards and he drew my attention to it again by stabbing at it with his finger. The name of the sender was written on the back."

"Do you remember it?"

"Yes, I do, because of his insistence."

"Good girl," said Alleyn quietly.

"It was 'Otto Brod' and the address was a theatre in Prague. I'm afraid I don't remember the name of the theatre or the street. I *ought* to remember the theatre. It was a French name, Theatre de—something. *Why* can't I remember!"

"You haven't done badly. Was there something in the envelope?"

"Yes. It wasn't anything fat. One sheet of paper I should think."

"And his manner was triumphant?"

"I thought so. He was just rather odd about it. He'd been drinking—brandy I thought—the tumbler was on the dressing-shelf and he made as if to put the flask behind his looking-glass."

"Did you think he was at all the worse for wear?"

"I wondered if it accounted for his queer behaviour."

"Can you tell me anything else he said? The whole conversation if you remember it."

Martyn thought back and it seemed she had journeyed half a lifetime in three days. There was the room. There was J. G. going out and leaving her with Bennington and there was Bennington staring at her and talking about the cigarette-case. There was also something else, buried away behind her thoughts of which the memory now returned. She was made miserable by it.

"He said, I think, something about the cigarette-case. That he himself hadn't given it to Miss Hamilton."

"Did he say who gave it to her?"

"No," Martyn said. "I don't think he said that. Just that *he* didn't."

157

"And was his manner of saying this strange?"

"I thought his manner throughout was—uncomfortable and odd. He seemed to me to be a very unhappy man."

"Yet you used the word triumphant?"

"There can be unhappy victories."

"True for you. There can, indeed. Tell me one thing more. Do you connect the two conversations? I mean do you think what he said about the cigarette-case had anything to do with what he said about the letter?"

"I should say nothing. Nothing at all."

"Oh, Lord!" Alleyn said resignedly and called out: "Have you got all that, Mike?"

"Coming up the straight, sir."

"Put it into longhand, now, will you, and we'll ask Miss Tarne to have a look at it and see if she's been misrepresented. Do you mind waiting a minute or two, Miss Tarne? It'll save you coming back."

"No, of course not," said Martyn whose ideas of police investigation were undergoing a private revolution. Alleyn offered her a cigarette and lit it for her. The consultation, she felt, was over and the famous surgeon was putting his patient at her ease.

"I gather from Lamprey's far-reaching conversation that you are a New Zealander," he said. "If I may say so, you seem to have dropped out of a clear sky into your own success story. Have you been long at the Vulcan, Miss Tarne?"

"A night and three days."

"Good Lord! And in that time you've migrated from dresser to what sounds like minor stardom. Success story, indeed!"

"Yes, but——" Martyn hesitated. For the first time since she walked into the Vulcan she felt able to talk about herself. It didn't occur to her that it was odd for her confidant to be a police officer.

"It's all been very eccentric," she said. "I only reached England a little over a fortnight ago and my money was stolen in the ship so I had to get some sort of job rather quickly."

"Did you report the theft to the police?"

"No. The purser said he didn't think it would do any good."

"So much," said Alleyn with a wry look, "for the police!"

"I'm sorry——" Martyn began and he said: "Never mind. It's not an uncommon attitude, I'm afraid. So you

158

had a rather unhappy arrival. Lucky there was your cousin to come to your rescue."

"But—no—I mean——" Martyn felt herself blushing and plunged on. "That's just what I didn't want to do. I mean I didn't want to go to him at all. He didn't know of my existence. You see——"

It was part of Alleyn's professional equipment that something in his make-up invited confidence. Mr. Fox once said of his superior that he would be able to get himself worked up over the life story of a mollusc provided the narrative was obtained first-hand. He heard Martyn's story with the liveliest interest up to the point where she entered the theatre. He didn't seem to think it queer that she should have been anxious to conceal her relationship to Poole or that she was stupid to avoid the Vulcan in her search for a job. She was describing her interview with Bob Grantley on Wednesday night when Sergeant Gibson's voice sounded in the passage. He tapped on the door and came in.

"Excuse me, sir," he said, "but could you see the night-watchman. He seems to think it's important."

He had got as far as this when he was elbowed aside by Fred Badger who came angrily into the room.

"'Ere!" he said. "Are you the guvnor of this 'owd'yerdo?"

"Yes," said Alleyn.

"Well, look. You can lay orf this young lady, see? No call to get nosy on account of what she done, see? I don't know nothink abaht the law, see, but I'm in charge 'ere of a night and what she done she done wiv my permission. Nah!"

"Just a moment——" Alleyn began and was roared down.

"Suppose it was an offence! What abaht it! She never done no 'arm. No offence taken where none was intended, that's correct ain't it! Nah ven!"

"What," Alleyn said turning to Martyn, "is this about?"

"I'm afraid it's about me sleeping in the theatre that first night. I'd nowhere to go and it was very late. Mr. Badger very kindly—didn't turn me out."

"I see. Where did you sleep?"

"Here. In this chair."

"Like a charld," Fred Badger interposed. "Slep' like a charld all night. I looked in on me rahnds and seen 'er laying safe in the arms of Morpus. Innercent. And if anyone tells you different you can refer 'im to me. Badger's the name."

"All right, Badger."

"If you put me pot on with the management for what I done, leaving 'er to lay—all right. Aht! Finish! There's better jobs rahnd the corner."

"Yes. All right. I don't think we'll take it up."

"Awright. Fair enough." He addressed himself to Martyn. "And what was mentioned between you and me in a friendly manner needn't be mentioned no more. Let bygones be bygones." He returned to Alleyn. "She's as innercent as a babe. Arst 'is nibs."

Alleyn waited for a moment and then said: "Thank you." Gibson succeeded in removing Fred Badger but not before he had directed at Martyn that peculiar clicking sound of approval which is accompanied by a significant jerk of the head.

When he had gone Alleyn said: "I think I'd better ask you to interpret. What *was* his exquisite meaning?"

Martyn felt a dryness in her mouth. "I think," she said, "he's afraid he'll get into trouble for letting me sleep in here that night and I think he's afraid I'll get into trouble if I tell you that he showed me how the murder in the Jupiter case was accomplished."

"That seems a little far-fetched."

Martyn said rapidly: "I suppose it's idiotic of me to say this but I'd rather say it. Mr. Bennington very naturally resented my luck in this theatre. He tackled me about it and he was pretty truculent. I expect the stage-hands have gossiped to Badger and he thinks you might—might——"

"Smell a motive?"

"Yes," said Martyn.

"Did Bennington threaten you?"

"I don't remember exactly what he said. His manner was threatening. He frightened me."

"Where did this happen?"

"Off-stage, during the first dress-rehearsal."

"Was anyone present when he tackled you?"

The image of Poole rose in Martyn's memory. She saw him take Bennington by the arm and twist him away from her.

"There were people about," she said. "They were changing the set. I should think it very likely—I mean it was a very public sort of encounter."

He looked thoughtfully at her and she wondered if she had changed colour. "This," he said, "was before it was decided you were to play the part?"

160

"Oh, yes. That was only decided half an hour before the show went on."

"So it was. Did he do anything about this decision? Go for you, again?"

"He didn't come near me until I'd finished. And knowing how much he must mind, I was grateful for that."

Alleyn said: "You've been very sensible to tell me this, Miss Tarne."

Martyn swallowed hard. "I don't know," she said, "that I would have told you if it hadn't been for Fred Badger."

"Ah, well," Alleyn said, "one mustn't expect too much. How about that statement, Mike?"

"Here we are, sir. I hope you can read my writing, Miss Tarne."

When she took the paper, Martyn found her hands were not steady. Alleyn moved away to the table with his subordinate. She sat down again and read the large schoolboyish writing. It was a short and accurate résumé of the incident of the letter from Prague.

"It's quite right," she said. "Am I to sign it?"

"If you please. There will be statements for most of the others to sign later on but yours is so short I thought we might as well get it over now."

He gave her his pen and she went to the table and signed. P.C. Lamprey smiled reassuringly at her and escorted her to the door.

Alleyn said: "Thank you so much, Miss Tarne. Do you live far from here?"

"Not very far. A quarter of an hour's walk."

"I wish I could let you go home now but I don't quite like to do that. Something might crop up that we'd want to refer to you."

"Might it?"

"You never know," he said. "Anyway you can change now." Lamprey opened the door and she went to the dressing-room.

When she had gone Alleyn said: "What did you make of her, Mike?"

"I thought she was rather a sweetiepie, sir," said P.C. Lamprey. Fox, in his disregarded corner, snorted loudly.

"That was all too obvious," said Alleyn. "Sweetness apart did you find her truthful?"

"I'd 1ave said so, sir, yes."

"What about you, Br'er Fox? Come out of cover and declare yourself."

Fox rose, removed his spectacles and advanced upon them. " There was something," he observed, " about that business of when deceased went for her."

" There was indeed. Not exactly lying, wouldn't you think, so much as leaving something out?"

" Particularly in respect of whether there was a witness."

" She had her back to you but she looked at this portrait of Adam Poole. I'd make a long bet, Poole found Bennington slanging that child and ordered him off."

" Very possibly, Mr. Alleyn. He's sweet on the young lady. That's plain to see. *And* she on him."

" Good Lord!" Mike Lamprey ejaculated. " He must be forty! I'm sorry, sir."

Mr. Fox began a stately reproof but Alleyn said: " Go away, Mike. Go back to the stage. Wake Dr. Rutherford and ask him to come here. I want a change from actors."

III

Dr. Rutherford, on his entry into the greenroom, was a figure of high fantasy. For his greater ease in sleeping he had pulled his boiled shirt from its confinement and it dangled fore and aft like a crumpled tabard. Restrained only by his slackened braces, it formed a mask, Alleyn conjectured, for a free adjustment of the doctor's trouser buttoning. He had removed his jacket and assumed an overcoat. His collar was released and his tie dangled on his bosom. His hair was tousled and his face blotched.

He paused in the doorway while Lamprey announced him and then, with a dismissive gesture, addressed himself to Alleyn and Fox.

" Calling my officers about me in my branched velvet gown," he shouted, " having come from a day-bed where I left Miss Gainsford sleeping, I present myself as a brand for the constabular burning. What's cooking, my hearties?"

He stood there, puffing and blowing, and eyed them with an expression of extreme impertinence. If he had been an actor, Alleyn thought, he would have been cast, and cast ideally, for Falstaff. He fished under his shirt tail, produced his snuff-box, and helped himself, with a parody of regency deportment, to a generous pinch. " Speak!" he said. " Propound! I am all ears."

" I have nothing, I'm afraid, to propound," Alleyn said cheerfully, " and am therefore unable to pronounce. As for

162

speaking, I hope you'll do most of that yourself, Dr. Rutherford. Will you sit down?"

Dr. Rutherford, with his usual precipitancy, hurled himself into the nearest arm-chair. As an afterthought he spread his shirt tail with ridiculous finicking movements across his lap. " I am a thought down-gyved," he observed. " My points are untrussed. Forgive me."

" Tell me," Alleyn said. " Do you think Bennington was murdered?"

The doctor opened his eyes very wide, folded his hands on his stomach, revolved his thumbs and said: " No."

" No?"

" No."

" We do."

" Why?"

" I'll come to that when I'm quite sure you may be put into the impossible class."

" Am I a suspect, by all that's pettifogging?"

" Not if you can prove yourself otherwise."

" By God!" said Dr. Rutherford deeply, " if I'd thought I could get away with it, be damned if I wouldn't have had a shot. He was an unconscionable rogue, was Ben."

" In what way?"

" In every way, by Janus. A drunkard. A wife-terrorist. An exhibitionist. And what's more," he went on with rising intensity, " a damned wrecker of plays. A yeaforsooth knavish pander, by heaven! I tell you this, and I tell you plainly, if I, sitting in my O.P. box could have persuaded the Lord to stoop out of the firmament and drop a tidy thunderbolt on Ben, I would have done it with bells on. Joyously!"

" A thunderbolt," Alleyn said, " is one of the few means of dispatch that we have not seriously considered. Would you mind telling me where you were between the time when he made his last exit and the time when you appeared before the audience?"

" Brief let me be. In my box. On the stairs. Off-stage. On the stage."

" Can you tell me exactly when you left your box?"

" While they were making their initial mops and mows at the audience."

" Did you meet anyone or notice anything at all remarkable during this period?"

" Nothing, and nobody whatever."

" From which side did you enter for your own call?"

" The O.P., which is actors' right."

"So you merely emerged from the stairs that lead from the box to the stage and found yourself hard by the entrance?"

"Precisely."

"Have you any witness to all this, sir?"

"To my knowledge," said the doctor, "none whatever. There may have been a rude mechanical or so."

"As far as your presence in the box is concerned there was the audience. Nine hundred of them."

"In spite of its mangling at the hands of two of the actors, I believe the attention of the audience to have been upon My Play. In any case," the doctor added, helping himself to a particularly large pinch of snuff and holding it poised before his face, "I had shrunk in modest confusion behind the curtain."

"Perhaps someone visited you?"

"Not after the first act. I locked myself in," he added, taking his snuff with uncouth noises, "as a precautionary measure. I loathe company."

"Did you come back-stage at any other time during the performance?"

"I did. I came back in both intervals. Primarily to see the little wench."

"Miss Tarne?" Alleyn ventured.

"She. A tidy little wench it is and will make a good player. If she doesn't allow herself to be debauched by the sissies that rule the roost in our lamentable theatre."

"Did you, during either of these intervals, visit the dressing-rooms?"

"I went to the usual office at the end of the passage if you call that a dressing-room."

"And returned to your box—when?"

"As soon as the curtain went up."

"I see." Alleyn thought for a moment and then said: "Dr. Rutherford, do you know anything about a man called Otto Brod?"

The doctor gave a formidable gasp. His eyes bulged, his nostrils wrinkled and his jaw dropped. The grimace turned out to be the preliminary spasm of a Gargantuan sneeze. A handkerchief not being at his disposal, he snatched up the tail of his shirt, clapped it to his face and revealed a state of astonishing disorder below the waist.

"Otto Brod?" he repeated looking at Alleyn over his shirt tail as if it was an improvised yashmak. "Never heard of him."

"His correspondence seems to be of some value," Alleyn

said vaguely but the doctor merely gaped at him. "I don't," he said flatly, "know what you're talking about."

Alleyn gave up Otto Brod. "You'll have guessed," he said, "that I've already heard a good deal about the events of the last few days: I mean as they concerned the final rehearsals and the change in casting."

"Indeed? Then you will have heard that Ben and I had one flaming row after another. If you're looking for motive," said Dr. Rutherford with an expansive gesture, "I'm lousy with it. We hated each others' guts, Ben and I. Of the two I should say, however, that he was the more murderously inclined."

"Was this feeling chiefly on account of the part his niece was to have played?"

"Fundamentally it was the fine flower of a natural antipathy. The contributive elements were his behaviour as an actor in My Play and the obvious and immediate necessity to return his niece to her squalid little *métier* and replace her by the wench. We had at each other on that issue," said Dr. Rutherford with relish, "after both auditions and on every other occasion that presented itself."

"And in the end, it seems, you won?"

"Pah!" said the doctor with a dismissive wave of his hand. "Cat's meat!"

Alleyn looked a little dubiously at the chaotic disarray of his garments. "Have you any objection," he asked, "to being searched?"

"Not I," cried the doctor and hauled himself up from his chair. Fox approached him.

"By the way," Alleyn said. "As a medical man, would you say that a punch on the jaw such as Bennington was given, could have been the cause of his fainting some time afterwards? Remembering his general condition?"

"Who says he had a punch on the jaw? It's probably a hypostatic discoloration. What do *you* want?" Dr. Rutherford demanded of Fox.

"If you wouldn't mind your taking your hands out of your pockets, sir," Fox suggested.

The doctor said: "Let not us that are squires of the night's body be called thieves of the day's beauty," and obligingly withdrew his hands from his trouser pockets. Unfortunately he pulled the linings out with them. A number of objects fell about his feet—pencils, his snuff box, scraps of paper, a pill-box, a programme, a note-book and a half-eaten cake of chocolate. A small cloud of snuff floated above this collection. Fox bent down and made a clucking sound of disapproval. He began to collect the scattered objects, inhaled snuff and was seized with a paroxysm of sneezing. The doctor broke into a fit of uncouth laughter and floundered damagingly among the exhibits.

" Dr. Rutherford," Alleyn said with an air of the liveliest exasperation, " I would be immensely obliged to you if you'd have the goodness to stop behaving like a pantaloon. Get off those things, if you please."

The doctor backed away into his chair and examined an unlovely mess of chocolate and cardboard on the sole of his boot. " But, blast your lights my good ass," he said, " there goes my spare ration. An ounce of the best rapee, by heaven!" Fox began to pick the fragments of the pill-box from his boot. Having collected and laid aside the dropped possessions, he scraped up a heap of snuff. " It's no good now, Dogberry," said the doctor with an air of intense disapproval. Fox tipped the scrapings into an envelope.

Alleyn stood over the doctor. " I think," he said, " you had better give this up, you know."

The doctor favoured him with an antic grimace but said nothing. " You're putting on an act, Dr. Rutherford, and I do assure you it's not at all convincing. As a red-herring it stinks to high heaven. Let me tell you this. We now know that Bennington was hit over the jaw. We know when it happened. We know that the bruise was afterwards camouflaged with make-up. I want you to come with me while I remove this make-up. Where's your jacket?"

" *Give me my robe. Put on my crown. I have immortal longings in me.*"

Fox went out and returned with a tail-coat that was in great disorder. " Nothing in the pockets, Mr. Alleyn," he said briefly. Alleyn nodded and he handed it to Dr. Rutherford who slung it over his shoulder.

Alleyn led the way down the passage where Gibson was still on guard and round the back of the stage to the dock. P.C. Lamprey came off the set and rolled the doors back.

Bennington had stiffened a little since they last looked at him. His face bore the expression of knowledgeable acquiescence that is so often seen in the dead. Using the back of a knife-blade, Alleyn scraped away the greasepaint from the left jaw. Fox held a piece of card for him and he laid smears of greasepaint on it in the manner of a painter setting his palette. The discoloured mark on the jaw showed clearly.

" There it is," Alleyn said, and stood aside for Dr. Rutherford.

" A tidy buffet, if buffet it was. Who gave it him?"

Alleyn didn't answer. He moved round to the other side and went on cleaning the face.

" The notion that it could have contributed to his death," the doctor said, " is preposterous. If as you say, there was an interval between the blow and the supposed collapse. Preposterous!"

Fox had brought cream and a towel with which Alleyn now completed his task. The doctor watched him with an air of impatience and unease. " Damned if I know why you keep me hanging about," he grumbled at last.

" I wanted your opinion on the bruise. That's all, Fox. Is the mortuary van here?"

" On its way, sir," said Fox who was wrapping his piece of card in paper.

Alleyn looked at the doctor. " Do you think," he said, " that his wife will want to see him?"

" She won't want to. She may think she ought to. Humbug, in my opinion. Distress herself for nothing. What good does it do anybody?"

" I think, however, I should at least ask her."

" Why the blazes you can't let her go home, passes my comprehension. And where do *I* go, now? I'm getting damn' bored with Ben's company."

" You may wait either on the stage or, if you'd rather, in the unoccupied dressing-room. Or the office, I think, is open."

" Can I have my snuff back?" Dr. Rutherford asked with something of the shamefaced air of a small boy wanting a favour.

" I think we might let you do that," Alleyn said. " Fox, will you give Dr. Rutherford his snuff-box?"

Dr. Rutherford lumbered uncertainly to the door. He stood there with his chin on his chest and his hands in his pockets.

" See here, Alleyn," he said, looking from under his eyebrows at him. " Suppose I told you it was I who gave Ben that wallop on his mug. What then?"

" Why," Alleyn said, " I shouldn't believe you, you know."

CHAPTER X

SUMMING UP

Alleyn saw Helena Hamilton in her dressing-room. It was an oddly exotic setting. The scent of banked flowers, of tobacco smoke and of cosmetics was exceedingly heavy, the air hot and exhausted. She had changed into her street clothes and sat in an arm-chair that had been turned with its back to the door so that when he entered he saw nothing of her but her right hand trailing near the floor with a cigarette between her fingers. She called: "Come in, Mr. Alleyn," in a warm voice as if he was an especially welcome visitor. He would not have guessed from this greeting that when he faced her he would find her looking so desperately tired.

As if she read his thoughts she put her hands to her eyes and said: "My goodness, this is a long night, isn't it?"

"I hope that for you, at least, it is nearing its end," he said. "I've come to tell you that we are ready to take him away."

"Does that mean I ought to—to look at him?"

"Only if you feel you want to. I can seen no absolute need at all; if I may say so."

"I don't want to," she whispered and added in a stronger voice: "It would be a pretence. I have no real sorrow and I have never seen the dead. I should only be frightened and confused."

Alleyn went to the door and looked into the passage where Fox waited with Gibson. He shook his head and Fox went away. When Alleyn came back to her she looked up at him and said: "What else?"

"A question or two. Have you ever known or heard of a man called Otto Brod?"

Her eyes widened. "But what a strange question!" she said. "Otto Brod? Yes. He's a Czech or an Austrian, I don't remember which. An intellectual. We met him three years ago when we did a tour of the Continent. He had written a play and asked my husband to read it. It was in German and Ben's German wasn't up to it. The idea was that he should get someone over here to look at it but he was dreadfully bad at keeping those sorts of promises and I don't think he ever did anything about it."

168

" Have they kept in touch, do you know?"

" Oddly enough, Ben said a few days ago that he'd heard from Otto. I think he'd written from time to time for news of his play but I don't suppose Ben answered." She pressed her thumb and fingers on her eyes. " If you want to see the letter," she said, " it's in his coat."

Alleyn said carefully: " You mean the jacket he wore to the theatre? Or his overcoat?"

" The jacket. He was always taking my cigarette-case in mistake for his own. He took it out of his breast-pocket when he was leaving for the theatre and the letter was with it." She waited for a moment and then said: " He was rather odd about it."

" In what way?" Alleyn asked. She had used Martyn's very phrase and now when she spoke again it was with the uncanny precision of a delayed echo: " He was rather strange in his manner. He held the letter out with the cigarette-case and drew my attention to it. He said, I think, ' That's my trump card.' He seemed to be pleased in a not very attractive way. I took my case. He put the letter back in his pocket and went straight out."

" Did you get the impression he meant it was a trump card he could use against somebody?"

" Yes. I think I did."

" And did you form any idea who that person could be?"

She leant forward and cupped her face in her hands. " Oh, yes," she said. " It seemed to me that it was I myself he meant. Or Adam. Or both of us. It sounded like a threat." She looked up at Alleyn. " We've both got alibis, haven't we? If it was murder."

" *You* have, undoubtedly," Alleyn said and she looked frightened.

He asked her why she thought her husband had meant that the letter was a threat to herself or to Poole but she evaded this question, saying vaguely that she had felt it to be so.

" You didn't come down to the theatre with your husband?" Alleyn said.

" No. He was ready before I was. And in any case——" She made a slight expressive gesture and didn't complete her sentence.

Alleyn said: " I think I must tell you that I know something of what happened this afternoon."

The colour that flooded her face ebbed painfully and left it very white. She said: " How do you know that? You

169

can't know." She stopped and seemed to listen. They could just hear Poole in the next room. He sounded as if he was moving about irresolutely. She caught her breath and after a moment she said loudly: "Was it Jacko? No, no, it was never Jacko."

"Your husband himself——" Alleyn began and she caught him up quickly. "Ben? Ah, I can believe that. I can believe he would boast of it. To one of the men. To J. G.? Was it J. G.? Or perhaps even to Gay?"

Alleyn said gently: "You must know I can't answer questions like these."

"It was never Jacko," she repeated positively and he said: "I haven't interviewed Mr. Doré yet."

"Haven't you? Good."

"Did you like Otto Brod?"

She smiled slightly and lifted herself in her chair. Her face became secret and brilliant. "For a little while," she said, "he was a fortunate man."

"Fortunate?"

"For a little while I loved him."

"Fortunate indeed," said Alleyn.

"You put that very civilly, Mr. Alleyn."

"Do you think there was some connection here? I mean between your relationship with Brod and the apparent threat when your husband showed you the letter?"

She shook her head. "I don't know. I don't think Ben realised. It was as brief as summer lightning, our affair."

"On both parts?"

"Oh, no," she said as if he had asked a foolish question. "Otto was very young, rather violent and dreadfully faithful, poor sweet. You are looking at me in an equivocal manner, Mr. Alleyn. Do you disapprove?"

Alleyn said formally: "Let us say that I am quite out of my depth with——"

"Why do you hesitate? With what?"

"I was going to say with a *femme fatale*," said Alleyn.

"Have I been complimented again?"

He didn't answer and after a moment she turned away as if she suddenly lost heart in some unguessed-at object she had had in mind.

"I suppose," she said, "I may not ask you why you believe Ben was murdered?"

"I think you may. For one reason: his last act in the dressing-room was not consistent with suicide. He refurbished his make-up."

" That's penetrating of you," she said. " It was an unsym-
pathetic make-up. But I still believe he killed himself. He
had much to regret and nothing in the wide world to look
forward to. Except discomfiture."

" The performance to-night, among other things, to regret?"

" Among all the other things. The change in casting, for
one. It may have upset him very much. Because yesterday
he thought he'd stopped what he called John's nonsense
about Gay. And there was his own behaviour, his hopeless,
hopeless degradation. He had given up, Mr. Alleyn. Believe
me he had quite given up. You will find I'm right, I promise
you."

" I wish I may," Alleyn said. " And I think that's all at
the moment. If you'll excuse me, I'll get on with my job."

" Get on with it, then," she said and looked amused. She
watched him go and he wondered after he had shut the
door if her expression had changed.

II

Adam Poole greeted Alleyn with a sort of controlled impatience. He had changed and was on his feet. Apparently
Alleyn had interrupted an aimless promenade about the room.

" Well?" he said. " Are you any further on? Or am I
not supposed to ask?"

" A good deal further, I think," Alleyn said. " I want a
word with you, if I may have it and then with Mr. Doré. I
shall then have something to say to all of you. After that
I think we shall know where we are."

" And you're convinced, are you, that Bennington was
murdered?"

" Yes, I'm quite convinced of that."

" I wish to God I knew why."

" I'll tell you," Alleyn said, " before the night is out."
Poole faced him. " I can't believe it," he said, " of any
of us. It's quite incredulous." He looked at the wall between
his own room and Helena's. " I could hear your voices in
there," he said. " Is she all right?"

" She's perfectly composed."

" I don't know why you wanted to talk to her at all."

" I had three things to say to Miss Hamilton. I asked
her if she wanted to see her husband before he was taken
away. She didn't want to do so. Then I told her that I
knew about an event of yesterday afternoon."

171

"What event!" Poole demanded sharply.

"I mean an encounter between her husband and herself."

"How the hell did you hear about that?"

"You knew of it yourself, evidently."

Poole said: "Yes, all right. I knew," and then, as if the notion had just come to him and filled him with astonishment, he exclaimed: "Good God, I believe you think it's a motive for *me*." He thrust his hand through his hair. "That's about as ironical an idea as one could possibly imagine." He stared at Alleyn. An onlooker coming into the room at that moment would have thought that the two men had something in common and a liking for each other. "You can't imagine," Poole said, "how inappropriate *that* idea is."

"I haven't yet said I entertain it, you know."

"It's not surprising if you do. After all, I suppose I could, fantastically, have galloped from the stage to Ben's room, laid him out, turned the gas on and doubled back in time to re-enter! Do you know what my line of re-entry is in the play?"

"No."

"I come in, shut the door, go up to Helena, and say: '*You've guessed, haven't you? He's taken the only way out. I suppose we must be said to be free.*' It all seems to fit so very neatly doesn't it? Except that for us it's a year or more out of date." He looked at Alleyn. "I really don't know," he added, "why I'm talking like this. It's probably most injudicious. But I've had a good deal to think about the last two days and Ben's death has more or less put the crown on it. What am I to do about this theatre? What are we to do about the show? What's going to happen about——" He broke off and looked at the wall that separated his room from Martyn's. "Look here, Alleyn," he said. "You've no doubt heard all there is to hear and more about my private life. And Helena's. It's the curse of this job that one is perpetually in the spotlight."

He seemed to expect some comment on this. Alleyn said lightly: "The curse of greatness?"

"Nothing like it, I'm afraid. See here, Alleyn. There are some women who just can't be fitted into any kind of ethical or sociological pigeon-hole. Ellen Terry was one of them. It's not that they are above reproach in the sense most people mean by the phrase, but that they are outside it. They behave naturally in an artificial set-up. When an attachment comes to an end, it does so without any regrets or recrimination. Often, with an abiding affection on both sides. Do you agree?"

"That there are such women? Yes?"

"Helena is one. I'm not doing this very well but I do want you to believe that she's right outside this beastly thing. It won't get you any further and it may hurt her profoundly if you try to establish some link between her relationship with her husband or anyone else and the circumstances of his death. I don't know what you said to each other but I do know it would never occur to her to be on guard for her own sake."

"I asked her to tell me about Otto Brod."

Poole's reaction to this was surprising. He looked exasperated. "There you are!" he said. "That's exactly what I mean. Otto Brod! A fantastic irresponsible affair that floated out of some midsummer notion of Vienna and Strauss waltzes. How the devil you heard of it I don't know though I've no doubt that at the time she fluttered him like a plume in her bonnet for all to see. I never met him but I understand he was some young intellectual with a pale face, no money and an over-developed faculty for symbolic tragedy. Why bring him in?"

Alleyn told him that Bennington, when he came down to the theatre, had had a letter from Brod in his pocket and Poole said angrily: "Why the hell shouldn't he? What of it?"

"The letter is not to be found."

"My dear chap, I suppose he chucked it out or burnt it or something."

"I hardly think so," said Alleyn. "He told Miss Hamilton it was his trump card."

Poole was completely still for some moments. Then he turned away to the dressing-shelf and looked for his cigarettes.

"Now what in the wide world," he said with his back to Alleyn, "could he have meant by a trump card?"

"That," said Alleyn, "is what, above everything else, I should very much like to know."

"I don't suppose it means a damn' thing, after all. It certainly doesn't to me."

He turned to offer his cigarettes but found that Alleyn had his own case open in his hands. "I'd ask you to have a drink," Poole said, "but I don't keep it in the dressing-room during the show. If you'd come to the office——"

"Nothing I'd like more but we don't have it in the working hours either."

"Of course not. Stupid of me." Poole glanced at his dress for the ball and then at his watch. "I hope," he said, "that my business-manager is enjoying himself with my guests at my party."

"He rang up some time ago to inquire. There was no message for you."

"Thank you." Poole leant against the dressing-shelf and lit his cigarette.

"It seems to me," Alleyn said, "that there is something you want to say to me. I've not brought a witness in here. If what you say is likely to be wanted as evidence I'll ask you to repeat it formally. If not, it will have no official significance."

"You're very perceptive. I'm damned if I know why I should want to tell you this but I do. Just out of earshot behind these two walls are two women. Of my relation with the one, you seem to have heard. I imagine it's pretty generally known. I've tried to suggest that it has come to its end as simply, if that's not too fancy a way of putting it, as a flower relinquishes its petals. For a time I've pretended their colour had not faded and I've watched them fall with regret. But from the beginning we both knew it was that sort of affair. She didn't pretend at all. She's quite above any of the usual subterfuges and it's some weeks ago that she let me know it was almost over for her. I think we both kept it up out of politeness more than anything else. When she told me of Ben's unspeakable behaviour yesterday, I felt as one must feel about an outrage to a woman whom one knows very well and likes very much. I was appalled to discover in myself no stronger emotion than this. It was precisely this discovery that told me the last petal had indeed fallen and now——" He lifted his hands. "Now, Ben gets himself murdered, you say, and I've run out of the appropriate emotions."

Alleyn said: "We are creatures of convention and like our tragedies to take a recognisable form."

"I'm afraid this is not even a tragedy. Unless——" he turned his head and looked at the other wall. "I haven't seen Martyn," he said, "since you spoke to her. She's all right, isn't she?" Before Alleyn could answer he went on: "I suppose she's told you about herself—her arrival out of a clear sky and all the rest of it?"

"Everything, I think."

"I hope to God—— I want to see her, Alleyn. She's alone

174

in there. She may be frightened. I don't suppose you understand."

" She's told me of the relationship between you."

" The *relationship*——" he said quickly. " You mean——"

" She's told me you are related. It's natural that you
should be concerned about her."

Poole stared at him. " My good ass," he said, " I'm
eighteen years her senior and I love her like a boy of her
own age."

" In that case," Alleyn remarked. " You can *not* be said
to have run out of the appropriate emotions."

He grinned at Poole in a friendly manner, and accompanied by Fox, went to his final interview—with Jacques
Doré.

III

It took place on the stage. Dr. Rutherford elected to
retire into the office to effect, he had told Fox, a few
paltry adjustments of his costume. The players, too, were
all in their several rooms and Clem Smith had been wakened,
re-examined by Fox, and allowed to go home.

So Jacko was alone in the tortured scene he had himself
designed.

" What do we talk about?" he asked and began to roll
himself a cigarette.

" First of all," Alleyn said, " I must tell you that I am
asking for a general search through the clothes that have
been worn in the theatre. We have no warrant at this stage
but so far no one has objected."

" Then who am I to do so?"

Fox went through his pockets and found a number of
curious objects—chalk, pencils, a rubber, a surgeon's scalpel
which Jacko said he used for wood carving, and which was
protected by a sheath, a pocket-book with money, a photograph of Helena Hamilton, various scraps of paper with
drawings on them, pieces of cotton-wool and an empty
bottle smelling strongly of ether. This, he told Alleyn, had
contained a fluid used for cleaning purposes. " Always they
are messing themselves and always I am removing the mess.
My overcoat is in the junk room. It contains merely a
filthy handkerchief, I believe."

Alleyn thanked him and returned the scalpel, the pocket-book and drawing-materials. Fox laid the other things aside, sat down and opened his note-book.

"Next," Alleyn said, "I think I'd better ask you what your official job is in this theatre. I see by the programme——"

"The programme," Jacko said, "is euphemistic. 'Assistant to Adam Poole' is it not? Let us rather say: Dogsbody in Ordinary to the Vulcan Theatre. Henchman Extraordinary to Mr. Adam Poole. At the moment, dresser to Miss Helena Hamilton. Confidant to all and sundry. Johannes Factotum and not without bells on. *Le* Vulcan, *c'est moi,* in a shabby manner of speaking. Also: *j'y suis, j'y reste.* I hope."

"Judging by this scenery," Alleyn rejoined, "and by an enchanting necklace which I think is your work, there shouldn't be much doubt about that. But your association with the management goes further back than the Vulcan, doesn't it?"

"Twenty years," Jacko said, licking his cigarette paper, "for twenty years I improvise my role of Pantaloon for them. Foolishness, but such is my deplorable type. The eternal doormat. What can I do for you?"

Alleyn said: "You can tell me if you still think Bennington committed suicide?"

Jacko lit his cigarette. "Certainly," he said. "You are wasting your time."

"Was he a vain man?"

"Immensely. And he knew he was artistically sunk."

"Vain of his looks?"

"But yes, *yes!*" Jacko said with great emphasis, and then looked very sharply at Alleyn. "Why, of his looks?"

"Did he object to his make-up in this play? It seemed to me a particularly repulsive one."

"He disliked it, yes. He exhibited the vanity of the failing actor in this. Always, always he must be sympathetic. Fortunately Adam insisted on the make-up."

"I think you told me that you noticed his face was shiny with sweat before he went for the last time to his room?"

"I did."

"And you advised him to remedy this? You even looked into his room to make sure?"

"Yes," Jacko agreed after a pause, "I did."

"So when you had gone he sat at his dressing-table and carefully furbished up his repellant make-up as if for the curtain call. And then gassed himself?"

176

"The impulse perhaps came very suddenly." Jacko half-closed his eyes and looked through their sandy lashes at his cigarette smoke. "Ah, yes," he said softly. "Listen. He repairs his face. He has a last look at himself. He is about to get up when his attention sharpens. He continues to stare. He sees the ruin of his face. He was once a coarsely handsome fellow, was Ben, with a bold rake-helly air. The coarseness has increased but where, he asks himself, are the looks? Pouches, grooves, veins, yellow eyeballs and all emphasised most hideously by the make-up. This is what he has become, he thinks, he has become the man he has been playing. And his heart descends into his belly. He knows despair and he makes up his mind. There is hardly time to do it. In a minute or two he will be called. So quickly, quickly he lies on the floor, with trembling hands he pulls his coat over his head and puts the end of the gas-tube in his mouth."

"You knew how he was found then?"

"Clem told me. I envisaged everything. He enters a world of whirling dreams. And in a little while he is dead. I see it very clearly."

"Almost as if you'd been there," Alleyn said lightly. "Is this, do you argue, his sole motive? What about the quarrels that had been going on? The change of cast at the last moment? The handing over of Miss Gainsford's part to Miss Tarne? He was very much upset by that, wasn't he?"

Jacko doubled himself up like an ungainly animal and squatted on a stool. "Too much has been made of the change of casting," he said. "He accepted it in the end. He made a friendly gesture. On thinking it over I have decided we were all wrong to lay so much emphasis on this controversy." He peered sideways at Alleyn. "It was the disintegration of his artistic integrity that did it," he said. "I now consider the change of casting to be of no significance."

Alleyn looked him very hard in the eye. "And that," he said, "is where we disagree. I consider it to be of the most complete significance: the key, in fact, to the whole puzzle of his death."

"I cannot agree," said Jacko. "I am sorry."

Alleyn waited for a moment and then—and for the last time—asked the now familiar question.

"Do you know anything about a man called Otto Brod?"

There was a long silence. Jacko's back was bent and his head almost between his knees.

177

"I have heard of him," he said at last.

"Did you know him?"

"I have never met him. Never."

"Perhaps you have seen some of his work?"

Jacko was silent.

"*Können Sie Deutsch lesen?*"

Fox looked up from his notes with an expression of blank surprise. They heard a car turn in from Carpet Street and come up the side lane with a chime of bells. It stopped and a door slammed.

"*Ja wohl,*" Jacko whispered.

The outside doors of the dock were rolled back. The sound resembled stage-thunder. Then the inner and nearer doors opened heavily and someone walked round the back of the set. Young Lamprey came through the prompt entrance. "The mortuary van, sir," he said.

"All right. They can go ahead."

He went out again. There was a sound of voices and of boots on concrete. A cold draught of night air blew in from the dock and set the borders creaking. A rope tapped against canvas and a sighing breath wandered about the grid. The doors were rolled together. The engine started up and, to another chime of bells, Bennington made his final exit from the Vulcan. The theatre settled back into its night-watch.

Jacko's cigarette had burnt his lips. He spat it out and got slowly to his feet.

"You have been very clever," he said. He spoke as if his lips were stiff with cold.

"Did Bennington tell you how he would, if necessary, play his trump card?"

"Not until after he had decided to play it."

"But you had recognised the possibility?"

"Yes.'

Alleyn nodded to Fox who shut his note-book, removed his spectacles and went out.

"What now?" Jacko asked.

"All on," Alleyn said. "A company call. This is the curtain speech, Mr. Doré."

IV

Lamprey had called them and then retired. They found an empty stage awaiting them. It was from force of habit, Martyn supposed, that they took up, for the last time their

178

after-rehearsal positions on the stage. Helena lay back in her deep chair with Jacko on the floor at her feet. When he settled himself there, she touched his cheek and he turned his lips to her hand. Martyn wondered if he was ill. He saw that she looked at him and made his clown's grimace. She supposed that, like everybody else, he was merely exhausted. Darcey and Gay Gainsford sat together on the small settee and Parry Percival on his upright chair behind them. At the back, Dr. Rutherford lay on the sofa with a newspaper spread over his face. Martyn had returned to her old seat near the prompt corner and Poole to his central chair facing the group. "We have come out of our rooms," Martyn thought, "like rabbits from their burrows." Through the prompt entrance she could see Fred Badger, lurking anxiously in the shadows.

Alleyn and his subordinates stood in a group near the dock doors. On the wall close by them was the baize rack with criss-crossed tapes in which two receipts and a number of commercial cards were exhibited. Fox had read them all. He now replaced the last and looked through the prompt corner to the stage.

"Are they all on?" Alleyn asked.

"All present and correct, sir."

"Do you think I'm taking a very risky line, Br'er Fox?"

"Well, sir," said Fox uneasily. "It's a very unusual sort of procedure, isn't it?"

"It's a very unusual case," Alleyn rejoined and after a moment's reflection he took Fox by the arm. "Come on, old trooper," he said. "Let's get it over."

He walked on to the stage almost as if, like Poole, he was going to sum-up a rehearsal. Fox went to his old chair near the back entrance. Martyn heard the other men move round behind the set. They took up positions, she thought, outside the entrances and it was unpleasant to think of them waiting there, unseen.

Alleyn stood with his back to the curtain and Poole at once slewed his chair round to face him. With the exception of Jacko who was rolling a cigarette, they all watched Alleyn. Even the doctor removed his newspaper, sat up, stared, groaned and returned ostentatiously to his former position.

For a moment, Alleyn looked round the group and to Martyn he seemed to have an air of compassion. When he began to speak his manner was informal but extremely deliberate.

"In asking you to come here together," he said, "I've

179

taken an unorthodox line. I don't myself know whether I am justified in taking it and I shan't know until those of you who are free to do so have gone home. That will be in a few minutes, I think.

"I have to tell you that your fellow-player has been murdered. All of you must know that we've formed this opinion and I think most of you know that I was first inclined to it by the circumstance of his behaviour on returning to his dressing-room. His last conscious act was to repair his stage make-up. While that seemed to me to be inconsistent with suicide it was, on the other hand, much too slender a thread to tie up a case for homicide. But there is more conclusive evidence and I'm going to put it before you. He powdered his face. His dresser had already removed the pieces of cotton-wool that had been used earlier in the evening and put out a fresh pad. Yet after his death there was no used pad of cotton-wool anywhere in the room. There is, on the other hand, a fresh stain near the gas-fire which may, on analysis, turn out to have been caused by such a pad having been burnt on the hearth. The box of powder has been overturned on the shelf and there is a deposit of powder all over that corner of the room. As you know, his head and shoulders were covered, tentwise, with his overcoat. There was powder on this coat and over his fingerprints on the top of the gas-fire. The coat had hung near the door and would, while it was there, have been out of range of any powder flying about. The powder, it is clear, had been scattered after and not before he was gassed. If he was, in fact, gassed."

Poole and Darcey made simultaneous ejaculations. Helena and Gay looked bewildered, and Percival incredulous. Jacko stared at the floor and the doctor groaned under his newspaper.

"The post-mortem," Alleyn said, "will of course settle this one way or the other. It will be exhaustive. Now, it's quite certain that the dresser didn't go into the room after Mr. Bennington entered it this last time and it is equally certain that the dresser left it in good order—the powder-pad prepared, the clothes hung up, the fire burning and the door unlocked. It is also certain that the powder was not overturned by the men who carried Mr. Bennington out. It was spilt by someone who was in the room after he was on the floor with the coat over his head. This person, the police will maintain, was his murderer. Now, the question arises, doesn't it, how it came about that he was in such a condition—

comatose or unconscious—that it was possible to get him down on the floor, put out the gas-fire, and then disengage the connecting tube, put the rubber end in his mouth and turn the gas on again, get his fingerprints on the wing tap and cover him with his own overcoat. There is still about one sixth of brandy left in his flask. He was not too drunk to make-up his own face and he was more or less his own man, though not completely so, when he spoke to Miss Tarne just before he went into his room. During the second interval Mr. Darcey hit him on the jaw and raised a bruise. I suppose it is possible that his murderer hit him again on the same spot—there is no other bruise—and knocked him out. A closer examination of the bruise may show if this was so. In that case the murderer would need to pay only one visit to the room: he would simply walk in, a few minutes before the final curtain, knock his victim out and set the stage for apparent suicide.

"On the other hand it's possible that he was drugged."

He waited for a moment. Helena Hamilton said: "I don't believe in all this. I don't mean, Mr. Alleyn, that I think you're wrong: I mean it just sounds unreal and rather commonplace like a case reported in a newspaper. One knows that probably it's all happened but one doesn't actively believe it. I'm sorry I interrupted."

"I hope," Alleyn said. "You will all feel perfectly free to interrupt at any point. About this possibility of drugging. If the brandy was drugged, then of course we shall find out. Moreover it must have been tinkered with after he went on for his final scene. Indeed, any use of a drug, and one cannot disregard the possibility of even the most fantastic methods, must surely have been prepared while he was on the stage during the last act. We shall, of course, have a chemical analysis made of everything he used—the brandy, his tumbler, his cigarettes, his make-up and even the grease-paint on his face. I tell you, quite frankly, that I've no idea at all whether this will get us any further."

Fox cleared his throat. This modest sound drew the attention of the company upon him but he merely looked gravely preoccupied and they turned back to Alleyn.

"Following out this line of thought it seems clear," he said, "that two visits would have to be made to the dressing-room. The first, during his scene in the last act and the second, after he had come off and before the smell of gas was first noticed: by Mr. Parry Percival."

Percival said in a high voice: "I knew this was coming."

181

Gay Gainsford turned and looked at him with an expression of the liveliest horror. He caught her eye and said: "Oh, don't be fantastic, Gay darling. *Honestly!*"

"Mr. Percival," Alleyn said, "whose room is next to Mr. Bennington's and whose fire backs on his, noticed a smell of gas when he was about to go out for the curtain-call. He tells us he is particularly sensitive to the smell because of its associations in this theatre and that he turned his own fire off and went out. Thus his fingerprints were found on the tap."

"Well, naturally they were," Parry said angrily. "Really, Gay!"

"This, of course," Alleyn went on, "was reminiscent of the Jupiter case but in that case the tube was not disconnected because the murderer never entered the room. He blew down the next-door tube and the fire went out. In that instance the victim was comatose from alcohol. Now, it seems quite clear to us that while this thing was planned with one eye on the Jupiter case, there was no intention to throw the blame upon anyone else and that Mr. Percival's reaction to the smell was not foreseen by the planner. What the planner hoped to emphasise was Mr. Bennington's absorption in the former case. We were to suppose that when he decided to take his own life he used the method by which he was obsessed. On the other hand," Alleyn said, "suppose this hypothetical planner was none other than Bennington himself?"

V

Their response to this statement had a delayed action. They behaved as actors do when they make what is technically known as a "double take." There were a few seconds of blank witlessness followed by a sudden and violent reaction. Darcey and Percival shouted together that it would be exactly like Ben: Helena cried out inarticulately and Poole gave a violent ejaculation. The doctor crackled his newspaper and Martyn's thoughts tumbled about in her head like dice. Jacko, alone, stared incredulously at Alleyn.

"Do you mean," Jacko asked, "that we are to understand that Ben killed himself in such a way as to throw suspicion of murder upon one of us? Is that your meaning?"

"No. For a time we wondered if this might be so but the state of the dressing-room, as I'd hoped I'd made clear, flatly contradicts any such theory. No. I believe the planner based the method on Bennington's preoccupation with the other case and hoped we would be led to some such conclusion. If powder had not been spilt on the overcoat we might well have done so."

"So we are still—in the dark," Helena said and gave the commonplace phrase a most sombre colour.

"Not altogether. I needn't go over the collection of near-motives that have cropped up in the course of our interviews. Some of them sound far-fetched, others at least possible. It's not generally recognised that, given a certain temperament, the motive for homicide can be astonishingly unconvincing. Men have been killed from petty covetousness, out of fright, vanity, jealousy, boredom or sheer hatred. One or other of these motives lies at the back of this case. You all, I think, had cause to dislike this man. In one of you the cause was wedded to that particular kink which distinguishes murderers from the rest of mankind. With such beings there is usually some—shall I say, explosive agency, a sort of fuse—which, if it is touched off, sets them going as murder-machines. In this case I believe the fuse to have been a letter written by Otto Brod to Clark Bennington. This letter had disappeared and was probably burnt in his dressing-room. As the powder-pad may have been burnt. By his murderer."

Poole said: "I can't begin to see the sense of all this." and Helena said drearily: "Dark. In the dark."

Alleyn seemed to be lost in thought. Martyn, alone of all the company, looked at him. She thought she had never seen a face as withdrawn and—incongruously the word flashed up again—compassionate. She wondered if he had come to some crucial point and she watched anxiously for the sign of a decision. But at this moment she felt Poole's eyes upon her and when she looked at him they exchanged the delighted smiles of lovers. "How *can* we," she thought, and tried to feel guilty. But she hadn't heard Alleyn speak and he was half-way through his first sentence before she gave him her attention.

". . . So far about opportunity," he was saying. "If there were two visits to the dressing-room during the last act I think probably all of you except Miss Hamilton could have made the earlier one. But for the second visit there is a more restricted field. Shall I take you in the order in which you are sitting? Miss Tarne, in that case, comes first."

Martyn thought: "I ought to feel frightened again."

"Miss Tarne has told us that after she left the stage,

and she was the first to leave it, she stood at the entry to the dressing-room passage. She was in a rather bemused state of mind and doesn't remember much about it until Mr. Percival, Mr. Darcey and Mr. Bennington himself came past. All three spoke to her in turn and went on down the passage. It is now that the crucial period begins. Mr. Doré was nearby and after directing the gun-shot, took her to her dressing-room. On the way, he looked in for a few seconds on Mr. Bennington who had just gone to his own room. After Miss Tarne and Mr. Doré had both heard Mr. Darcey and Mr. Percival return to the stage, they followed them out. They give each other near alibis up to this point and the stage-hands extend Miss Tarne's alibi to beyond the crucial time. She is, I think, out of the picture."

Gay Gainsford stared at Martyn. "That," she said, " must be quite a change for you."

" Miss Gainsford comes next." Alleyn said as if he had not heard her. " She was in the greenroom throughout the crucial period and tells us she was asleep. There is no witness to this."

" George!" said Gay Gainsford wildly and turned to Darcey, thus revealing for the first time in this chronicle, his Christian name. " It's all right, dear," he said. " Don't be frightened. It's all right."

" Mr. Percival and Mr. Darcey are also in the list of persons without alibis. They left the stage and returned to it together, or nearly so. But they went of course to separate rooms. Mr. Percival is the only one who noticed the smell of gas. Dr. Rutherford," Alleyn went on, moving slightly in order to see the doctor, " could certainly have visited the room during this period, as at any other stage of the performance. He could have come down from his box, passed unobserved round the back of the scenery, taken cover and gone in after these four persons were in their own rooms."

He waited politely but the doctor's newspaper rose and fell rhythmically. Alleyn raised his voice slightly. " He could have returned to his O.P. stairs when the rest of you were collected on the prompt side and he could have made an official entry in the character of Author." He waited for a moment. The others looked in a scandalised manner at the recumbent doctor but said nothing.

" Mr. Poole has himself pointed out that he could have darted to the room during his brief period off-stage. He could not, in my opinion, have effected all that had to be

184

done and if he had missed his re-entry he would have drawn immediate attention to himself.

"Mr. Doré is in a somewhat different category from the rest," Alleyn said. "We know he came away from her dressing-room with Miss Tarne but although he was seen with the others on the prompt side, he was at the back of the group and in the shadows. Everyone's attention at this period was riveted on the stage. The call-boy checked over the players for the curtain-call and noticed Mr. Bennington had not yet appeared. Neither he nor anyone else had reason to check Mr. Doré's movements."

Jacko said: "I remind you that Parry said he smelt gas while I was still with Miss Tarne in her room."

"I have remembered," Alleyn answered, "what Mr. Percival said." He looked at Helena Hamilton. "And while all this was happening," he concluded, "Miss Hamilton was on the stage holding the attention of a great cloud of witnesses in what I think must have been a most remarkable play."

There was a long silence.

"That's all I have to say," Alleyn's voice changed its colour a little. "I'm going to ask you to return to your rooms. You'll want to do so in any case to collect your coats and so on. If you would like to talk things over among yourselves you are quite free to do so. We shall be in the greenroom. If each of you will come in and leave us an address and telephone number I'll be grateful." He looked round them for a moment. Perhaps deliberately he repeated the stage-manager's customary dismissal: "Thank you, ladies and gentlemen. That will be all."

CHAPTER XI

LAST ACT

Alleyn stood in front of Adam Poole's portrait and looked at his little group of fellow-policemen.

"Well," he said. "I've done it."

"Very unusual," said Fox.

Bailey and Thompson stared at the floor.

Gibson blew out a long breath and wiped his forehead.

P.C. Lamprey looked as if he would like to speak but knew his place too well. Alleyn caught his eye. "That, Mike," he said, "was an almost flawless example of how an investigating officer is not meant to behave. You will be good enough to forget it."

"Certainly, sir."

"What do you reckon, Mr. Alleyn?" Fox asked. "A confession? Brazen it out? Attempt to escape? Or what?"

"There'll be no escape, Mr. Fox," Gibson said. "We've got the place plastered outside. No cars without supervision within a quarter of a mile and a full description."

"I said 'attempt,' Fred," Mr. Fox pointed out majestically.

"If I've bungled," Alleyn muttered, "I've at least bungled in a big way. A monumental mess."

They looked uneasily at him. Bailey astonished everybody by saying to his boots, with all his customary moroseness: "That'll be the day."

"Don't talk Australian," Mr. Fox chided immediately but he looked upon Bailey with approval.

A door in the passage opened and shut.

"Here we go," said Alleyn.

A moment later there was a tap at the greenroom door and Parry Percival came in. He wore a dark overcoat, a brilliant scarf, yellow gloves and a green hat.

"If I'm still under suspicion," he said, "I'd like to know but I suppose no one will tell me."

Fox said heartily: "I shouldn't worry about that if I were you, sir. If you'd just give me your address and phone number. Purely as a reference."

Parry gave them and Lamprey wrote them down.

"Thank you, Mr. Percival," Alleyn said. "Good night." Parry walked to the door. "They all seem to be going home in twos except me," he said. "Which is rather dreary. I hope no one gets coshed for his pains. Considering one of them seems to be a murderer it's not too fantastic a notion though I suppose you know your own business. Oh, well. Good night."

Evidently he collided with Gay Gainsford in the passage. They heard her ejaculation and his fretful apology. She came in followed by Darcey.

"I couldn't face this alone," she said and looked genuinely frightened. "So George brought me."

"Perfectly in order, Miss Gainsford," Fox assured her.

Darcey, whose face was drawn and white, stood near the door. She looked appealingly at him and he came forward and gave their addresses and telephone numbers. His voice sounded old. "I should like to see this lady home," he said and was at once given leave to do so. Alleyn opened the door for them and they went out, arm in arm.

Poole came next. He gave a quick look round the room and addressed himself to Alleyn. " I don't understand all this," he said, " but if any member of my company is to be arrested, I'd rather stay here. I'd like to see Martyn Tarne home—she lives only ten minutes away—but if it's all right with you, I'll come back." He hesitated and then said quickly, " I've spoken to Jacques Doré."

Alleyn waited for a moment. " Yes," he said at last, " I'd be glad if you'd come back."

" Will you see Helena now? She's had about all she can take."

" Yes, of course."

" I'll get her," Poole said and crossed the passage. They heard him call: " Ella?" and in a moment he reopened the door for her.

She had put a velvet beret on her head and had pulled the fullness forward so that her eyes were shadowed. Her mouth drooped with fatigue but it had been carefully painted. Fox took her address and number.

" Is the car here?" she asked and Fox said: " Yes, Madam, in the yard. The constable will show you out."

" I'll take you Ella," Poole said. " Are you sure you'd rather be alone?"

She turned to Alleyn. " I thought," she said, " that if I'm allowed, I'd rather like to take Jacko. If he's still about. Would you mind telling him? I'll wait in the car."

" There's no one," Alleyn asked, " that you'd like us to send for? Or ring up?"

" No, thank you," she said. " I'd just rather like to have old Jacko."

She gave him her hand. " I believe," she said, " that when I can think at all sensibly about all this, I'll know you've been kind and considerate."

Poole went out with her and Lamprey followed them.

A moment later, Martyn came in.

As she stood at the table and watched Fox write out her address she felt how little she believed in herself here, in this quietly fantastic setting. Fox and his two silent and soberly dressed associates were so incredibly what she had always pictured plain-clothes detectives to be, and Alleyn, on the contrary, so completely unlike. She was much occupied with this notion and almost forgot to give him her message.

187

"Jacko," she said, "asked me to say his address is the same as mine. I have a room in the house where he lodges." She felt there might be some ambiguity in this statement and was about to amend it when Alleyn asked: "Has Mr. Doré gone?"

"I think he's waiting for Miss Hamilton in her car."

"I see," Alleyn said. "And I believe Mr. Poole is waiting for you. Good-bye, Miss Tarne, and good luck."

Her face broke into a smile. "Thank you *very* much," said Martyn.

Poole's voice called in the passage. "Where are you, Kate?"

She said good night and went out.

Their steps died away down the passage and across the stage. A door slammed and the theatre was silent.

"Come on," said Alleyn.

He led the way round the back of Jacko's set to the prompt corner.

Only the off-stage working lights were alive. The stage itself was almost as shadowy as it was when Martyn first set foot on it. A dust-begrimed lamp above the letter rack cast a yellow light over its surface.

In the centre, conspicuous in its fresh whiteness, was an envelope, that had not been there before.

It was addressed in a spidery hand to Chief Detective-Inspector Alleyn.

He took it from the rack. "So he did it this way," he said and without another word, led them on to the stage.

Jacko's twisted stairway rose out of the shadows like a crazy ejaculation. At its base, untenanted chairs faced each other in silent communion. The sofa was in the darkest place of all.

Young Lamprey began to climb the iron steps to the switchboard. The rest used their flashlamps. Five pencils of light interlaced, hovered and met at their tips on a crumpled newspaper. They advanced upon the sofa as if it housed an enemy but when Alleyn lifted the newspaper and the five lights enlarged themselves on Dr. Rutherford's face, it was clearly to be seen that he was dead.

The little group of men stood together in the now fully-lit stage while Alleyn read the letter. It was written on official theatre paper and headed: "The Office. 1.45 a.m."

DEAR ALLEYN,

I cry you patience if this letter is but disjointedly patched together. Time presses and I seem to hear the clink of constabular bracelets.

Otto Brod wrote a play which he asked Clark Bennington to vet. Ben showed it to the two persons of his acquaintance who could read German and had some judgment. I refer to Doré and myself. The play we presented last night was my own free adaptation of Brod's piece made without his consent or knowledge. Base is the slave that pays. In every way mine is an improvement. Was it George Moore who said that the difference between his quotation and those of the next man was that he left out the inverted commas? I am in full agreement with this attitude and so, by the way, was Will Shakespeare. Doré, however, is a bourgeois where the arts are in question. He recognised the source, disapproved, but had the grace to remain mum. The British critics, like Doré, would take the uncivilised view and Ben knew it. He suspected the original authorship, wrote to Brod and three days ago got an answer confirming his suspicions. This letter he proposed to use as an instrument of blackmail. I told Ben, which was no more than the truth, that I intended to make things right with Brod who, if he's not a popinjay, would be well-content with the honour I've done him and the arrangement I proposed. Ben would have none of this. He threatened to publish Brod's letter if a certain change was made in the casting. The day before yesterday, under duress, I submitted and no longer pressed for this change. However, owing to Miss G.'s highstrikes, it was, after all, effected. Five minutes before the curtain went up on the first act, Ben informed me, with, Ho, such bugs and goblins in my life, that at the final curtain, he intended to advance to the footlights and tell the audience I'd pinched the play. Knowing Ben meant business, I acted: in a manner which, it appears, you have rumbled and which will be fully revealed by your analysis of the grease-paint on his unlovely mug.

He powdered his face with pethidine-hydrochloride, an effective analgesic drug, now in fashion, of which the maximum therapeutic dose is 100 mg. Ben got about 2 gm. on his sweaty upper lip. I loaded his pre-pared powder-pad with pethidine (forgive the nauseating alliteration) while he was on in the last act and burnt the pad when I returned, immediately before the curtain-call. He was then comatose and I doubt if the gassing was necessary. However, I wished to suggest suicide. I overturned his powder box in opening out his overcoat. My own vestment being habitually besprinkled with snuff was none the worse but the powder must have settled on his coat after I had covered his head. Unfortunate. I fancy that with unexpected penetration, you have in all respects hit on the *modus operandi*. Pity we couldn't share the curtain-call.

It may interest you to know that I have formed the habit of pepping up my snuff with this admirable drug and had provided myself with a princely quantity in the powder form used for dispensing purposes. One never knew which way the cat would jump with Ben. I have been equipped for action since he threatened to use his precious letter. By the way it would amuse me to know if you first dropped to it when I trampled on my pethidine box in the greenroom. Dogberry, I perceived, collected the pieces.

My other spare part is secreted in the groove of the sofa. I shall now return to the sofa, listen to your oration and if, as I suspect, it comes close to the facts, will take the necessary and final step. I shall instruct the moronic and repellent Badger to place this letter in the rack if I am still asleep when the party breaks up. Pray do not attempt artificial respiration. I assure you I shall be as dead as a door-nail. While I could triumphantly justify my use of Brod's play I declined the mortification of the inevitable publicity, more particularly as it would reflect upon persons other than myself. If you wish to hang a motive on my closed file you may make it vanity.

Let me conclude with a final quotation from my fellow-plagiarist.

" *Sometimes we are devils to ourselves*
When we will tempt the frailty of our powers
Presuming on their changeful potency."

I hear the summons to return. Moriturus, to coin as
Miss G. would say, a phrase, te saluto, Cæsar.
   Your etc. on the edge of the viewless winds.
                                        John James Rutherford

III

Alleyn folded the letter and gave it to Fox. He walked
back to the sofa and stood looking down at its burden for
some time.
   " Well, Fox," he said at last, " he diddled us in the end,
didn't he?"
   " Did he, Mr. Alleyn?" asked Fox woodenly.
   Bailey and Thompson moved tactfully off-stage. Young
Lamprey came on with a sheet from one of the dressing-
rooms. Fox took it and dismissed him with a jerk of his
head. When the sheet was decently bestowed, Alleyn and
Fox looked at each other.
   " Oh, let us still be merciful!" Alleyn said, and it is
uncertain whether this quotation from the doctor's favourite
source was intended as an epitaph or an observation upon
police procedure.

IV

Poole switched off his engine outside Jacko's house. Martyn
stirred and he said: " Do you want to go in at once? We
haven't said a word to each other. Are you deadly tired?"
   " No more than everybody else but—yes. Aren't you?
You must," she said drowsily, " be so dreadfully puzzled
and worried."
   " I suppose so. No. Not really. Not now. But you must
sleep, Martyn. 'Martyn.' There, now, I've used your Christian name again. Do you know that I called you Kate
because I felt it wasn't time yet, for the other? That astonished me. In the theatre we be-darling and be-Christian name
each other at the drop of a hat. But it wouldn't do with you."
   He looked down at her. She thought: " I really must rouse
myself," but bodily inertia, linked with a sort of purification
of the spirit flooded through her and she was still.
   " It isn't fair," Poole said, " when your eyelids are so
heavy, to ask you if I've made a mistake. Perhaps to-morrow
you will think you dreamed this, but Martyn, before many

more days are out, I shall ask you to marry me. I do love you so very much."

To Martyn his voice seemed to come from an immensely long way away but it brought her a feeling of great content and refreshment. It was as if her spirit burgeoned and flowered into complete happiness. She tried to express something of this but her voice stumbled over a few disjointed words and she gave it up. She heard him laugh and felt him move away. In a moment he was standing with the door open. He took her keys from her hand.

" Shall I carry you in? I must go back to the theatre."

The cold night air joined with this reminder of their ordeal to awaken her completely. She got out and waited anxiously beside him while he opened the house door.

" Is it awful to feel so happy?" she asked. " With such a terror waiting? Why must you go to the theatre?" And after a moment. " Do you *know*?"

" It's not awful. The terrors are over. Alleyn said I might return. And I think I do know. There. Good night. Quickly, quickly, my darling heart, good night and good morning."

He waited until the door shut behind her and then drove back to the theatre.

The pass-door into the foyer was open and the young policeman stood beside it.

" Mr. Alleyn is in here, sir," he said.

Poole went in and found Alleyn with his hands in his pockets in front of the great frame of photographs on their easel.

" I'm afraid I've got news," he said, " that may be a shock to you."

" I don't think so," Poole said. " Jacko spoke to me before I left. He knew about the play: I didn't. And we both thought John's sleep was much too sound."

They stood side by side and looked at the legend over the photographs.

" Opening at this Theatre on Thursday, May 14
'THUS TO REVISIT'
A New Play by John James Rutherford."

THE END